LOVE ME FOR ME

Sarah Ettritch

Norn Publishing
Kingston, Canada

ISBN: 978-1-927369-64-7

Published byNorn Publishing
Kingston, Ontario, Canada
www.nornpublishing.com

V1.0

1

Erin entered the bustling lobby of the Hunt and Bishop office tower and crossed to the executive elevator, her flat dress shoes ringing on the gleaming tiled floor. While she waited for the elevator to arrive, she mentally rehearsed what she'd say to Dad, assuming she'd correclly guessed the reason for his terse text, summoning her to see him at 11 a.m. sharp. He hadn't invited her to his office since their last argument. Over breakfast, she'd skimmed one of the company documents he'd sent her to review. She'd even read a paragraph while she brushed her teeth. But would that be enough to stall him? Again.

The elevator arrived and whisked her up to the 50th floor, which contained only two offices: Aaron Hunt's and Royce Bishop's. She stepped onto plush carpet, turned left, passed through the glass door with Aaron Hunt emblazoned across it in black letters. Nobody was in the cozy waiting room. Erin would have sunk into one of the leather chairs, but Katie, Dad's assistant, beamed at her. "Nice to see you, Erin. He's ready for you. You can go right in."

"Thanks." Dad's door was open. Erin tapped on it and strode inside.

"I need it tomorrow," Dad said into his cell phone. He motioned for Erin to sit, but she wandered over to the wall of fame, as she thought of it, and surveyed the framed photos she'd viewed hundreds of times. Dad with city politicians, Dad with provincial and federal politicians, Dad with sports figures, Dad with journalists, Dad with CEOs of companies large and small, Dad with local celebrities, and some not so local. Shaking hands, slapping backs, thumbs up, wide smiles. In a few of them, Dad was sticking a shovel into the ground, flanked by beaming department heads, the mayor at the time, and the local city councillor.

"Get back to me by the end of today," Dad barked. What sounded like his phone thudded to the desk.

Erin turned to him.

"Sit," he said, motioning to one of the guest chairs again.

"I'm okay standing." She didn't want him towering over her.

"Suit yourself." He leaned forward in his chair and rested his elbows on his desk. "I have a job for you."

That was the last thing she'd expected him to say. "We agreed I'd come work with you after I'd had some time off."

Irritation flashed across his face, but he didn't lash out. "This is a temporary job, and don't tell me you don't have the time because you're busy." He picked up his phone, swiped a few times, and held it out to her. "Katie took it on her way in yesterday. It was on a pole near a bus stop."

She studied the photo on the phone's display. A poster. Printed on it in green block letters:

Come out and
Save McMillan Park

Saturday, May 22nd, 2 pm, south gate

Say no to luxury housing
Say no to Hunt and Bishop
Green, NOT Greed

Citizens for Responsible Housing

She handed Dad his phone and gave him a questioning look.

"The city rezoned the park at our request, but only a few people here and at city hall are supposed to know that. We're about to purchase it. The land."

Erin didn't know anything about McMillan Park. "Where is it?"

"In the Iron Court area."

A low-income area. "You don't usually build there."

"That's not the point. Someone is leaking information to this group. More specifically, to Lily Altree."

"Never heard of her."

"If you showed any interest in the business, you'd know who she is." Dad waved a dismissive hand. "She hasn't stopped any projects yet, but she tries. Sometimes we have to jump through extra hoops because of the fuss she's causing, just so the city can say it did its due diligence. She's like a mosquito buzzing around my head. I always manage to crush it." He banged his fist on his desk. "But it's still annoying."

"She heads this Citizens for Responsible, uh . . ."

"Housing group? Yes. I want to know who's betraying me."

Erin didn't envy the person. Knowing Dad, they'd be fired—and more.

"You're about the right age and would blend in."

"What do you mean?"

"You're going to that protest."

"What?"

"Show up, wave the signs or whatever they do, and see what you can find out."

Erin dropped into one of the guest chairs. "I don't think I'm the right person for this. I've never been to a protest before." She'd certainly never been to the Iron Court area. "Can't you hire a PI, or ask someone else to do it?"

"I don't want anyone to know someone's shafting me. I want this kept in the family."

"How am I supposed to find out who told them about the park? They're not just going to tell me."

"I'm sure you'll figure something out. Either that, or you can tell me you're ready to come to work with me. No more lazing around." Dad folded his arms and leaned back in his chair, a smirk on his face. "So which is it? Are you going to find out who's leaking info, or should I send you down to human resources to fill out some forms?"

Erin raised her hands in surrender. "All right, all right. I'll go to the protest."

"Good."

"I'll have to earn their trust first. It might take some time."

"Then it takes some time. Now that Altree's got her teeth into this project, this won't be the last protest. Be the best little protestor they've got and find out whose balls I have to break." Dad looked at his watch. "I have an 11:15."

Dismissed, then. Erin stood. "Mom said if you're free for lunch, to call her."

His face brightened. "I just might do that."

She waited to see if he'd invite her to go with them, then wandered toward the door. "Bye, then."

"I'll see you later," Dad said, already focused on the monitor sitting on his desk.

～

As soon as Erin got home, she went into her private apartment within her parents' house, plunked into her office chair, and fired up her laptop, determined to find out everything she could about Lily Altree and the Citizens for Responsible Housing. A search found the group's one-page website. She scanned the About section, which described a grassroots group of locals who kept tabs on the real estate developments taking place around the city. If they didn't agree with one, they protested. No names, though, and a generic contact email.

She studied the handful of pics. Around fifteen to twenty people were in each one. As Dad had said, most were around her age, but not all. Erin couldn't find the name Lily Altree anywhere on the site, but searching the internet for that name yielded results. A few newspaper articles mentioned Altree when reporting on previous protests. A couple of social media profiles also popped up. Erin studied the profile picture attached to one. Altree had short curly red hair and appeared pale, but not anemic. A few freckles dotted her cheeks. She wasn't wearing any makeup.

Erin's gaydar dinged, but it had about an eighty percent success rate, so she could be wrong. And she wasn't going to the protest to make friends. She was going to find out who was betraying Dad. If she succeeded, maybe he'd get off her back for a while.

Spring was here, with summer soon to follow, which meant ideal viewing conditions here on the ground. She already knew when she'd go out, where she'd set up her telescope, what photos she hoped to take. The last place she wanted to be was stuck in an office, in boring meetings about developments she couldn't care less about. If she found out who was betraying Dad, she might be able to wheedle a few more months out of him, promise to take her place at his side in the fall.

To unmask the traitor, she needed a plan, starting with a fake name, one she'd easily remember so it would roll off her tongue. She examined herself in the full-length mirror standing in the corner of her bedroom. Bartlett. Mom's maiden name. She adopted what appeared to be a relaxed pose, winked at herself, and said, "Bartlett. Erin Bartlett." It felt right. One decision made.

Next, she threw open the doors of her walk-in closet and eyed the blazers and dress pants hanging on the left, and the blouses and turtlenecks hanging on the right. She needed jeans and t-shirts. And a pair of sneakers wouldn't hurt.

Assuming it would take more than one protest for someone in the grassroots group to spill his or her guts about an informant, she also needed a phone for Erin Bartlett, so she'd have a contact number.

What about social media profiles? It would look weird if she wasn't anywhere online, but it would be suspicious if she created new profiles. Anyone looking her up would notice the creation dates and wonder. Maybe she could claim to be tech-challenged. No, that didn't feel right. Maybe she'd deleted all her profiles because she'd realized she was addicted to social media. Better. If anyone asked, she'd run with that.

Should she drive her Mercedes to this protest, or take a cab or the bus? Going to the Iron Court area of the city would be like going to a foreign country. She'd feel safer in her own car, but showing up in a Mercedes wouldn't be the best idea. She'd drive part of the way and take a cab for the rest.

She sat at her desk again and worked on creating a history for Erin Bartlett. Someone—probably Dad—had once told her the best lies were mainly the truth, so if you ever had to tell a big lie, stick to the truth as much as possible. Too many fibs were difficult to remember. If anyone asked, she was taking some time off before she went to work for her father, lived with her parents, and was interested in real estate developments. She didn't have to explain that her interest was completely different from theirs. Essentially, she'd be herself. Only her name would change.

When Dad had suggested she go to the protest, Erin had thought he was nuts. But now she looked forward to it. Operation Informant would almost be fun if she wasn't terrified of letting Dad down.

Her stomach grumbled. She went in search of Michael, the Hunts' combined chef, butler, and pool boy. After lunch, she'd go clothes shopping, then pick up Christina, Royce Bishop's daughter and her assumed-to-be future wife. That evening, they'd attend a reception the mayor was holding, one in which businessmen like Dad would be toasted. One that would remind her of how much she must disappoint him.

∽

ERIN LIFTED A GLASS of champagne from the silver tray the waiter presented to her and watched Christina do the same. They clinked glasses. "Cheers." Erin sipped her bubbly. The voices of those chatting around her in civilized tones mixed with the classical music played by a string quartet. The mayor's receptions for local investors and entrepreneurs were always the same. If Dad hadn't insisted on her presence tonight, Erin would be at home on her bedroom balcony.

Christina had already drained half her glass. She set it on the table they shared with their parents in the reception hall at one of the city's finest hotels. "I wish there was dancing."

Erin snorted. "Here?" Most of the couples were her parents' age. Not that they didn't dance, but she'd only seen them do so at weddings.

"Sure, why not? My parents are taking ballroom dancing lessons."

"Seriously?" She couldn't imagine Royce Bishop dancing. He was a quiet, thoughtful man, the one behind the scenes at Hunt and Bishop Property Investments. Erin's dad was the boisterous one, the brash investor who snapped up properties from under other investors and twisted arms to get what he wanted. Business partners for many years, their two fathers' personalities complemented each other, but their opinions sometimes clashed. Royce—she felt funny calling him Royce, even though he'd told her she could—was a more "by the book" person and had tried to persuade Dad to build affordable housing in addition to the swanky condos Hunt and Bishop was known for, but Dad was having none of it. "There's no money in it," Erin had heard him say many times.

"They thought maybe we'd want to join them sometime," Christina said, bringing Erin back to the reception. "They're private lessons," she added.

"Why would we want to learn how to ballroom dance?"

Christina cocked her head. "It could be fun."

Erin hesitated. "I'll think about it."

"Whenever you say that, you mean no."

"No, I don't."

"Yes, you do. You never stop thinking about it. You—"

"Good evening, ladies."

Erin turned toward the voice. A man in his thirties smiled nervously at them and lifted a camera. Before she could protest, a flash blinded her.

"Thank you." He went to move away, but Dad stormed over and blocked his path. He snatched the camera from the journalist's hand.

"Hey, that's my camera."

"It's mine now," Dad snapped.

"I'll report you to the police."

"Go ahead. I don't recognize you. New in town?"

The man squared his shoulders. "I'm Christopher Birmingham, the society reporter for the Standard."

"I don't care if you're the editor-in-chief. Everyone knows photos of my daughter are off limits."

Birmingham smirked. "She's not a child."

"Let me phrase this another way, Mr. Birmingham," Dad said contemptuously. "I can let you keep your job with the understanding that you will never try to photograph my daughter again, or I can make a few calls and destroy your life. Which is it?"

Erin stepped forward. "Dad."

His hand shot toward her, palm out. She stepped back.

"Well?" he said to Birmingham. "Do I call the owner of the Standard and the chief of police, or not?"

Birmingham glared at him. "No."

"Good." Dad scowled as he checked the camera and pressed a couple of buttons. "I'm not an unreasonable man. You can take a photo of me and my lovely wife." He handed the camera back to the cowed society reporter. "I'm pretty sure I deleted the photo in the cloud too, but in case I haven't, I can make those calls anytime. Understand?"

Birmingham scowled and straightened his blazer's collar. "Yes. Sir."

"Fine. Wait for me over there." He pointed to a spot that would be out of earshot.

Birmingham did what he was told, his tail tucked between his legs. A security guard who'd arrived to see what the fuss was about trailed after him.

Dad blew out some air. "Idiot."

"He said I'm not a child, and he's right," Erin said.

"You're not in the business yet, Erin. When you are, you'll be fair game. Until then, you're a private person." His voice softened. "I'd never forgive myself if something happened to you because of the business."

His words warmed Erin. Dad rarely got sentimental.

"Don't forget to show up for that protest. Don't let me down."

The warmth died. Erin opened her mouth to say he could count on her, but Dad had already turned away and headed over to where the journalist was sulkily waiting for him.

Christina raised her brows and drank the rest of her champagne in one go. She set her glass down. "Your father scares me sometimes."

"He's only trying to protect me."

"What did he mean? What protest?"

"Something he asked me to do. I'll tell you about it another time." She sipped her drink. "I don't really want to do it, but it was that or start work with him right now. He's running out of patience."

A dimple formed in the middle of Christina's forehead when she grimaced. "You've been holding him off for almost a year. He's been pretty patient."

"Whose side are you on?"

"Nobody's. But are you sure you want to work with him? You say you do, but . . ."

What else would she do? Dad expected her to take over the business one day. If Erin had siblings, she'd defer to one of them.

But she didn't. Mom and Dad had tried for years to get pregnant and had finally managed it. Here she was. They'd tried again, then tried IVF, then accepted that Erin would be it. She wouldn't disappoint them, especially Dad, who'd probably wanted a son.

"Tell me to shut up if you want, but you don't want to spend your life living for other people."

Erin stared at Christina, at her perfectly coiffed blonde hair, the dress that fit her so snuggly she must have had it custom made, her long fingers with their manicured nails painted pink, the luxury designer bag sitting next to her glass. Christina was hardly in a position to dole out sage advice when it came to not worrying about what others thought of one's choices, especially the important ones.

Not for the first time, she wondered if love would ever grow between them. They'd known each other all their lives. Their dads had already been in business together when they'd come along. They'd gone to the same private daycare, same private school, played together, participated in the same afterschool activities. When Christina had come out and Mom and Dad hadn't freaked, Erin had plucked up the courage to reveal her own truth to them. To their credit, they'd embraced her as they'd embraced Christina, but suddenly there was an implicit assumption that she and Christina would eventually ride off into the sunset together. Both families spoke about them as if they were a couple.

Arranged matches weren't unusual in their social circle. Erin could do much worse than Christina. They didn't share many interests, but Erin enjoyed her company and Christina was easy on the eyes. "That's how most couples around here start out," a family friend had said to Erin at the country club once, when one of the members had walked in with her new husband on her arm. "She told me she doesn't love him yet, but boy, what a match!" Nobody would deny that she and Christina were also a great match. They had plenty of time to find their spark. For now, they held hands—occasionally—and bided their time.

Christina's voice cut into her thoughts. "Are you listening to me, or is your head in the clouds again?"

Not the clouds. The stars. But she wouldn't quibble. "I'm not living my life for other people. I want to work at the company, work with Dad. But once I do, it'll be more than nine to five. You know how much our dads work. I'm not ready for that yet."

Christina appeared dubious. "When do you think you'll be ready?"

The sound of a clinking glass saved Erin from answering. Along with everyone else, she turned in the direction of the clinking.

"I'd like to say a few words," the mayor said, wearing the chain of office around his neck. "I love hosting these receptions and rubbing elbows with the best this city has to offer. With your dedication and your determination, our city . . ."

Erin tuned him out. Christina was right. Dad wouldn't wait forever. She'd go home tonight and pick up those company documents again. She'd prove to him she was serious.

Two hours later, Erin peered through her telescope at the twinkling stars while the company documents sat ignored on her desk.

2

Erin waited for the light to turn green so she could cross the street and join the group she'd eyed hanging around outside McMillan Park. Now that she was here, she went back to thinking Dad was crazy for having her do this. What if the protestors saw right through her? What if she accidentally said her real name?

To calm herself, she counted the cars idling at the intersection. Usually she was driving, like that dude in the red convertible, with a blonde half his age in the passenger seat. Erin rolled her eyes. Sure, the blonde was interested in him for his riveting conversation, and not for his sports car. They reminded her of the couple she'd passed just a few minutes ago, right after a cab had dropped her off three blocks away. The guy's shoes were scuffed and his jeans were ripped, yet he was on the arm of a woman in a business suit. Amazing how people with money and power fooled themselves into thinking they got the girl or guy because they were interesting, especially when that girl or guy was half their age or broke.

Erin would never be the guy in the red convertible or the woman with the gold digger on her arm. Been there, done that. In university, she'd fallen hard for Kerry. They'd met at a coffee shop, a chance meeting, or so Erin had thought. Cute, funny, attentive Kerry, who shared every one of Erin's interests. They'd enjoyed long lazy afternoons in bed when neither of them had classes. Erin had imagined their engagement, their wedding, their vacations in Europe and exotic locales, seen them watching the sun set together on a swinging bench on their front porch, imagined what Kerry's hair would look like when it was gray. Until the day she'd received a text from Kerry. As usual, her heart had leapt, until she'd realized Kerry had accidentally texted her.

Kerry: It's going great. She's really into me. Not really my type, but hey, the moula more than makes up for it. Bought me a bike yesterday. Has a rich friend. Want me to hook you up?

Erin: ????

Kerry: Crap.

Erin: WTF?

Kerry: We weren't serious, right? It was just a bit of fun.

Erin had wept for weeks over that bit of fun. She'd learned her lesson. She wanted someone who wanted her for her, not for her money. The problem was how to tell. The only sure way was to stick to dating others with moula.

Both she and Christina were wealthy. When they walked into the country club together, nobody raised a brow and whispered about that idiot Erin. She wasn't the guy in the red convertible.

The light changed. Erin went with the herd and crossed to the other side. The group was just ahead now. Her hands were clammy. She wished she was wearing her power clothes, not jeans, a plain lavender t-shirt and blazer, and sneakers. And no Rolex. She felt naked without her Rolex.

Wanting a few extra seconds before she made contact, she peered through the iron-barred fence set about five feet back from the sidewalk. What she could see of McMillan Park, which occupied an entire large city block, didn't seem worth saving. Patchy grass, dead or dying trees, a tired-looking play area with a swing set, teeter totter, old-style merry-go-round, and a sandbox with dirty sand. The fence Erin peered through was rusty and its paint was peeling. But there were people in the park, two sitting on a worn bench and kids on the swings that weren't broken. Still,

Erin couldn't understand why the people in the neighbourhood would want this over a modern apartment building surrounded by manicured green space. Time to talk to the protestors.

Only a couple of them held signs. The rest were milling about, as if waiting for something to happen. Deep breath. She wouldn't force a smile because it would look fake, but she needed to pull her shoulders out of her ears. Consciously relaxing them, she approached the woman closest to her.

"Hi," Erin said, a little too loudly.

The woman turned to her. "Hey."

"Is this where the protest against the new development is happening?"

"You got it." The woman's face brightened. "I'm Shawna."

"Erin."

Shawna's eyes narrowed. "Haven't seen you at any of our other events."

"Yeah, this is my first one. I finally decided to take an interest in local issues, not just read about them."

"Well, this is certainly a local issue." Shawna swept her arm toward the fence from where she stood in the five-foot cement area between the sidewalk and the park. "The only green space around here, and a greedy developer will destroy it and build a monstrosity."

A monstrosity. Not the way Erin would have described a twenty-storey modern apartment building. Laundry and a fireplace in every suite, high ceilings, solar panels on the roof, along with a swimming pool.

"How did you hear about the protest?" Shawna asked.

"I saw a poster near a bus stop." She searched those gathered for a redhead but came up empty. "Are you in charge?"

"Me?" Shawna chuckled. "I'm terrible at organizing. No, that's Lily." She glanced around. "But she's not here yet, and she has the rest of our signs."

Erin didn't care about signs. "How do you track what developers are doing?" she asked, hoping she sounded like a wide-eyed innocent in awe of these heroic protectors standing against big bad developers. "I thought a lot of that information was private, especially when they're still negotiating with the city over the land or plans."

"Lily follows it all." An old blue Toyota pulled up to the curb. Shawna pointed to it. "And here she is."

Everyone swarmed toward the car, as if a celebrity had arrived. Erin hung back a bit, watched Lily Altree jump out, scurry to her trunk, and open it. With the amount of rust pockmarking the car's body, Erin wouldn't have been surprised if the trunk lid fell off. It must be hanging on by a thread, and a rusty one at that.

A woman climbed out of the passenger seat and elbowed her way next to Altree. The girlfriend, maybe? Altree still dinged her gaydar in person. Her short red hair was fierier than her photo had done it justice, she wore a checked blouse and jeans, and Erin had glimpsed comfortable shoes—sneakers—before everyone had surrounded her.

She forced herself forward and joined those getting a sign. Here was her chance. If she was lucky, she'd introduce herself, ask Altree a few seemingly innocent questions, hang around for ten minutes and then get the hell out of here. But Shawna turned away from Altree with two signs.

"Here you go," she said, handing one to Erin.

Normally Erin would be grateful someone was looking out for her at a strange event, but not right now. She forced a smile and accepted her sign. *Green over Greed.* Written in green marker, of course. Shawna's read *Say No to Condos.* That was going to change minds for sure.

The others lined up in front of the fence. Erin joined them. "Where'd Lily go?" she asked Shawna. Altree and her car had disappeared while Erin was checking out her sign.

"She didn't want to get a parking ticket." Shawna hoisted her sign above her head and chanted. "Save McMillan Park. Green not greed. Save McMillan Park. Green not greed."

Erin lifted her sign and joined in.

~

LILY HUSTLED BACK TO the protest, wishing she'd found a closer parking spot. Saturday mornings were better for parking, but Sandy had said more people would see them if they tried an afternoon, and Lily had agreed. Still, she'd stifled her disappointment when she'd pulled up to the curb and counted twelve people, not including herself and Sandy. Twelve. From a population of over 300,000. Didn't anyone care that developers were gobbling up green space and building housing that was unaffordable for most of them? When she saw housing advocates on the news talking about the lack of affordable housing, she wanted to scream. Where were they today?

On days like this, she felt like giving up, shredding the placards and letting someone else worry about what was built in this city. But her life had to mean something, or what had happened to Jay-Jay wouldn't make sense. Lily was on this earth for a reason, though sometimes she wondered if this cause was it. Then she reminded herself not to let the bastards get her down, especially since it was McMillan Park on the line. Now was the time to make noise, while the city still owned the land.

She rounded the corner and jogged up to the line that had formed outside the park, the one Hunt and Bishop wanted to buy so another eyesore could be erected. Patrick had carried five extra signs from the trunk to the sidewalk. When Lily reached the pile, there were still five there. She sighed, joined the line, and glanced down it. She hadn't really noticed who was there when she'd quickly counted, wanting to hand out signs as quickly as possible so she could park the car and get back here.

Angie, Patrick, Don, Maria, Sue, Sandy, Peter, Donna, Doug, Shawna, Ryan, and someone she didn't know. A brown-haired slender woman in jeans and a blazer. Damn, if she hadn't arrived late, she'd have made a point of talking to her.

She squeezed between Sandy and Patrick and bobbed her sign in the air. "Save our parks," she shouted. "Save our parks."

"Did you see the agenda for the city council meeting next month?" Patrick raised his voice so she could hear him. "Someone from Hunt and Bishop is presenting. You know what that means."

It meant whatever they presented to council would be accepted, because Hunt and Bishop Property Investments wouldn't present to council unless it knew its plans to purchase the park site and build an apartment were in the bag. How many councillors had they paid off this time?

Patrick lowered his sign. "I'm not even sure why we're out here."

Fury shot through Lily. She wanted to swat him with her sign. "It's not over until it's over," she said through clenched teeth.

She hoisted her sign higher and shouted even louder. "Save our parks! Save our parks!" It would take more than the cowards at city hall and the pigs at Hunt and Bishop to stop her from standing here. She thrust her sign toward the sky that was threatening rain and shouted at the top of her lungs. "Save our parks!" For the residents of the Iron Court neighbourhood. For Jay-Jay.

~

HALF AN HOUR LATER, Erin was already flagging. Her arms ached from holding the sign aloft, and she was thirsty from all the chanting. She'd have a new appreciation for protestors now, even though they rarely changed anything. They certainly wouldn't stop Dad from buying the land behind her and building an apartment building.

Someone driving by honked their horn. The person in the passenger seat gave them a thumbs up. Better than the finger. So far, she'd say it was about 50% thumbs up and 50% go fuck yourselves. One guy had even yelled it out the window, in case they couldn't see his rude gesturing. She agreed with something a woman had shouted. There was nothing wrong with progress. This city had a housing crisis that was constantly in the news. These protestors were part of the problem.

A raised voice to her left drew her attention, one that wasn't chanting any of the slogans Erin had learned. ". . . get a job instead of standing here making trouble." A man in a suit stood in front of Altree, screaming at her. "Get a fucking job, morons. The cops should just throw you all in jail."

Altree's reply was too low for Erin to hear.

The guy stepped closer, his face only inches from Altree's. "Bitches like you need a good slap."

Without thinking, Erin was in motion, closing the distance between her and Altree in seconds. "Back off, buddy."

He turned toward Erin. "Another one who needs slapping."

Erin shifted her weight slightly so she could take the guy down if she had to. Dad had been right to insist she take a self-defence course every year. The moves were always fresh in her mind. "Do you always threaten to hit women who don't agree with you?"

"Fuck you."

"What a brilliant comeback! Move along."

"Or what?"

"Or I'll . . . I'll be forced to make you move along. So you'd better go now."

Altree nodded. "We're exercising our right to—"

"He doesn't care about rights," Erin said. "He's upset about his own pathetic loser life and has to take it out on others. Especially women."

The guy's body stiffened and his jaw set. Fear snaked through Erin, but she continued to stare at him. "Move along," she said, her voice strong and steady, much to her relief. "Or you'll be the one the police come for."

"You're a waste of time, anyway," he muttered. But he moved along.

She let out her pent breath and turned to Altree. "Are you okay?"

Altree's eyes bulged. "Of course I'm okay. Do you think that's the first man who's told me I need a good beating, that I should be at home like a good little woman, not shit disturbing? I can take care of myself."

Erin was taken aback. She hadn't expected thanks, not exactly, but still.

"I didn't need you marching over here and taking over. I was handling it."

"Sorry," Erin mumbled, taking in Altree's blazing brown eyes, the freckles dotting her cheeks and nose, the ones she could barely see right now because Altree was flushed. Her throat suddenly tightened, the same way it had tightened in Grade 11 when she saw Patsy Goodson sashaying down the corridor and felt as if she'd been hit by a lightning bolt. She'd had crushes on girls before, but Patsy had kept her up at night, filled her head with fantasies she would never have dared share, and made her drive by Patsy's house three or four times a day. She'd breathed and dreamed Patsy for months. The non-relationship had eventually petered out, but for a while, it had been Patsy, Patsy, Patsy.

She was older now—mid-twenties—and wiser. She wasn't so naïve about relationships, wasn't like the guy in the red convertible with someone drooling over his money. Someone like Altree would never work. Someone who was ungrateful, to boot.

Erin whirled, went back to her place in the line, and lifted her sign.

~

LILY'S ANGER AT BEING treated like someone who needed rescuing quickly died when the newbie marched away. Yes, she'd had run-ins with hundreds of people like that guy and didn't need her hand held. But the newbie didn't know that and was probably wondering why nobody else had stepped in. *Because I've snapped at all of them for doing so at one time or another.* They knew to stand back. Now she'd lashed out at someone new, someone who'd come to help. Given the meagre turnout today, she needed everyone she could get. She'd have to apologize—sort of.

Sandy elbowed her. "She stood up for you. How chivalrous." She smirked. "You're blushing."

"I am not blushing. I'm mad."

"I hope she comes for coffee with us afterwards. If it rains on the way, she'll probably whip off her blazer and cover any puddles, so your feet won't get wet. And if anyone threatens you, she'll be, what did she say? Forced to do something to them." Sandy chuckled. "You should sit next to her."

"Drop it, okay."

Sandy's eyes danced. She looked past Lily, at Patrick. "Let's go for coffee in about twenty minutes. Pass it down the line."

He quickly did so, to Lily's dismay. Was she the only one who'd stand here for days? She'd once stared down a bulldozer when trying to stop a developer who only cared about money from destroying one of the few green spaces in the west end. The cops had eventually come and the developer had grudgingly agreed that Lily be fined, rather than charged. Easy for the developer to do, because it had gotten exactly what it wanted. It didn't help that the city councillors were in the developers' pockets.

"I'll make a point of inviting your saviour along," Sandy said. "She's new. We should welcome her."

"Just give the word and we'll pack up for the day," Patrick said.

Lily sighed and lifted her sign.

~

ERIN CARRIED HER REGULAR coffee to the tables Altree's group had claimed. She'd kill for a latte, but had noticed everyone else had ordered regular old coffees and had decided it would be better to go along with the crowd. When the coffee idea had travelled down the line, she'd groaned to herself, even though it was the perfect opportunity to pick up a few tidbits of information. At least Altree's girlfriend had made a point of inviting her to go with them. Erin didn't feel like she was crashing the gathering. Hopefully everyone would be more relaxed here, and it would give her a chance to redeem herself for upsetting Altree—Lily. On the stroll here, Erin had learned everyone's name and had to stop thinking of her as Altree.

The only empty place at the two tables they'd pushed together was next to Lily, which was both good and bad. Erin set her coffee on the table and dropped into the empty chair. Fortunately Lily was busy talking.

". . . might not be this year," she was saying.

"Why not?" Maria said.

Lily shrugged. "Some unanticipated expenses have come up. I'm thinking maybe another year or two."

"You're always pushing it off. What's going on this time?"

"Nothing."

"I thought you took on more shifts so you could apply this year."

"What are we talking about?" Erin asked, genuinely curious.

Sandy answered the question. "Law school."

Erin turned to Lily. "You're applying to law school?" she blurted. Then she inwardly cringed. She'd sounded too surprised, as if someone like Lily would be the last person she'd expect to go to law school.

Lily didn't seem to notice. "Someone has to hold these bastards to account, and apparently standing in the street protesting and bombarding councillors with emails isn't doing it."

Erin couldn't help but admire Lily's conviction and determination, even though she disagreed with her position when it came to real estate developments. "The city and developers have the best law firms working for them," she felt compelled to say.

Lily squared her shoulders. "That doesn't scare me. What are you saying? That we shouldn't even try, because we don't have a hope in hell of winning against the big guys?"

Erin thought quickly on her feet. "There are better ways to go about it than meeting them head on. You could find people sympathetic to your cause who work for them, for example. Find out information that way and use it against them."

Lily's expression didn't change, and neither did her body language. "At some point, it would have to be fought in the courts, anyway."

Not exactly a denial that someone at city hall or Hunt and Bishop was feeding her information.

Sandy started blabbing about something that had happened to her at work the day before, probably to change the subject. Erin listened politely along with the others and drank her coffee, wishing she could leave, but knowing she had to stay.

An hour later, the silences between topics were growing longer and a few people had already left. Erin doubted she'd get any information today, but she'd made contact, and now she had to make sure she was on Lily's radar.

"Well, I guess I'll head out," she said, before a new topic of conversation made it difficult to leave without appearing rude.

"Thanks for coming out," Sandy said.

The others murmured their agreement.

"Will you be holding another protest?" she asked.

"Of course," Lily said, to chuckles. "We're far from finished with McMillan Park. And there will always be another short-sighted twit wanting to bulldoze a park or tear down a perfectly good building that's stood there for more than a hundred years."

Erin bit her tongue. She really, really wanted to point out that people who weren't obsessed with the same things as them weren't necessarily twits. But she didn't want to blow what she considered a stellar performance at the last minute. Instead, she smiled and nodded and tried not to crush the empty coffee cup in her hand.

"I guess I'll see you at the next protest, then," she said. "I'll keep my eye out for it."

A chorus of "See you" and "Bye" rose.

Erin left the table, and had just tossed her cup into the recycling section of the waste station when someone tapped her shoulder. She whirled, then masked her surprise.

"I just wanted to say thanks, for coming out, and for when you stood up to that guy." Lily wasn't smiling, but her voice had softened.

"No problem." Lily's prickly manner didn't stop Erin from admitting she was cute.

"I shouldn't have reacted the way I did. It's just that I'm capable of handling those situations myself."

Not exactly an apology, but not an easy thing to say for someone as stubborn as the woman in front of her.

"How did you find out about the protest?" Lily asked.

Erin's heart pounded. Did Lily suspect something? "I saw one of your posters near a bus stop." Please don't let her ask where because Dad hadn't told her the location. She continued speaking before Lily could say anything. "If you hold another protest, I'd like to go. I can give you my phone number."

"That's why I came over." Lily pulled out her phone and tapped in the number Erin gave her. "I'll text you the details of our next protest when I know them."

"I'm between jobs right now, so my availability is good."

Lily grunted and pocketed her phone. "I won't keep you from the rest of your Saturday. See you."

"Yeah, see you," she said to Lily's back.

She left the shop feeling deflated and not quite understanding why, whether it was Lily's dismissive attitude toward her or Lily's failure to offer her phone number in return. Neither reason made sense to Erin. She would never call Lily, and who cared what the woman thought of her? She was here to find out who was betraying Dad.

Of course. Now she understood the reason for her downer mood. She didn't have much to report except that she'd made contact and left her number. Now that she'd met Lily, she knew she'd have to build trust with her if she wanted Lily to reveal her informant's name. Next time she met with them—assuming there was a next time—she'd try to find out if anyone else knew who it was. Sandy was a good candidate and was friendlier and more talkative than Lily.

Erin rounded the nearest corner, and after glancing over her shoulder at least three times, arranged for a cab. One arrived almost instantly.

Ten minutes later, she was walking through the underground garage where she'd parked her car. She pressed a button on her key fob as she approached her black Mercedes sedan. With a sigh of relief, she slid behind the steering wheel and leaned back against the leather seat. This was more like it.

She tuned in to an internet rock station and headed home.

~

BY THE TIME ERIN was driving up the winding tree-lined road leading to the Hunts' main house, she was having misgivings about seeing Lily's group again. They weren't bad people, and they didn't have a hope in hell of winning against Dad. Now that she'd had some time away from them and had thought it over, she felt a bit icky about lying to them. At the same time, she didn't want to let Dad down, and the thought of showing up for work at Hunt and Bishop made her want to puke.

Inside the house, she bounded up the stairs to the second floor, sure she'd find Dad in his home office. She didn't bother to knock, just walked right in and threw herself into one of the comfortable armchairs.

Dad looked up from his laptop and raised his brows. "So?"

"You don't have anything to worry about."

He tapped away at the laptop's keys for a few seconds, then closed it. "Tell me about it."

"Not many showed up, for one thing."

"How many?"

"Counting me? Fourteen."

"Ha!"

"But it might not be quantity, but quality. Lily Altree is pretty passionate."

"Passion can only carry one so far. She can yap all she wants. It won't stop the project from going forward. I'm more interested in who's leaking information."

Erin's shoulders slumped. "I don't know yet. They're not going to tell a person they don't know."

"Then they should get to know you. I hope you gave them a reason to expect you again."

"Lily—Altree has my number, the number I'm using for this."

A smile crept across Dad's face. "Good. We already have our eyes on two other sites. I don't want any surprises."

"Can't you hack her accounts or something? Whoever it is must have emailed her or talked to her on the phone. You've got guys in IT who know how to do black hat stuff."

"I'd rather you try first before I move on to methods that could land us in hot water. It's not as if you're busy."

Her jaw tightened.

"Plus, having you in with them might turn the tables for a bit. We can find out about protests before they happen."

"What could you do? Organize a counter-protest?"

"You never know what information is going to be valuable." He tapped his right temple. "Remember that."

She mentally added it to her list of Dad's pearls of wisdom.

The scent of lilac wafted into the office. A second later, Mom walked into the room. "Good, you're back," she said to Erin. "I thought perhaps you'd forgotten dinner." She shifted her attention to Dad. "Both of you. We're leaving in an hour." She looked down at Erin. "I hope you're not going in those clothes."

Erin could hear the sniff in her voice.

"Why don't you put on that new blouse and blazer we bought when we were out last week, and do lose the sneakers. Oh, I told Christina you'd pick her up."

Christina. Seeing Mr. Red Convertible had reminded her of why she and Christina were a good match. Christina liked her for her, and not for her Rolex and Mercedes. There were days when Erin believed that was more important than love, which could grow over time. Yes, Lily was cute, and strong, and confident, but there was no way Erin would date her, even if she were available. The moment Lily found out who she really was, she'd quickly get over any surprise and cling to her like a leech. A rust bucket for a car, having to work extra shifts to scrape the money together for law school. Erin would be her saviour, in a bad way. Maybe that was why the adults in her life were pushing her towards Christina. Better to stick to someone who also had a Rolex than fall for someone who couldn't see beyond one.

She leaped to her feet. "I'll go take a shower, then."

"I think that would be a good idea, dear."

Time to forget about her undercover operation for Dad and focus on transforming herself back into Erin Hunt, daughter of Aaron Hunt of Hunt and Bishop Property Investments.

~

A FEW DAYS LATER, Erin squinted along the length of her golf club, to get a sense of at which angle to hit the ball. Then she straightened, assumed her golf stance, swung the club a few inches back, and hit the ball. It rolled through the spokes of the first wheel, then the second, hit one of the wooden borders and sped off in a different direction, travelled through a clown's open mouth, hit another border, rolled toward the hole and . . .

"Yes!" She pumped her fist into the air.

Christina rolled her eyes. "I still beat you." She handed Erin the notepad they'd used to keep score. "See."

"I don't care. It's mini putt, not the Master's Tournament. I play for fun." One of the reasons she'd suggested they play a round of mini putt in the course her parents had built for her behind the house. She doubted they expected her to still be using it in her twenties, but playing relaxed her.

"I'm not saying I wanted to go with your parents to the country club to play for real. Your mom takes no prisoners when she plays." Christina brushed a piece of fake grass off her golf pants.

Erin felt silly in her polo shirt, white pants, and golfing shoes, but Christina had insisted they dress suitably for their game.

"So carry on with what you were saying before my win became official," Christina said.

"Oh yeah." Erin fell into step with Christina and strolled to the nearby shed. "I told Dad he didn't have anything to worry about. Not that I think he's worried about them. He's steaming about whoever's leaking information."

"I wouldn't want to be that person."

"Me, either."

"So you're just going to hang out with these people until one of them gives you a name."

"That's the plan."

Christina was silent while she entered the shed and hung her club on the rack meant for the mini-putt clubs. "I'm not sure I could do that."

"What?" Erin hung her club next to Christina's.

"Lie to everyone. Spy on people who are just doing what they think is right."

Erin faced her. "I'm not spying on them."

"What would you call it? If they say anything your dad needs to know about, you'll tell him."

"I doubt they'll tell me anything he doesn't already know, except when they're planning a protest. And I'm not telling a huge lie. I've changed my last name, that's all."

Christina gave her a long look.

"Okay, I'm coming across as a between jobs regular person. But that's it. I tell the truth about everything else."

"It's a big lie, Erin. If they knew who you really are, they wouldn't want anything to do with you. You're the fox in the henhouse."

"That's a bit dramatic, don't you think?" Erin said, despite the little voice inside her agreeing with Christina. "I'm not trying to stop them from protesting or anything. And once they give me a name, I'm out of there."

"Just like that? What if you make friends with them?"

"I won't." But Erin wasn't sure that was true. While she hadn't exactly enjoyed her time at the coffee shop, she had learned a bit about those in Lily's group and hadn't felt uncomfortable with them. It had been a while since she'd been out with a group and just talked. She spent most of her time with her parents and the Bishops, especially Christina. She'd lost touch with the few friends she'd made in university.

"I guess your dad would be upset with you if you told him you didn't want to do it."

Erin snorted. Understatement of the year. She met Christina's eyes to tell her she'd stated the obvious, but what she saw in them gave her pause. Sympathy? Or pity? "Do you want to stay for dinner?" she asked, wanting to change the subject.

"I'd like to, but I'm meeting with my designer tonight."

They headed back to the house. "What designer?"

"The one who's designing my dress for the country club ball."

"That's not for a while."

"It's never too early to plan what to wear." Christina gave her a sidelong glance. "I suppose you'll be wearing a tux again."

"I was planning on it."

"I see." Christina's tone said it all.

Erin stifled a grin.

They skirted around the house and strolled to the driveway. Dad's Porsche was there. Already back from the country club, then.

Christina pecked Erin on the cheek, then slid into the driver's seat of her Jaguar sports car. "Talk tomorrow?"

"For sure." Erin waved goodbye and watched Christina drive up the road leading to the main gate. Her mind went back to the part of their conversation about lying to Lily's group. She wished the group hadn't welcomed her, that they'd been hardasses who railed against the greedy one percent and called for the deaths of anyone with an investment account. But they were just a group of regular people trying to make the city a better place as they saw it, though why they'd go through the trouble of saving McMillan Park, she didn't understand. The site was a dump.

Guilt was still nagging at her when she went downstairs to the recreation room, where she knew she'd find her parents. Mom was there, but not Dad. "Who won?"

Mom gave her a withering look. Poor Dad. "Where's Dad?"

"Up in his office, returning a phone call." Mom was behind the bar, mixing herself a drink. "Do you want a drink?"

"Not right now."

"Where's Christina?"

"She's meeting with her dress designer tonight."

Mom didn't ask for details, but then she used a designer all the time.

"Can I ask you something?" Erin said.

"Go ahead."

"Do you think pretending I'm someone I'm not with Lily Altree's group is spying on them?"

Mom sipped her Margarita and set her glass on the bar. "Yes."

Erin gaped.

"But you're not doing anything wrong. You're not going to call the police on them, or destroy their group. You're there to find out who's shafting your father, and by extension, who's shafting me and you."

Erin hadn't thought of it like that, but it didn't completely assuage her guilt. "Still, if they knew who I am," she said, parroting Christina's words.

"But they don't. And you'll keep it that way. Your loyalty is to your father, Erin, not to them. Don't worry, sweetheart. Nothing bad will happen to them. Your father is only interested in who's betraying him."

"I guess so." She jerked her thumb over her shoulder. "I'm going to change."

She bounded up to the second floor and into her apartment suite. As she changed, she caught a glimpse of herself in the mirror. Okay, sure, Lily and her group would be horrified to know they'd sat and chatted and had coffee with one of the evil Hunts, but Erin meant them no harm. She wasn't after them. Sure, she'd drop them like a hot potato once she had the informant's name, but it wasn't as if they were best buddies. She wasn't anything to them.

A loud chime made her jump. What the hell? It sounded like a phone, but her phone didn't make that noise.

Wait. Her undercover phone. She scrambled over to her desk, pulled open the drawer, and checked the phone. A text. Erin sat on the end of her bed and read it.

It's Lily, from the protest last weekend. I need a partner for a project on Friday afternoon. You free? Text me back and I'll call you. No worries if you aren't.

Erin read the text again. Showing up for a protest or two was one thing. Doing something with Lily alone both terrified and intrigued her. She wasn't playing this game to make friends, and Christina's reframing of her undercover operation as spying had given her pause. But seeing Lily alone would be a golden opportunity, one she might not get again. She could ask questions, hopefully get a name, and her operation would be over. No harm done.

It was either that, or going to Dad's office and saying, "Sorry, Dad, I've decided not to see Altree's group again. I'm ready to come work with you."

She tapped in her reply. *Sure, I'm free. Give me a call.*

3

Erin gripped the clipboard with the petition sheets clipped to it and mentally reviewed the rules. Don't step on mall property. Don't badger anyone. Don't engage with assholes. Lily had thrust the clipboard into her hand as soon as Erin had met her on the sidewalk close to the entrance of a popular mall, and had barked the rules when Erin had told her she'd never gathered signatures before. They hadn't talked much before Lily had chosen a "prime spot." She stood several feet away from Erin now, holding her clipboard out every time someone passed by and saying, "Save McMillan Park. Sign the petition." She was taking the people approaching from the west, and Erin from the east.

Her phone, her real phone in her back pocket, not her fake undercover one, vibrated again. That was the third time since she'd left home, but it would have to wait. She couldn't juggle the clipboard and the phone, and she wanted to make a good impression, be the best little helper Lily could have, as Dad would say.

Oh, someone was coming in her direction. Mimicking Lily, she held out her clipboard, and raised her voice so she'd be heard over the sounds of the traffic rushing by. "Save McMillan Park. Sign the petition." The guy carried on past her as if she didn't exist.

Lily stepped over to her. "Most people won't sign. The petition is online too, but a lot of people won't sign online because they end up on a mailing list. And I think real signatures hold more weight. You get people from all over the world signing the online ones. Nobody cares that some guy in Australia wants to save McMillan park." She went back to her spot.

Erin had seen calls on social media to sign online petitions, but never bothered because she wasn't sure they accomplished anything. The one she held in her hand wouldn't go anywhere, either. Guilt stirred. Going to work with Dad loomed. She raised her clipboard again when two people headed her way. "Save McMillan Park. Sign the petition."

The woman kept going, but the man stopped. "What's happening with McMillan Park?"

"Someone's going to build apartments there."

He grinned. "Good. The park's a rundown piece of shit."

Erin watched his back as he walked away. The worst part: she agreed with him.

"Did I hear you say they're going to build an apartment building at McMillan Park," another man said.

Erin nodded, then tried not to appear too surprised when the guy grabbed the clipboard from her, filled in his name, address, and phone number, and signed. After he'd left, she checked to make sure he hadn't used an obviously fake name.

Twenty minutes later, she was starting to get a sense of the rhythm of successes versus failures. About one out of every twenty to twenty-five people at least stopped for more information, and most of those who did signed.

She stole a glance at Lily, who was having a discussion with someone. When Lily had called her about the project, she'd explained they were the only two available during the day. Everyone else worked or had classes. Wanting to stick to business, Erin hadn't asked why Lily was available during the day. She knew Lily worked. At the coffee shop, Maria had mentioned her taking on more shifts. Maybe she had Fridays off. Erin was determined to strike up a conversation with her when they called it quits.

"Save McMillan Park. Sign the petition," she said to a guy in a gray business suit. He stopped directly in front of her, glanced to his left, then to his right, then leaned in. "Be careful. McMillan Park isn't safe," he hissed.

Erin backed away from him. "What do you mean?"

He glanced to his left again. "UFOs. Unidentified flying objects. I've seen them land there. At night. It's the lights. Bright lights."

Was he having her on? He didn't look like he was crazy. His hair was neat, his suit was impeccable, his shoes shined. "Uh, thanks for warning me."

"You won't thank me when they come for you. Now you know. Protect yourself." He strode away.

Erin stared after him, then shook her head and focused on the woman pushing a baby stroller heading her way.

An hour and a half later, she'd filled up quite a few petition pages. She was trying to figure out whether she should consider that a success (for Lily) or a failure (for Dad) when Lily closed the distance between them.

"I think we've done enough for today," Lily said.

Erin quickly agreed. Her feet were sore, and she was tired of saying, "Save McMillan Park. Sign the petition."

Lily took the clipboard Erin offered her and flipped through the pages. "Not bad. I only have to cross out one."

"Cross out one?"

Lily pointed at a name near the top of the second page. First name *Queen*. Last name *of England*.

"That—that must have been when three people signed one after the other," Erin stammered. "I didn't have time to check."

"No worries. You did great."

A burst of warmth flooded through Erin.

"We got a bunch of signatures and nobody threatened to punch me," Lily continued. "That's a first. It's why I never do this alone."

"Has someone ever actually punched you?"

"I've been shoved a couple of times."

Erin wasn't sure what she would have done if she'd felt physically threatened. "Some guy told me McMillan Park is a hot spot for UFOs."

Lily chuckled. "Well, thanks again for showing up for this."

Erin's heart sank. She knew a "see you later" when she heard one. "Yeah, no problem." Her mind raced, trying to come up with a question that wouldn't sound odd when they were saying goodbye, but she drew a blank.

"We'll do another protest at the park soon. I'll text—"

A familiar tune played over the noise of the passing cars and trucks. Lily's face lit up. "Oh, hell, yeah. You want to go get ice cream?"

"Sure."

Lily shoved the clipboards into her backpack, slung it onto her back, and headed in the direction of the ice cream truck. Erin hurried after her. The truck had parked itself right outside the main entrance to the parking lot.

A line had already formed. "What are you going to get?" Erin asked Lily.

"A chocolate dip cone. You?"

A chocolate dip cone sounded good to her, considering she didn't know what was on offer and wouldn't want to hold up the line. This was only the second or third time she'd get ice cream from a truck like this. "The same."

"My treat."

Erin turned to her. "I can pay for my own."

"Let me pay. Consider it a thanks for coming. Seriously."

She wanted to protest again. Having someone like Lily pay for something, even an ice cream, didn't sit right. But she was undercover, so she forced a smile. "Thanks."

The line moved quickly. Erin waited while Lily ordered their cones and paid, and accepted the cone and napkin Lily handed to her, which Lily did while she was already licking some of the chocolate dip off her ice cream.

They strolled along the sidewalk. Erin didn't know where they were going, and didn't care. This was a golden opportunity to use one of the conversation openers she'd thought up on the way to the mall. "So . . . at the coffee shop, you said you're planning to go to law school?"

Lily nodded. "That's the plan."

"You want to take developers to court."

"Also the plan. How about you? What do you do?"

"I'm between jobs right now. But I'm going to work with my father. He owns his own business." One of Dad's pearls of wisdom floated into her consciousness. One that was surfacing quite a lot lately. Only lie when you have to. It'll make the times when you have to lie sound more like the truth and you'll have less to remember, so less chance to trip yourself up. "I'm not ready yet though. I told him it'll be the end of the summer, and he was cool with that." In an alternate reality, maybe.

Lily licked her cone. "You sound like me."

"In what sense?"

"I've been saying I want to go to law school for at least three years."

"Three years?" Erin couldn't help exclaiming. Lily's answer exhilarated her. "To be honest, I'm not sure I want to work with my father," she said, the words tumbling out. "I've started to read some of his business documentation, but I don't digest anything and it's to the point where just the thought of opening a document makes me want to throw up. He's in investments." Another almost truth. "Investments don't excite me."

"Then why work with him? Why not do something else?"

"I could ask you the same thing." Erin said, having sensed that Lily wasn't all that enthusiastic about law school.

"You could, but I'm asking you."

Erin ate more of the ice cream's chocolate coating. Maybe, just this once, she'd admit the truth. After all, once she found out who the informant was, she'd never see Lily again. "I don't want to let my father down. I'm a big disappointment to him already. Is it the same for you?" she quickly added, feeling exposed. She'd never said it so bluntly before, and she wasn't sure she wanted to hear Lily's thoughts on the matter. What if Lily said, "Fuck your father." What if she didn't? "Do your parents want you to go to law school?" Erin said to her.

"It has nothing to do with my parents." Lily bit into her cone and swallowed more ice cream. "I guess it's something I'm having trouble letting go of."

"You mean you wanted to go at some point, but now you don't?"

"I don't think I ever wanted to go to law school per se. I've always thought of it as a means to an end?"

"What end?"

Lily took her time answering. "I got it into my head that maybe courts could help stop developers from decimating neighbourhoods, that lawsuits would be more effective than protests and petitions. I figured I could be the lawyer, and at first the idea appealed to me. But I've realized I don't want to be a lawyer. I haven't told everyone yet, though. It's hard to reverse course when you've been saying something for a while and people are encouraging you, though I think they're starting to wonder whether I'll ever do it. I won't. It's not a good fit for me."

"What would be a good fit?" Erin asked, surprising herself. She usually didn't pepper someone she hardly knew with personal questions. When she was introduced to someone at a reception or the country club, it was, "How do you do? Pleased to meet you. Have you tried the red wine?"

Lily didn't seem to mind. "Something I don't see a path to doing.

Erin wanted to say, "What can't you do? What?" Because even though she barely knew her, she already believed Lily could do anything she set her mind to. But there was a limit to demanding answers to personal questions from an almost stranger.

"What about you?" Lily asked. "What would you rather do than investments with your father?"

"I don't know," she mumbled.

"You have no idea?"

"Nothing that would make my parents happy."

Lily stared at her. Erin faced forward and focused on finishing off her cone, aware of Lily's eyes on her and waiting for the scorn. She risked another look at her.

Lily was still staring. She pointed at Erin's mouth. "You have a little chocolate, just below your mouth there."

Erin dabbed at her chin in the area Lily seemed to be pointing to.

"A little to the left," Lily said.

She tried again.

Lily moved closer and lifted her napkin. "Uh, let me . . ." She dabbed at Erin's chin. "Got it."

Their eyes met. Blood rushed to Erin's cheeks at the same time Lily's face turned a deep red.

Lily stepped back, cleared her throat. "I'm thinking we'll protest again next weekend, maybe at the north gate this time," she said briskly.

"Sounds good," Erin said, even though she couldn't care less about protesting. She wanted to get more chocolate on her chin so Lily could dab it off and—uh-uh. Nope. Guy in the red convertible, plus Lily was taken, and so was she. And if that wasn't enough, she wasn't here to socialize and gaze into anyone's bright brown eyes. She was here to find out who was betraying Dad. It was time to take a risk. "I searched for information about Hunt and Bishop and McMillan Park, but I couldn't find any."

"That's because the damn media is in the developers' pockets. We're lucky if we get three lines in the last page of the newspaper. The TV news people don't cover us at all."

"I meant I couldn't find any connection between Hunt and Bishop and the park, anywhere. No official announcements, nothing. I checked city hall, I checked Hunt and Bishop's information section. I wanted to learn more about it, but there's nothing online. How did you find out Hunt and Bishop is planning to build an apartment there?" Erin held her breath.

Lily stopped walking and turned to face her, making a passing pedestrian give her a dirty look. "I'm going to trust you, okay. You can't tell anyone outside the group."

Trying not to appear too interested, Erin nodded.

"I got an email from someone telling me about Hunt and Bishop's intention to purchase the land, build the apartment, everything."

The obvious question popped into Erin's head, the one with the answer that would make Dad happy. But she hesitated, for a really dumb reason. Once she had a name, she'd have no reason to see Lily, someone she'd known for all of five minutes and who'd hate her if she knew the truth. Just because they were both having problems getting their working lives on track and Lily was easy to talk to and was cute, to boot, was no reason to imagine they could ever be friends. Erin needed to get a grip and remember why she was here. Whatever desire she felt to be with Lily would pass.

"Who sent you the email?" Once again, she tried not to appear as if the answer meant everything.

Lily swallowed the last of her cone. "I have no idea."

Erin blinked at her, glad she'd already finished her cone, or she might have dropped it.

"It's someone who calls himself—or herself—White Knight. The email came out of the blue. I even wondered if it was spam, but it went to my Inbox and the subject line was intriguing. Hunt and Bishop are buying McMillan Park. I couldn't resist opening that, right?"

Erin found her voice. "You have no idea who it is?"

"Nope. Maybe someone at city hall."

Dad would prefer that answer over it being one of his people.

"I hope they keep emailing me."

"Didn't you wonder if the information is true? They could have been feeding you a lie."

"Why would someone do that?"

"I don't know, to make you look bad," Erin said, genuinely concerned.

"It's the sort of thing Hunt and Bishop does. They swoop in, buy land that has been miraculously rezoned for apartments or condos or a housing subdivision, and build, giving zero shits about how it affects the neighbourhood or anything else. If it turns out to be false information, no harm done really because our opposition never gets any media coverage. But you can bet the moment the land purchase goes through, there will be glowing news reports about it."

Well, Dad did know the owners of the two local newspapers and the heads of the local TV stations. Perhaps Lily didn't appreciate that her small group didn't merit the attention of the local media. It wasn't as if thousands of people were marching in protest against Dad's projects.

"You need to make more noise," she said, feeling a bit strange. She shouldn't be helping Lily fight Dad.

"Easier said than done. There are too many other causes higher on people's priority lists."

Erin didn't know what to say to that, because it was true.

The silence stretched out. "I should get going," Lily said. "I have to work tonight."

"What do you do?"

"I wait tables at the Golden Goose."

"The restaurant on Drummond?" Erin had driven by it a few times.

"Yeah. Do you need a ride anywhere?"

Lily's offer surprised Erin. She hadn't offered earlier, before the ice cream truck had shown up. "Thanks, but no. I'm in the mood to stroll for a bit." Disappointment stabbed through her, but her car was waiting for her in a parking lot not too far away. "I'll walk back with you to your car, though."

As they strolled along the sidewalk—they'd been walking around the block, Erin realized—

she felt compelled to fill the silence, even though it wasn't uncomfortable. Like an idiot, she said the first thing that sprang into her mind. "It must be difficult for you and Sandy, with her working days and you working nights."

"Why would it be difficult?"

She wanted to kick herself. Of all the things she could have blurted out. "Well, uh, you know, it means you don't get to see each other much, and, uh, I imagine . . ."

Lily slowed down and turned to look at her.

Erin continued to flail. Her brain seemed to have abandoned her and her mouth wasn't cooperating either. "I mean, uh . . ." She trailed off when Lily laughed. "What?"

"You think we're a couple. Me and Sandy."

"No, I mean, maybe. Yes. I don't know."

Lily's eyes danced. "Sandy's going to love this when I tell her."

"You don't have to tell her."

"Are you kidding? Of course I have to tell her. She'll get a chuckle out of it." Lily paused. "Sandy and I are close, but not that way. We've known each other since elementary school."

They weren't a couple, then. Erin tried to ignore the elation that managed to burst forth, even though she felt mortified. "I'm so sorry. I don't even know why I asked. It's none of my business."

Lily dismissed her apology with a wave of her hand. "I like that you just brought it up in conversation, like you would if Sandy was a guy. She's straight by the way. Sandy."

Erin still wasn't sure her gaydar was right about Lily, and she certainly wasn't going to ask now.

"Your assumption about me is right, though," Lily said, answering Erin's unsaid question. "I'd say I bat for the other team." She quirked a brow. "But I'm guessing we're on the same team. Am I right?"

"Yeah," Erin said, a little taken aback by Lily's bluntness.

Lily nodded. "Glad we got that out of the way. And just as we reached the car. Good timing." She tossed her backpack into the back seat and opened the driver-side door. "I'll text you when I know what our next move is. Probably another protest, like I said. Have a good one." She climbed into the car, fired up the engine, and drove away.

Erin watched the receding car until she couldn't see it anymore. She set out in the direction of the parking lot where her Mercedes waited for her. Lily didn't know the identity of the informant, which would not please Dad. Erin should be disappointed too, but she wasn't. For the first time in her life, not feeling disappointed made her uncomfortable. She felt even more uncomfortable when she checked her phone and listened to the two voicemails Christina had left.

4

Eᴙɪɴ ʀᴇʟᴀxᴇᴅ ɪɴ ᴀ poolside lounge chair and waited for Dad to finish swimming his laps. She'd walked through the house and outside to the pool area with a spring in her step, even though she still didn't have a name for the informant. At least she had some new information. Too many meetings with Lily and her group without progress would lead to only one destination: taking her place at Dad's side at Hunt and Bishop. Unfortunately, handing Dad the identity of the informant would lead to the same place, but at least she would have succeeded in his eyes for once.

Dad pulled himself out of the pool and accepted the towel Michael handed him. He padded over to Erin and dried his face. "How'd it go?"

"We got quite a few signatures."

He scowled down at her and patted his chest with the towel.

"I made a tiny bit of progress."

"Spit it out."

"The informant contacted her by email and calls himself White Knight. But she doesn't know who it is."

"Shit. And White fucking Knight. What an asshole!"

"I guess he sees himself as doing good."

"He'll have plenty of time to do good when I find out who it is and fire his ass."

"Lily thinks it could be someone at city hall."

"One thing we agree on."

Maybe the only thing. "He probably got her email address off her website."

Dad grunted. "You have to get me one of those emails."

"She's only gotten one so far, telling her about McMillan Park."

"So get that one."

"Why?"

"Pete in IT might be able to figure out who sent it. Something about an IP address. He talked to me about it once, but I only half listened."

Like when Dad talked to her about Hunt and Bishop. Erin sighed, for two reasons. "I'll try, but I can't exactly say, 'Hey, Lily, forward me your email.' I'll have to earn more of her trust before that happens."

"Then earn more of her trust. I'm sure she'll keep trying to shut down the park project."

Erin nodded. "She's planning another protest."

Dad snorted. "Good. Let her keep spinning her wheels." He handed the towel to Michael, who'd stood at a discreet distance. "We're going to the club for dinner. You want to come?"

Normally Erin would agree, but dinner at the country club led to other activities and a late night home. She'd try to bow out early, but Mom would persuade her to stay. "It's a clear sky tonight, and a new moon."

"Meaning what? You're going to spend all night on your balcony? I don't understand what you see up there. It's the same old sky."

"But it's not. The stars you can see change depending on the date. I can show you photos," she said eagerly.

Dad was already on his way into the house. "Some other time. I have to change. I'll let your mother know you're not coming."

Michael peered down at her. "What would you like for dinner?"

Her shoulders slumped. "Pasta, I guess."

"I'll do your favourite." He strode into the house.

She stared at the still pool water glistening in the late afternoon sun. Hanging out with Lily's group was one thing. Manipulating Lily into forwarding her an email from White Knight was another. When she'd agreed to go undercover for Dad, she'd created Erin Bartlett, average woman on the street. Fake name, stick to the truth most of the time, wear jeans and sneakers, don't show up in her Mercedes, leave the Rolex at home. She'd thought she'd covered every contingency. But she'd missed one when it came to meeting Lily Altree. She hadn't expected to like her.

~

AT TABLE NUMBER SEVEN, Lily gathered the dirty glasses and plates onto the tray she deftly held and carried them into the kitchen. Time for her break. She left through the back entrance into a burst of warm air, which felt hotter than it was because she'd spent all night in the air-conditioned restaurant.

She wasn't alone in the back alley. She moved away from the smokers on break from the hotel next door and checked her phone, which had vibrated a couple of times as she'd served drinks and meals. Sandy, but she hadn't left a message. Lily called her, in case something was up.

"So how'd it go today with the newbie?" Sandy asked cheerfully after they'd exchanged greetings and Lily had reminded her she was on break and didn't have much time to talk.

"Fine. We gathered a decent amount of signatures."

"You did, or she helped too?"

"No, she actually helped. She wasn't like that other woman who showed up a couple of months ago in her dress and stilettos and lasted all of five minutes before she took off." In fact, Erin had impressed her. She'd stood for almost two hours without complaining once. Just got down to business and did what needed to be done. She was earnest, and came across a little . . . innocent wasn't the word. Sheltered, maybe, but that didn't quite capture it either. Whatever it was, Lily felt comfortable with her, enough to not brush off personal questions.

"She thought we were a couple," she said to Sandy, then smiled when Sandy snorted and giggled.

"You know what I always say. If I was gay, we probably would be."

Lily chuckled, going along with her like she usually did, even though she didn't think it was true. She loved Sandy, truly she did. But there was no attraction there, maybe because she knew Sandy was off limits and she would never do anything to threaten their friendship. But she didn't think so. They just didn't have any chemistry. And they were too alike in too many ways. They'd drive each other crazy.

"Is she gay?" Sandy asked. "I thought she might be, but my guesses are never as good as yours."

Lily inwardly sighed. If she could keep Erin's sexual orientation out of it, she would. "Yeah."

Sandy shrieked. "Ask her out."

"No! Do you ask out every straight guy?"

"I ask the cute ones. Come on. You haven't dated anyone in a while."

"I'm happy being single, okay?"

"You don't have to marry her. Just have a fling."

She wasn't the fling type. Sometimes she wished she was.

"I know, I know, you won't. And if there's no attraction there, then I agree, there's no point. I'm just teasing." Sandy gasped. "Unless you do like her that way."

She hesitated. "I don't." Erin was pleasant to look at, yes. She was easy to talk to. Lily wouldn't mind seeing her again. But attracted to her? Nah. Nope. Uh-uh.

"Oh, well. You'll run into someone who'll make you forget about how happy you are being single."

"Or maybe I'll always be happy being single. It's not a disease." Lily checked the time. "Anyway, I have to go. I want to check my email before I go in."

"Just a second."

"What?"

Sandy didn't reply right away, and Lily could tell her phone was no longer at her ear. "I just looked her up online," Sandy finally said.

"Who?"

"Erin. Bartlett, right? There's nothing that matches her. No social media, nothing. I mean, sure, I've found stuff for Erin Bartlett, but none of them are her."

"Maybe she doesn't use her real name for her profiles, or only her first name or something. Maybe she's a Luddite. I have accounts at most places, but I don't go on very often."

"Yeah, but you're weird."

"Maybe she's weird too. Anyway, I have to go. Call me tomorrow."

They disconnected. Erin's lack of presence on social media didn't concern Lily at all. Like she'd told Sandy, she had accounts, but she rarely checked them. Too busy, and she wasn't interested in everyone's fake wonderful lives. She'd soured on social media when she'd spent an afternoon practically talking a university friend out of committing suicide, then seen the same friend on social media that night, posting a photo of herself "having a blast at the beach" with another friend. All smiles, all "look at my wonderful life." The suicide crisis hadn't been fake, but the post that evening certainly was.

Last she'd heard, the friend was still alive and kicking. Or rather, former friend. Lily hadn't hung out with her much after that afternoon. If there was one thing she hated, it was people who cared more about what everyone else thought about them than they did about themselves. And fake crap. She could not abide dishonesty about the important stuff.

Hoping Sandy wouldn't ask Erin about her online presence, Lily switched to her email. Adrenaline shot through her when she saw a new one from White Knight. She opened it and skimmed the short paragraph, then read it again.

Holy crap.

They'd sent documents. Actual internal documents. The rezoning application that had been approved, the purchase agreement waiting to be signed, and the architectural drawings for the apartment building. This was a gold mine.

Who was White Knight? She wished they'd contact her directly so they could work together, but she'd take what she could get. She hadn't planned on going to the upcoming council meeting, since it would just be the usual rigged charade that would end with everything rubber stamped. But now that she had these documents, she could show up prepared. Hunt and Bishop would prevail in the end like it always did, but she'd make them work for their fucking victory.

~

A COUPLE OF BLOCKS away from McMillan Park, Erin paid her cab fare and included a generous tip. She hopped out of the cab, turned the corner onto Dorchester Street, and strolled to the park's south gate. The protest a couple of weeks ago had taken place here. Lily's group would gather at the north gate today, and Erin would be among them, holding a sign and chanting the chant, but she wanted to walk through the park first, hoping to get more of a sense of what Lily and the others wanted to save beyond her glimpse through the iron fence last time.

She took a few steps into McMillan Park and surveyed her surroundings. The patchy grass desperately needed a drink. Dead trees towered into the sky along with those still alive. Two swings belonging to the swing set closest to her were dangling from one chain, and the plastic bars had seen better days. Erin walked along the pockmarked cement path with weeds poking through the cracks. One of the sides of the sandbox to her left was threatening to topple over, and the sand appeared dirty. The merry-go-round groaned as two children around ten years old struggled to get it moving.

The seesaws were a mess. One of the three seesaws had detached from the support frame and lay next to it. If Erin brought kids here, she'd force them to wear protective gear. Why would Lily bother saving this place? Green space? This was more like brown space. Was it a matter of principle and it didn't matter what was here as long as it wasn't something from Hunt and Bishop or another developer?

The park and equipment didn't improve as she progressed toward the north gate. She arrived there as baffled as when she'd entered by the south, but it was time to pretend she wanted this park to survive. This time, Lily was already here, but at the end of the line the group had formed just inside the inner edge of the sidewalk. Erin had figured out that Lily took that position because people were more likely to stop and talk to a person at the end than with someone in the middle, faced with multiple protestors.

"Hey," Sandy said, waving to her from next to Lily. Patrick also said hi and pointed to several signs propped up against the fence. Erin grabbed one. *Not Another Apartment.* Not a great slogan. The sign underneath the one she'd taken said *Parks are for kids, not pigs.* With clenched teeth, she joined the line and hoisted her sign above her head. "Save McMillan Park. Save McMillan Park."

A couple of hours later, she joined the group for coffee after an unremarkable protest. This time nobody had yelled in Lily's face, but nobody had seemed all that interested either, except for a couple of mothers with their children who'd stopped to talk to Lily and given the group the thumbs up. Erin had also noticed that only eight people had shown up today, including herself. She should be pleased for Dad, but she kind of felt bad for Lily. What was the harm in a protest, especially when it wouldn't change anything? Then again, if thirty or forty people had shown up and more people had stopped to chat, or honked their horns as they drove by, she'd be worried for Dad.

She ordered the same old regular coffee and sat in one of the remaining vacant seats, disappointed that Sandy and Maria were flanking Lily. Curiosity quickly replaced her disappointment when she tuned in to the ongoing conversation.

". . . will help at the council meeting," Lily was saying. "I wasn't going to go until the documents arrived."

"I wonder who sent them to you," Patrick murmured.

"Someone who wants to help, obviously."

"What documents?" Erin said.

Her heart jumped when Lily met her eyes. "Sorry, I guess we started this while you were getting your coffee. I heard from our informant again. This time they sent documents. The rezoning application. The tentative purchase agreement for the park. Drawings of the apartments Hunt and Bishop plans to build."

Erin clutched her coffee tighter and consciously controlled her breathing. "Are you sure they're legit?" she said evenly.

"They look legit."

If they were the real deal, Dad would freak. Erin wanted to ask if she could see them, but she didn't want to appear too interested. "I didn't think the public were allowed to speak at council meetings." She'd observed a few with Dad.

"We can't," Lily said. "But there's usually a local reporter there, and I can always hold a sign. I want to go over the documents with a fine-toothed comb, see if there's anything juicy to latch onto that would make for a good sound bite or quote."

"Two sets of eyes would help," Sandy said. "Two perspectives, and you can go through the documents faster." When Lily nodded, she continued. "Erin seems really interested. Why don't you go through the documents together?"

Erin's face flushed when Lily turned to Sandy and glared at her, but she seized the opportunity Sandy had given her. "Sure, I'd like to help."

"Perfect," Sandy said.

Lily didn't look like she thought it was perfect. Erin wasn't surprised. Lily came across as an independent woman who liked to do things herself and wouldn't appreciate being told she needed help. But Erin wouldn't offer to bow out. She needed to see those documents.

"Anyone else want to help?" Lily asked. Erin could hear the sigh in her voice.

"Two should be enough," Sandy said. "Too many and you'll be stepping on each other's toes. And you two seem the most interested."

Lily's gaze took in the group, but nobody else volunteered. "Okay. Erin and I will work on it."

Erin wanted to whoop, but she gulped down some coffee. Hopefully Dad wouldn't shoot the messenger. She wouldn't tell him until after she'd had a look at the documents.

The rest of the conversation was one huge round of small talk. When it was dwindling, Lily got up to throw her coffee cup into the recycling bin and motioned for Erin to join her. "You don't have to help if you don't want to," she said. "Sandy shouldn't have volunteered you like that."

"I'd like to help. Unless you really don't want me to," she added, knowing it was risky, but not wanting to antagonize Lily by forcing herself on her. She'd figure out another way to get a look at the documents.

Lily hesitated a beat. "I shouldn't turn down help when it's offered. Did you notice the smaller crowd today? I like your enthusiasm."

Erin ignored the guilt snaking through her and smiled.

"I'm not working on Thursday. Are you free then?"

"Yep."

"Why don't you come to my place? I have some errands to run in the afternoon, though, and I don't want a late night. I'm covering for someone Friday morning." She frowned in thought. "Come for dinner."

"Sure."

"What do you like to eat? What's your favourite food?"

Erin didn't have to think about it. "Italian."

"Any allergies?"

"No." She wondered if Lily would cook or order takeout.

They arranged for Erin to show up around 5:30 and returned to the others. The group was breaking up. Erin said goodbye to everyone and left with Lily's address in her phone. Okay. Things were progressing, but once Dad found out about the documents, he'd really want her to get an email. White Knight better have a plan for what would happen when Dad came after them.

With an extra spring in her step, she strode to where she felt she could safely climb into a cab. She was having dinner with Lily! To look at the documents, of course. It would be a working dinner. Still, she'd give some thought about what wine to bring. It couldn't be a bottle from the wine cellar because if Lily looked it up, she'd wonder why Erin had brought a two-hundred-dollar bottle, but she didn't want to show up with something cheap. She wanted the dinner to go well. For her undercover operation, of course.

~

"Perfect timing," Christina said, when Erin walked into what Christina called her pamper room at the Bishop residence. A few crumpled white towels were piled in the hamper, new age music played from the in-wall speakers, and the scent of sage incense wrinkled Erin's nose. She'd always declined Christina's invitations to join her for a spa afternoon, to the point that Christina had stopped asking. She perched on the edge of the chair that Christina's manicurist had just left. Erin had passed her in the hallway.

Christina lounged back in the chaise, held out her left hand to Erin, and wiggled her fingers. "What do you think?"

Erin peered down at the painted nails. "Green. I like it."

"Not green. Emerald."

Exactly. Green. But then Erin failed when it came to makeup, jewelry, nail polish, and anything else considered feminine. She wore her Rolex and sometimes gold studs in her ears, and that was it.

Christina's eyes slid shut. "How goes the investigation?"

"The inv—oh, you mean for Dad. Lily Altree's group. It's going."

"What does that mean? Are you still trying to figure out who White Knight is?"

When she'd had dinner with Christina before the last protest, Erin had told her about White Knight. "Yeah."

"What's the end game?"

"I guess Dad will deal with whoever it is," Erin drawled.

"No, when will your role in it be done? I know he wants a name. How is he expecting you to get one when Lily Altree doesn't even know it?"

"Right now, he wants an email from the informant, so I'm hoping Lily will forward one to me soon."

"What's an email going to do?"

Erin recalled the conversation with Dad about that very subject. "If we get one, he can pass it along to IT and they can figure out where it was sent from, and maybe even pinpoint it to a specific person."

Christina cracked an eye open. "They probably weren't dumb enough to use their own computer. In the movies, they always use some other computer to send dodgy emails, not their own."

She hadn't considered that and was sure Dad hadn't, either. "Even if we can narrow it down to a city block or something, we might be able to figure out who it is."

"They might have used their phone."

True, meaning the person could have sent the email from anywhere. Suddenly Dad's plan wasn't looking so great. "Well, that's my goal right now. Getting an email. I'm hoping she trusts me enough to forward me one."

"Lily?"

"Yeah. I'm seeing her again on Thursday, having dinner with her. I have to keep seeing her to gain her trust."

"And you don't feel the least bit guilty about that?"

Erin swallowed. "No."

Christina opened both her eyes and locked them on Erin's face. "You're not your father."

She withered under Christina's scrutiny. "Maybe a little."

Christina continued to stare at her, then shifted her attention to the ceiling and closed her eyes again. "Did you know my dad wanted to build affordable housing on that site?"

"Where, the park?"

"Uh-huh. Your dad shot him down. Wouldn't even listen or look at the proposal my dad had drawn up. Aaron does that with everything my father proposes lately. He treats him like his bitch."

"No, he doesn't," Erin reflexively said. Then she realized she hadn't seen Royce much lately. He and his wife had used to come over every once in a while, meet up with Mom and Dad at the country club, hang with them at receptions. But not lately. When had that happened?

"Choosing the projects has always been my dad's domain," she said to Christina.

"Choosing the projects has been your dad's domain lately. My dad has always proposed projects, and your dad even agreed to build a few of them. But he hasn't lately. My dad always offers input on your dad's projects. Your dad used to listen, but he doesn't anymore. It's as if he owns the company and my dad works for him."

"Your dad is the behind-the-scenes wizard. The one who executes the plan."

"That doesn't mean none of his ideas are good."

"I know that. I'm just saying that's the way they've always—usually—worked things."

Silence, then, "That's one way to spin it, I guess."

Erin recognized Christina's tone. "Let's not be irritated with each other because of what our fathers do. The sins of the fathers aren't the sins of the sons, or daughters, or something like that."

"You're right. It's just that Dad seems more irritated about things lately."

Dad had mentioned something similar about Royce. Erin hoped there wasn't a chasm developing between the two partners. Their two dads had worked well together for almost thirty years and completed some amazing projects. "We can't do anything about it. It's up to them to sort it out."

"As long as a family feud doesn't develop. We'd be caught in the middle."

Erin chuckled. "I doubt things will get that bad."

"They're already bad, Erin. We have to hope they don't get worse." Christina opened her eyes again and studied her nails, then sat up and twisted to face Erin. "You said you're seeing Lily on Thursday?"

She nodded.

"Then I might give Julia a call, see if she wants to see a movie."

"Good idea." Julia was a mutual friend of theirs, straight, moved in the same social circle.

"Dinner on Saturday, then?"

"Sure." Erin hesitated. "In a couple of weeks, I want to go see an exhibit at a gallery downtown."

Christina's face brightened. "Who's the artist?"

"It's not art. Not exactly. It's an astrophotography exhibit. Members of a local club—" the club she wished she had the courage to join "—are showing their photos, along with a pretty well-known photographer. He's sent a few of his photos to be exhibited."

Now Christina's face scrunched up. "I'll pass. That's more your thing, like this," she waved her nails under Erin's nose, "is more my thing. If I go, I'll just be bored, and you'll sense it."

"That's okay. I'll go alone." Again.

"I think it's time for a drink. Should we have one here or go out?"

"Whatever you like."

"Let's go out. I feel like stretching my legs. I'll go change."

Erin followed her from the pamper room but went downstairs to wait for her in the living room. Knowing Christina, she might have a long wait. She used the time to think of more questions she could ask Lily, so they wouldn't be sitting in awkward silence over dinner.

Her stomach clenched. Maybe she should call Lily and cancel. Showing up for protests was one thing. Sharing a meal with her was another, especially at her home. But Erin had already mentioned the dinner to Dad. He'd kill her if she cancelled. She needed an email, that was all. Once she had one and they'd uncovered the identity of White Knight, she'd drop from Lily's life. No harm done. Nobody hurt.

You're not your father.

Erin's shoulders sagged and she shrank in on herself. No. No, she wasn't.

5

Erin strode along the carpeted hallway to apartment 407, stepped inside, and waited for Lily to close the door. The aroma of baking lasagna filled her nostrils, making her mouth water. She held out the bottle of white wine she'd brought. "Here."

"Thanks," Lily murmured. She held the bottle out and read the label. "Haven't tried this one."

"It's pleasant." She'd spent too much time at the liquor store, until she'd finally recognized the label of a bottle her parents had ordered at a restaurant once. Not cheap, not expensive, and she didn't remember spitting it out.

"Have a seat. I'll open the wine."

The small entryway led straight into the living room. Erin sauntered over to the nearest bookcase and read the titles. Sci-fi, a little fantasy, and a few mysteries. Sci-fi movies. She approved. And she was sensing a theme. A couple of sci-fi movie posters hung on the walls, and another bookcase, a shorter one, contained a shelf of sci-fi action figures along with more books.

"Wine?" Lily shouted from the kitchen.

"Please." She examined an action figure from one of her favourite sci-fi shows but didn't touch it. She wouldn't touch it without permission.

Lily bustled into the living room. "Yeah, I'm an unabashed nerd," she said, handing Erin a wine glass.

"I think it's cool." She pointed at one of the figures. "What did you think of the episode when aliens stole his memory and he had to reconstruct it from the fragments he won in the arena?"

Lily nodded enthusiastically. "Loved that one." She motioned for Erin to sit down on the sofa and sat across from her in an armchair that had seen better days. "I wish they hadn't cancelled the series, and what did they put on instead? Some reality show."

Erin groaned. "I know, I know." She sipped her wine, then looked for somewhere to set her glass down but there was no coffee table or anywhere else to place her glass, except for the small square table with two chairs on either side of it near the window. A combination living room, dining room. Erin's bedroom was larger than this, but Lily's place was cozy.

She held on to her wine. "What are you streaming now?" She nodded at the shows Lily reeled off, having seen all of them except one, which she made a mental note to add to her list.

Before she knew it, twenty minutes had flown by. Worried about awkward silences, she'd come prepared with a list of questions and conversation starters, but hadn't needed a single one.

"Let me get the garlic bread going." Lily set her wine on the table. "Oh, shit, you've been holding your wine this entire time. Sorry. I have a little foldup table I use when people come over. I'll get it."

"It's fine," Erin said. "It's not heavy."

"No, I'll get it. We need something to put the documents on."

A minute later, she set up what appeared to be a folding games table and slapped a handful of papers onto it. "The documents. I printed them off."

"Have you read them?"

"I glanced at them when the email arrived. I've been working, and I figured I'd wait for you."

The woman confounded her. Erin would have thought she'd be eager to see whatever was inside. After all, making life difficult for companies like Hunt and Bishop was her life.

As soon as Lily went into the kitchen, Erin pulled the documents closer to her and spread them out on the table. She stifled a gasp. One of the architectural drawings for the apartment Dad planned to build at the park site. Her eyes went to the other documents. Proposal for the Rezoning of McMillan Park and Impact Analysis on the Iron Court Neighbourhood. The signatures, the seal on the drawing . . . Erin had seen enough of these documents in passing that in her opinion, they were genuine.

Lily returned and dragged the armchair over to the games table. She surveyed the documents, then pointed at the impact analysis and barked a laugh. "Impact analysis. Like they give a crap."

Erin was still reeling from seeing the ultra-sensitive documents sitting on Lily's table. This was serious stuff few people would know about at this stage. Dad was going to freak. "They just arrived by email?"

Lily nodded.

"White Knight again?"

"Yep."

More like a knight of the apocalypse as far as Dad would be concerned. But just seeing these documents narrowed down the list of possible traitors. Erin wanted the email too, but she didn't want to raise Lily's suspicions by asking for it right now. "Dumb question, but how will these help you at the council meeting?"

"They'll help when I talk to the reporter." She pointed at the drawing, which was tiny because it had been shrunk, but still readable. "When I say it's a 20-storey building, I'll mean it. When I say it'll have an underground parking garage that's going to make the traffic on Dorchester Street even worse, I can wave this in his face. And I'm sure we'll find something in the impact analysis, because I doubt they did one."

Erin was fairly certain Hunt and Bishop had done one, though the document would spin everything in its favour. "Why not just call the media, then?"

Lily gave her an indulgent smile. "Like I haven't tried. They ignore my calls. No matter. A photo of me inside the council chamber holding a sign will be great, and better than me talking at the meeting."

"Which you can't do anyway."

"Right. Doesn't matter. People won't be there to listen, and they're more likely to look at a photo than read an article." She flipped over the title page on the impact analysis. "I wonder what it says about the traffic."

While Lily read the analysis, Erin studied the drawing. She couldn't deny that she was mystified about why Lily and her group wanted to save the park. Okay, traffic, yes. Maybe the streets around the apartment would become more congested. But the plan included an area of green space anyone could use. It said so right here in the rezoning application. Erin would bet the new garden area would be better maintained than the park. Unless the city had thrown a ton of funding at it, which it obviously hadn't been interested in doing because it had sold the land, there would always have been tired old swings with tired old seesaws, sandboxes with decaying borders, patchy grass, and rust. Lots of rust. Maybe it had been neglected because the city had wanted to sell it for a while.

A bell dinged. Lily leaped to her feet. "That's my cue."

Erin sipped her wine, the only one she'd drink tonight because she'd driven here in her own car. If Lily asked for some reason, she'd taken the bus. The car was parked around the corner, near a bus stop.

Lily carried in a basket of garlic bread and set it on the table. She swept her arm toward it. "Dinner is almost served. Have a seat."

Erin moved her wine to her place. Feeling a bit warm, she was in the middle of removing her blazer when Lily deftly set two plates of lasagna on the table.

Lily straightened, then theatrically did a double take. "So the blazers do come off. I was wondering."

Chuckling, Erin threw her blazer around the back of her chair. She'd worn one of her favourite blouses underneath, one that bolstered her confidence.

"Sit, sit." Lily pulled out her own chair.

Now seated, Erin surveyed the table, which was impeccably set. Of course, Lily was a waitress at a decent restaurant. Her meal was also presented well: baked lasagna garnished with parsley, gooey garlic bread. Her mouth watered again.

"So how many blazers do you have, anyway?"

Her mind flashed to her walk-in closet with the row of blazers taking up one side of it. "A few." She unfolded her napkin.

"I shouldn't talk. I pretty much wear the same thing most of the time."

Jeans, blouse, sneakers. Erin had noticed. She took a bite of her lasagna, chewed, and had to think fast to stop herself from giving away her identity. "This is fantastic," she said, after swallowing. It tasted as good as Michael's, which was a wonderful compliment, one she wished she could give to Lily. "It's as good as the lasagna I've had in fancy restaurants," she said instead. Not quite the same as saying, "This is as good as the lasagna a world-class chef has prepared for me," but it would have to do.

"Thanks. I'm glad you like it. I really enjoy cooking. I try to make myself a decent meal when I can. Avoid the processed stuff."

"My cooking skills cover how to press the right buttons on a microwave."

Lily covered her mouth and snickered. "It's a lost art. People are too busy, in too much of a hurry. I don't cook as much as I'd like to."

They made small talk through the rest of the meal, picking up their conversation about TV shows, movies, and books. Their opinions about something they'd seen or read usually, but not always, matched. When Lily cleared away their empty plates and brought in dessert—chocolate cake—Erin marvelled at how comfortable she was sitting at this table, chatting with Lily Altree, something she never would have imagined doing in a million years.

But things might start to get uncomfortable now. Erin needed to steer the conversation back to parks, developers, Hunt and Bishop. "Why did you get involved in what developers are doing around the city?" she asked, genuinely interested.

Lily gulped down a piece of cake and dabbed at her mouth with her napkin. "When I was in university, I was interested in someone and followed her around like a puppy dog. It makes me cringe looking back. I'd never do something like that now. But I wanted her to like me so I did everything she did, including protesting against real estate developments that didn't make sense. I eventually got it through my thick head that the chances of us dating were about the chances of me winning the lottery. But by then, I was interested in the cause. So I kept with it."

"What happened to the woman you were interested in?"

"I don't know. It was one of those times when someone drifts out of your life and you hardly notice. It was just a crush. A major crush, but it burned itself out pretty quickly."

"Do you push back on all developments?" Erin forked a piece of cake into her mouth.

"No. It wouldn't be possible, and I'm not anti-development. I only go after the ones that stink."

"Like McMillan Park."

"Yeah, like McMillan Park."

Erin chewed on another piece of the delicious cake, taking the time to choose her words carefully. "Apart from the traffic, what stinks about McMillan Park? I'll be honest. I hadn't seen it before I showed up for the protest. It seems a little . . ."

"Run down? Past its due date? An eyesore? Yeah."

Okay, now she was really confused.

"It doesn't mean an apartment should go there." Lily set down her fork. "McMillan Park is the only green space for blocks, the only place mothers can take their children to play outside or people can go to relax on a bench. The city should be fixing it up, not selling it, but when they need to find money in the budget, the Iron Court neighbourhood is the first place they take it from. The seesaws are the same ones I played on fifteen years ago."

"You used to live in the area."

Lily nodded. "Until I was about twelve. Lived in one of the buildings right next door. After that, we moved to the Prince Court area."

Prince Court was a lower middle-class neighbourhood. Dad had said so when he'd taken her to see one of his finished condo developments last year as part of his effort to excite her about the business.

"Are you free Sunday afternoon?" Lily asked.

"What?"

"You know. Available."

"I think so."

"Then let's visit the park. Let me show you what I see. I'll pick you up."

This undercover thing was becoming more difficult. "I have something going on in the early afternoon, so I'll meet you there. Around three?"

"Sure."

The conversation returned to safer topics, much to Erin's relief. She helped Lily clear the table, then followed her into the living room.

"All right." Lily clapped her hands. "Let's go through everything again with a fine-toothed comb. I want a few facts to tell the reporter. And something punchy to go on my sign."

"Sounds like a plan." Erin paused. "I'd go with you to the meeting, but unfortunately I'm busy that night." There was no way she could show her face at a council meeting. Too many there would recognize her, including the mayor.

"That's okay. I'm just going to sit and hold a sign."

They pored over the documents and made notes. Dad would be pleased. Erin had never read any of his business documents in such detail. He wouldn't be pleased that they would have put her to sleep if she'd been alone.

"The offer is generous," Lily said, when they were finished. "The city will take it. It's a rubber stamp job now for the council."

"But you'll still show up with your sign."

"Hell, yeah. I'll still show up with my damn sign."

Now Dad would kill her, because Erin wouldn't mind if Lily swayed the council to change its mind. Lily wouldn't. She didn't stand a chance. And that was why Erin's breath caught in her throat. Lily knew it, knew it was futile. But she'd go down fighting. Erin rarely thought of anything or anyone as noble, but that was the word that came to mind.

The conversation and evening had hit its natural end. Erin slipped on her blazer. "Thanks so much for dinner. It was lovely. I mean it. You're a talented cook."

A smile spread across Lily's face. "No problem. Thanks for looking over the documents with me."

"I don't think I helped much. You could have dealt with them on your own."

"I think Sandy's trying to set us up. That's why she suggested you come and help me out."

Erin managed to clamp her mouth shut but couldn't stop her brows from shooting up.

Lily chuckled. "Sorry to be blunt, but I value honesty. And she might keep trying, so I figured you should know."

"Thanks for the warning." *I value honesty.* The reason Erin felt like shit right now, especially given what she was about to say. "I wouldn't mind giving the documents another read. I don't suppose you'd forward the email to me?"

"Sure." Lily plucked her phone from the table. "What's your email address?"

Erin reeled off the account she'd created for her undercover persona. Lily tapped her phone a few times. "You should have it."

"Thanks." She confirmed it was there, then said goodnight. As she strolled to her car, she tried to rally herself. Success! She had the email. If it revealed the identity of White Knight, her role as Erin Bartlett was over. No more protests. No more gathering signatures. No more strategizing.

No more seeing Lily.

~

HALF AN HOUR LATER, Dad peered at the email on Erin's undercover phone. "I don't believe this. It's fucking insane!" He kicked one of the bar stools in the recreation room, toppling it over.

For a moment, Erin thought he was going to throw her phone across the room. She made a calming motion with her hands. "Put the phone down slowly, Dad. Put it down slowly."

He scowled, but set the phone on the bar. Mom moved it out of his reach and began mixing a drink.

Dad balled his fists. "Nobody knows about these documents. Nobody."

"I thought we went through this before, Aaron," Mom said from behind the bar. "All sorts of people know."

"We haven't even bought the site yet. It's a tentative purchase agreement, as this document shows. Jesus."

"How likely is it the purchase will be approved?" Erin asked, hoping to calm him down by talking business.

"Almost definite. There are a couple of councillors who aren't sure, but we'll twist their arms."

Erin wondered how much money he'd offer them. She'd heard whispers that Dad would sometimes stoop to blackmail, but she didn't want to believe them. "Maybe it's one of them."

"They'd be taking a great risk by crossing me like that." Dad lifted the drink Mom pushed toward him and gulped it down. "I could use a few more of those."

"One more," Mom murmured. She began mixing the next one. "If this wasn't alcoholic, I'd throw in a couple of tranquilizers for you."

Dad's face relaxed for the first time since Erin had handed him her undercover phone. "Good to know you still love me." His gaze shifted to Erin. "You got an email. That's my girl."

When she'd imagined this moment, she'd seen herself pumping her fist in the air, feeling all warm and fuzzy. It hadn't worked out that way. Yes, she was pleased that he was pleased. But everything felt muted. Wrong.

"I knew having you pretend to be one of them would work out."

"Can I ask a question about your proposed development?"

"Of course."

"It's a poor neighbourhood. Why aren't you building affordable housing?"

"Jesus, you sound like Royce. I'll tell you the same thing I told him. There's no money in it, and I believe in improving a neighbourhood, not letting it coast. Why did you ask me that? Is Altree brainwashing you?" He wagged his finger at her. "Don't get caught up in anything Altree says. We could buy a site she approves and build something she designed and she'd still find a reason to complain. Build downtown? Too many floors obstructing the waterfront. Build in the suburbs. An eyesore. Build out in the middle of nowhere. Upsetting wildlife. Knock down a building nobody has pissed in for three-hundred years. Destroying history. People like her are allergic to anything resembling progress and success. I don't want any of her rubbing off on you."

He grabbed the drink Mom had finished mixing, but this time he only took a couple of sips before setting it back on the bar. "What's Altree planning to do with these documents?"

Erin's mouth wouldn't work. Her hesitation to tell him surprised her.

"She must have told you."

She forced the words out. "She's going to show up at the council meeting with a sign and talk to the city reporter."

Dad grunted. "Nothing I can't handle."

"What are you going to do?" Her voice sounded shrill.

He ignored her question. "If IT figures out from the email whose balls I'm going to break, none of this will be your concern anymore. You'll have finished your little job. You should come to the office and learn the ropes, Erin. It's time."

Erin felt her shoulders stiffen. "I'm not ready yet. I was thinking of maybe doing another year of school, maybe get a Master's."

"Give me a fucking break. You don't want to go to school. I'm not an idiot."

"I know you're not," Erin mumbled. "All right. I don't know what I want to do."

Dad's tone hardened. "When will you know?"

"It *has* been a year now," Mom said. "You said you needed time, and you've had it. You can't do nothing forever."

Mom's voice was soft, non-judgemental, but it still felt critical. Sometimes Erin thought the fact that she didn't have to work was behind her inability to feel drawn to anything. If she had a sense of urgency, needed to put food on the table and pay the rent, maybe her path would become clear, but she was certain Mom and Dad wouldn't throw her out, even if she did end up a lady of leisure for the rest of her life. Being an only child had its advantages. And disadvantages. Dad desperately wanted her to follow in his footsteps so "his blood" would take over the business when he retired.

"Let me think about it," she said feebly.

Dad rolled his eyes. "I thought that's what you were doing."

"What's the problem, sweetie?" Mom asked. "What's holding you back?"

"Nothing. I just . . . I don't feel . . ."

They stared at her, waiting.

"I want to do something I enjoy, something that makes me get out of bed every morning looking forward to the day."

"And you don't think working with me would do that," Dad said flatly.

"I don't know."

"You won't know unless you try," Mom said.

She was afraid that once she was in Dad's clutches, she wouldn't be able to escape if she absolutely hated the work. Stalling was difficult enough when she hadn't tried. She couldn't imagine working for him—with him—and then having to tell him she hated it.

Lost in her thoughts and paralyzed by the prospect of disappointing or wounding Dad, she almost jumped when Mom slid her arm around her shoulders.

"Your undercover operation is working with Dad," she said, squeezing Erin. "Isn't that right, Aaron?"

Dad grudgingly nodded.

"We'll try not to pressure you," Mom said. "But you must be getting bored, so figure out what you want. You can do anything. We'll support you, whatever you choose."

Would Dad? Erin didn't think so. "I'll try," was all she could manage. What was wrong with her? Even Christina was talking about getting her real estate licence.

"I'll let you know what IT finds out," Dad said. "And I'll tighten who has access to our documents."

Erin nodded, then excused herself. She had plans, to binge watch something while stuffing her face with popcorn, so she could forget this conversation. She was disappointing them, and herself, and she didn't know how to fix it.

6

L ILY DROPPED A LOONIE into the tip jar at the coffee shop, something she made a point of doing when the cashier smiled and didn't make her feel rushed. She plunked her steaming coffee onto the table Sandy had found near a window and sat across from her.

Sandy blew on her coffee. "I don't know why I always feel so warm and fuzzy after seeing a romcom. We know they'll be together in the end. But I do. I'm such a wuss."

Lily shrugged. Romcoms weren't her thing, but it had been Sandy's turn to choose the movie. If it had been up to her, she would have chosen the latest sci-fi thriller and Sandy would have been the one watching something she would have skipped otherwise.

"Speaking of couples, you haven't said anything."

"About what?" Lily said, even though she knew what was coming.

"How did it go with Erin?"

"It went fine. We had dinner, we read the documents. I made a great sign yesterday."

Sandy frowned at her. "So nothing else happened."

Not overtly. "I'm meeting her at McMillan Park tomorrow."

"Why?"

"Because she sees a run-down park that would probably be better off being something else."

"Why the hell has she been showing up for the protests, then?"

"I don't think she'd seen the park before."

"Okay, that accounts for the first time, but what about the rest?"

"I assume she doesn't want an apartment there. And honestly, I can see her point of view about the state of the park. That's why I'll probably tell her about Jay-Jay."

Sandy's eyes widened. "You usually don't bring her up, or you stall for a bit."

Because siblings usually came up when she was making small talk. There were few other small talk killers like:

"Yes, I have a sister."

"Are you close?"

"She's dead."

Yep, she'd gotten over feeling guilty for saying, "Nope, no siblings," when she figured she'd never see the other person again or they'd only be an acquaintance, their conversations never extending beyond the impersonal and shallow. It was easier for everyone.

With those she thought might stick around for a while, she'd say, "A sister," and then quickly change the subject. Erin hadn't asked about siblings. Lily could easily get away with sticking to the terrible effect the McMillan Park development would have on the Iron Court neighbourhood. But she'd probably come clean tomorrow. And when she'd lain awake in bed the night Erin had come for dinner, wondering why she'd tell her about Jay-Jay, she'd realized it was because she hoped Erin would stick around for a while.

"Telling her will help explain why I want to save the park, even though it's past its due date," she said.

Sandy sipped her coffee, her eyes on Lily's face. "You should ask her out."

"No."

"Why not?"

Lily clutched her coffee but didn't drink it.

"You want to."

Yep, she did. Probably why she'd told Erin about Sandy setting them up, so she could watch Erin's reaction and gauge her chances. Unfortunately she hadn't gleaned much. Erin's reaction had been controlled. She hadn't said, "Good for Sandy. She's figured us out." But she also hadn't laughed hysterically at the idea. She'd appeared a little surprised, but revealed nothing.

"Why do you think I want to ask her out?" she said to Sandy.

"Because usually when I suggest you ask someone out, you're blasting me right about now."

"You've been trying to push us together since we met her." Lily shrugged. "It's old news now."

"Oh, please. And I keep trying to push you together because nobody's come along for a while that I can see you with."

"You don't even know Erin."

"Come on. You don't have to know people to see the possibilities. There's an ease between the two of you. A synergistic energy."

"Don't go all woo-woo on me."

Sandy's face tightened. "I mean you just fit, okay? And that doesn't happen too often so I wouldn't be so quick to dismiss her."

Lily gulped down some coffee. "I'm not. I just . . . I don't know." She didn't want to be rejected. Didn't want to ruin a friendship that was just getting off the ground. She hadn't made a new friend in a while. Mom said it got more difficult to make friends as you aged, that she'd met most of her friends in university. *"You'll make a lot of new acquaintances, but not friends that'll be there to hold your hand. Everyone's too busy with work and family. It's not like on TV where co-workers spend Christmas together, like they're all orphans, only children, and have spouses that don't mind telling their families they won't be home for Christmas. Who buys into that crap?"* Then Mom would say what always made Lily chuckle, given Mom's aversion to buying into crap. *"The only new person you'll meet who'll stick with you is your soul mate."*

Sandy shifted in her seat. "If you're not ready to ask her out, tell me you won't shut her out, that you'll see her again."

"I'm sure I will, with you trying to push us together."

"You can thank me at your wedding."

Lily barked a laugh.

"Seriously, I can see it."

"I hardly know her."

"But you want to."

Yeah, she did. "Let me deal with it."

Sandy's hands went to her cheeks. "Oh my god. You don't want me to screw things up. You really do like her. Call her."

"Didn't I just say to let me deal with it?" Lily shook her head at Sandy's overly contrite expression and changed the subject to the upcoming city council meeting, but her mind stayed with Erin. *Let me deal with it.* So far, dealing with it meant trying not to think about her—it—whatever. She was too busy for a relationship, and Erin already thought she was nuts for wanting to save McMillan Park. Lily had been down that path already, fallen for someone who didn't understand her need to raise her voice, to make the world a better place, to ensure her life counted for something. She wasn't about to do it again.

～

ERIN TOOK A CAB to the usual spot a couple of blocks away from McMillan Park. When she entered the north gate, it was easy to spot Lily in the park that barely had any tree cover. Lily was staring at a sandbox, her hands on her hips. Definitely a jeans and shirt type of gal. Wondering if the sandbox contained garbage, or worse, Erin squared her shoulders and strode over to her.

"Hi," she said, forcing herself to look at the sandbox. Her shoulders relaxed. There was nothing there except dirty sand.

Lily turned to her. "You made it."

Yeah. Erin surveyed the park again from this vantage point. She still didn't see whatever Lily saw.

"You're not impressed."

"The city has definitely let it go."

Lily nodded. "I used to live in that building over there." She twisted to her right and pointed to a tired-looking high rise. Even from this distance, Erin could tell the balconies hadn't seen paint for years.

"If you're sure the city's never going to put money into this park, why save it? Why not let Hunt and Bishop build an apartment?"

"Because it's the only green space around here. And they're not building affordable housing. Does it make sense to build anything but affordable housing here?"

"The vacancy rate is low. Raising it will bring new people into the neighbourhood."

Lily blinked at her. "And push the people who already live here out. Where do you propose they move to when they can no longer afford to live and shop here? Another low-income neighbourhood? They're packed, and because the city doesn't give a flying fuck about people in neighbourhoods like these, it would only be a matter of time before a company like Hunt and Bishop comes along and does the same thing all over again."

"You think one apartment is going to do that?"

Lily stared at her. She drew a deep breath and slowly exhaled. "Why are you here?"

"What?"

"Why are you here?"

"You invited me to come look at the park with you."

"No, why are you showing up at our protests to save the park?"

Erin's heart pounded. Had Lily found out who she was? Probably not. Erin didn't know Lily well, but she had the impression Lily was honest and blunt. If she knew she was standing next to Aaron Hunt's daughter, the conversation would be a much different one.

"I saw a poster at a—"

"Bus stop. I know. But you don't seem terribly interested in what we're doing."

Erin stopped herself from blurting out whatever came to mind. If she blew this, Lily would never trust her, and Dad would not be pleased. Yes, she'd gotten him an email, but until he had a name, her undercover operation wasn't over. "I don't feel passionate about saving historical buildings. Parks, maybe, but I'm not sure this one's worth saving. I see your point about upsetting the balance here, so I can see why maybe affordable housing would be better." She really did understand Lily's point. "So you'd be okay with an affordable apartment building?"

"No. And you still haven't answered my question. If you don't give a damn, what are you doing here?"

To give herself time to think, Erin walked to a nearby bench and sank onto the worn wood.

Lily stood in front of her and folded her arms. "So?"

Erin looked up at her. In a flash, she realized she could tell Lily the truth. Not about her identity, but about why she had so much time on her hands. Lily was a safe person. Lily didn't know anyone she knew. Lily wouldn't pressure her one way or the other, or make her feel inadequate and stupid. Lily wouldn't make her wonder what was wrong with her. She had no skin in the game.

"I'm flailing, Lily. I finished my B.A. a year ago, and I've been drifting ever since. My father's clearly disappointed in me because he wants me to work with him and I'm not sure it's what I want. I think my mother's disappointed too, but she's better at hiding it. And frankly, I'm disappointed with myself, but I can't seem to figure it out. I feel stuck, spinning my wheels. I want to do something. I want to contribute in some way. My parents are pressuring me to come up with a plan. But I can't figure it out." Damn, her eyes were moistening. She looked down at her lap and blinked a few times, then raised her head. "I need to figure out what I want to do with my life. Disappointing my parents, especially my father, terrifies me. I thought if I showed them I'm interested in something . . . Anything . . ."

"So you showed up at the protest to show your parents you're doing something," Lily said.

"Yes." Which was true. Sort of.

Lily was silent for a moment, then she unfolded her arms and dropped onto the bench next to Erin. "What did you do your B.A. in?"

"English."

"That doesn't help much. Unless you want to be a professor."

"I don't."

She grunted. "What are you interested in?"

That was the problem. She wasn't passionate about anything. Well, not quite true, but she doubted a degree in binge watching and star gazing would get her anywhere. "I don't know," she said softly. "How about you? You don't really want to go to law school." But she'd mentioned another path, one she seemed to think was unattainable. "What do you want to do?"

Lily gazed past Erin, her eyes distant. "I don't know."

She was lying, but Erin was skating on thin ice here and wasn't about to challenge her about it.

"Whatever I decide to do, I'll probably have to go back to school, which means tuition money. I know I should be saving. But I always find something else to do with what I earn."

"Like what?"

Lily shook her head. "Doesn't matter."

But it did. "I can't imagine you're gambling it away."

When Lily chuckled, Erin chuckled too.

"Sometimes I think I should blow it on lottery tickets," Lily said. "But no, I put it into this. Buying materials for signs. Photocopying. I hired a PI once."

"Really?"

"A story for another time. Let's just say he was expensive. Oh yeah, and I'm still paying off my student loan. Sometimes I think I should have used my degree as soon as I graduated, rather than thinking I'd work and save for law school. When I was still telling myself I wanted to go to law school."

"What's your degree in?"

"Education."

"You wanted to teach."

"I thought I did. But I realized halfway through that I didn't. I could have switched programs, I guess. At the time I thought, 'I'm not a quitter.' In hindsight, I probably should have switched to something else. But I could have stomached teaching for a few years until I saved enough money for something else. That's pesky hindsight talking." She gave Erin a wry smile. "You're not the only one trying to figure things out."

Except Lily was working and putting blood, sweat, and tears into something she believed in, and Erin was positive Lily would eventually end up doing something she was passionate about. She wasn't flailing in the same way. She didn't have parents breathing down her back. She didn't feel like a failure.

Lily slapped her legs and stood. "Okay, so you don't really give a shit about all this but you want to be doing something right now. I can live with that. I could really use the extra pair of hands. Especially with this project." Her voice dropped. "You've been honest with me, so I'll be honest with you. This park is really special to me. It's not just that I lived nearby and played here." She gazed at the nearby swing set. Her shoulders heaved. "I had an older sister. She was killed when she was eleven. Drunk driver."

A frisson of shock made Erin sit straighter on the bench. "I'm so sorry."

"I was six when she was killed. I hate that I don't remember a lot about her, but I do remember her taking me to the park and playing with me." Lily smiled wistfully. "The sandbox, the swings, the seesaw . . ." She blew out some air. "I come here sometimes, sit on this very bench, especially on her birthday. My parents visit her grave, but I prefer to go where she's alive to me."

But soon there would be no park to visit. Erin wanted to bury her head in her hands. "It must have been a rough time."

"It was, but we got through it, mainly because my parents are strong people and didn't turn on each other. I can't imagine what they went through, though. She went to get some milk from the corner store and never came back."

"What happened to the driver?"

"Slap on the wrist. Don't believe anything the powers that be say about wanting to stop impaired driving." Lily cleared her throat. "Anyway, I don't mean to get heavy on you, but I know the park is a mess. I guess I wanted to be transparent about why I'll keep fighting for it until I know it's a lost cause. I value honesty."

Erin squirmed, feeling two inches tall. "What was her name? Your sister?"

"Julie. I called her Jay-Jay." Lily swallowed. "I also think that if the park is going to be destroyed, it makes more sense to build affordable housing. I saw from the drawing White Knight sent that it won't be one of the luxury buildings Hunt and Bishop tend to build, but still. Not many people in the neighbourhood will be able to afford the rent."

"But you don't want anything built here. You want to preserve the park as it is." Because of her sister.

"Yes, and now you know why. What about you? Any brothers or sisters?"

"No. Only child." She wanted to change the subject, get the topic of conversation off family, but she didn't want to do it after what Lily had just told her. Fortunately, Lily walked toward one of the swing sets and examined the four sorry-looking swings, then sat on one and gripped its chains.

Erin went over to her and pointed at the swing. "Do you want me to push?"

Lily's eyes danced. "I think I'm capable of swinging on my own power. Not that I would," she said with a grimace. "I don't trust this swing." She slid off it. "Want to grab a coffee? I don't have to work until six."

"Sure," Erin said, a little surprised.

She fell into step with Lily. They walked in comfortable silence until they reached the corner and waited for a red light to change.

"I'm glad we understand each other's motivation here a little more," Lily said. "Thanks for being so honest with me."

Once again, Erin felt two inches tall. Why couldn't Lily have been a mean-talking bitch who didn't like sci-fi and action figures, didn't cook great lasagna, wasn't easy to talk to, and didn't have bright brown eyes that danced? This was not her life, but Erin Bartlett's, and Erin Bartlett would disappear as soon as Dad knew the identity of White Knight.

When Erin got home, she'd call Christina and see what she was up to. She was Erin Hunt. She did not drive a red convertible.

7

ERIN SAT AT DAD's desk in his office in the Hunt and Bishop tower, watching the grainy video advance agonizingly slow on his laptop's display. Riveting images of people arriving at and leaving the library branch on Parker Avenue. IT had examined White Knight's email and matched its point of origin with the library, much to Dad's chagrin. The owner of a convenience store across the street had sent over this CCTV footage. Erin wondered how much Dad had paid him for it. "Couldn't get any footage from the library," Dad had told her. The librarian had stood firm. Privacy issues.

She wondered when Dad would get back from his meeting. Her back was getting sore. She'd been in this position for at least half an hour, and shifting her weight hadn't helped. Then she sensed someone's eyes on her and looked up. Dad had returned and was staring down at her, an odd expression on his face.

"You look quite comfortable in that chair," he said.

She swallowed. Realistically, she wouldn't be able to stall him for much longer. "What would I do if I worked with you?"

He perched on the arm of one of the guest chairs. "Anything you want. Let me be clear. I'd like you to reach the point where you can take over from me. But there's time for that. Lots of time, I hope. Meaning you'll have time to learn."

"Where would you put me first? The mail room?"

He laughed. "Are you kidding? My daughter's not working in the mail room. No. I think I'd want you to see the entire process we go through, from idea to the ceremonial first shovel in the ground, to the ribbon cutting. I'd start you with Jean and Steve. They present me with potential acquisitions."

She tried to muster some excitement. "Sounds interesting."

"Don't get me wrong. I don't expect you to become an expert on everything. It's not possible. You want to let everyone do what they're good at and stay out of their way as much as you can. But I want you to know the process, to have an appreciation for it. It will help you ask better questions. Make better decisions." His eyes narrowed. "What are you saying? You coming to work with your old man?"

"I'm considering it."

"Ha!" He leaped up and held out his arms. "That's my girl."

She went to him and hugged him, savouring the pleasure she'd seen on his face and heard in his voice. "Let me finish this White Knight project, and then we'll set a start date," she murmured when they drew apart.

"You got it. I can't wait to tell your mother." He beamed at her. "I knew this is where you'd end up. You're a Hunt." He pointed to the leather office chair she'd just vacated. "You belong in that chair."

She nodded and managed a smile. Why fight it? Why not take the easy path? Nothing more enticing was calling out to her. She couldn't wait for months, years, before doing something with her life.

Dad rounded the desk and peered at his laptop display. "Recognize anyone?"

"From Lily's group? No. But why would I? If it's someone who knows Lily, they'd just tell her the information. Why would they want to be anonymous?"

"I don't recognize anyone, either. Damn it." He went to slam the laptop closed but stopped himself.

"It has to be someone in the footage, though, right?" Erin said, wanting to mollify him.

"There must have been thirty people going in and out. And no, it might not be any of them. The store guy was only willing to give us four hours. Maybe the traitor is already inside. Maybe he works at the library. We only know when the email was sent, not when he entered or left the library."

Erin paced the office, swinging her arms, trying to loosen her back.

"I didn't realize how much time had gone by," Dad said. "Sorry."

She flashed him a smile.

"Why don't you sit down?"

She accepted his offer, sat in his chair, and clicked the Play button. More people she didn't recognize.

Forty-five minutes later, Dad told her to stop the playback. He'd watched fifteen minutes from behind her, then he'd dragged one of the guest chairs over and sat beside her. Now he stood. He did not look happy.

"What now?" Erin said.

"Pete in IT said if we get more emails and more footage, we can see who shows up more than once."

"So you want me to get more White Knight emails from Lily? As far as I know, she's only received two, and you already have one of them."

"I'm sure there will be more. Whoever's doing this won't stop."

"I guess I'll keep showing up for Lily's events, then." She didn't add that she hoped there would be one soon.

"Do that."

"So what do you think will happen at the city council meeting?" she asked, keeping her voice even. "Do you think Lily being there will make a difference?"

"Don't worry about her. I've got it handled."

That was why she was worrying, but she knew pressing him for details wouldn't work. Dad's "I've got this" meant "subject closed."

"Let's go to lunch," he said. "Forget White fucking Knight. This is a fantastic day. You're going to come to work with me."

She'd said she was considering it, but she knew she was splitting hairs. She had to face up to it. She was Aaron Hunt's daughter. Working with Dad, eventually sitting in this leather chair, had been her destiny from the moment she'd been born.

~

LILY ENTERED THE AIRY council chamber carrying the placard she'd created using Bristol board, a black marker, and a piece of wood. She had her choice of seats. Only one other person sat in the public viewing area, and he was a regular who never spoke to anyone. He didn't appear to be homeless, so he wasn't sheltering from the rain showers that had pelted down all day. Maybe he loved city politics. She didn't see any reporters, but at least one should show up.

She sat in the front row where the sign she held would be difficult to miss and rested the placard against the seat next to her. Councillors were trickling in, and the mayor was slowly making his way to his chair, chatting to someone who walked alongside him. The other man looked familiar. Lily took a moment to think about where she'd seen him before. It suddenly hit her. Aaron Hunt.

He was a dead ringer for the professional photo on the Hunt and Bishop web site. She couldn't deny he was a striking figure in person. Tall, thick brown hair peppered with gray, clean shaven, broad shoulders, a suit that probably cost more than she made in a week, and a Rolex, probably real. Lily had attended other council meetings concerning Hunt and Bishop projects, but couldn't remember seeing him. She wondered if he had a special interest in the McMillan Park project, or if he wanted to watch the presentation by one of his underlings, the one that would persuade the council to go ahead and do what it intended to do anyway: rubber stamp the purchase.

The mayor stopped near the dais and laughed. Hunt smiled along with him. Oh yeah, that was how it worked. The two of them were best buddies, probably drank and golfed together. Deals were made and shaken upon at the fucking country club. All the documentation existed to satisfy the peasants. Hunt and the mayor were probably godfathers to each other's kids. Did Hunt even have kids? If he did, Lily felt sorry for them. Imagine having a greedy, self-centred, arrogant bastard for a father.

While she waited, her mind wandered to Erin and what she was doing. She'd said she was busy tonight, and Lily hadn't wanted to ask what she was doing, even though she'd wondered. Ask personal questions, don't ask personal questions . . . Lily couldn't deny that she wanted to see her again and didn't want to scare her off with too many questions. Even if the purchase agreement was approved tonight—Jesus, of course it would be approved—they could still protest the project. Hopefully Erin would remain interested and not find something else to satisfy her parents. Scratch that selfish thought. Ideally, Erin would find something that would satisfy herself.

The seats in the chamber were filling. Lily leaned over to grab her placard. She heard someone approaching and lifted her head, expecting to see another activist. Two burly security guards towered over her. "Excuse me, Miss, but you'll have to leave the chamber."

She gaped at them. "Why?"

"Disruptions of city council meetings are strictly forbidden."

"I'm not going to disrupt the meeting. I'm going to hold up a sign." She lifted her sign and pressed her lips closed, to demonstrate, then her mouth dropped open when one of the guards tore the sign from her fingers.

"Come with us now, or we'll have to involve the police."

Too shocked to feel enraged, she mentally ran through her choices: stay and risk a scene, a huge scene that could land her at the police station, or leave with her tail tucked between her legs. A scene would attract a lot of attention, but the wrong kind. Unlike all their peaceful protests, it would hit the media and be spun in the worst possible light. She'd lose credibility regarding McMillan Park.

If she left, she could still talk to the reporter. Holding a sign would only have been a small show of defiance to make her feel better anyway. She could already hear the rubber stamp coming down.

"Fine, I'll leave." She reached for her sign, but the guard jerked it away from her. Asshole. "But I have a petition to present to council. I have that right."

The guard who hadn't grabbed the sign held out his hand. She handed him the papers with the signatures she and Erin had collected.

As they escorted her from the chamber, she stole a glance at Hunt, to see if he was smirking. Security guards marching an activist out had caught the attention of most councillors, but Hunt, sitting in an area reserved for dignitaries, was gazing straight ahead, making her feel like an ant, a fucking invisible ant. At least the guard handed her petition to the city clerk as they marched by the wide-eyed woman.

The guards left her on the sidewalk outside city hall's main entrance. A shower was in full swing. She huddled under the canopy keeping the area outside the entrance dry and waited for the reporter. A few minutes later, a face she recognized from the Standard strode toward her.

She moved to block his path. "Excuse me."

His pace slowed. He veered toward her.

"I have some information about the McMillan Park project that I think you'll . . ."

She followed him with her eyes as he picked up his pace and blew right past her into city hall. For a second, she considered dashing after him, but one of the guards who'd dumped her here was just inside the entryway, his eyes locked on her.

Her shoulders slumped. The chill damp air made her shiver. She trudged to her car, parked just around the corner, and wanted to scream when she saw the piece of yellow paper under one of her windshield wipers, flapping in the breeze. No fucking way. She was legally parked.

She grabbed it, climbed into the car and read the ticket. She had not parked in a manner that obstructed the road, for fuck's sake. Why did she ever think she could win these battles? She was just a waitress who made a lot of noise. The rich and powerful could ignore her shouts. She couldn't ignore their security guards, their tickets, their indifference. She'd bet her entire bank account the clerk had tossed the petition in the trash. Sometimes she wondered if it was time to give it up. She wasn't making a difference. They just laughed at her. Laughed.

Tears blurred her vision. She rested her head against the steering wheel and let them flow.

8

Erin gazed out her bedroom window, wishing she could be on her balcony where she always lost track of time, but the weather was terrible for stargazing. She really needed something to keep her mind occupied. Ever since Dad had left for the council meeting, she'd felt antsy. Not for him. He'd be fine.

She blew out a sigh and picked up the astronomy magazine she'd tried to read. Maybe this time she'd follow what the article was saying and actually take in the photos. She flopped onto her bed and—

A phone rang. Her undercover phone. She leaped off the bed and grabbed it off her desk. Lily. "Hi."

"Hey. It's Lily."

It was only 8:20. There was no way the meeting was over. "Is the council meeting finished already?"

Silence, then, "God, I'm sorry. I know you're busy tonight. I'll call you tomorrow."

"No!" Erin said, concerned at the lack of vigour in Lily's voice. "It's okay. I can talk for a few minutes." She waited for Lily to respond, but the silence stretched out. "You okay? Why didn't you go to the meeting?"

"I did. They threw me out."

"Why? What did you do?"

"Nothing. The meeting hadn't even started. I was just sitting there and security told me I had to leave. Then I waited outside for the reporter, but he wanted nothing to do with me. As soon as I said McMillan Park, I suddenly had the plague. To top it all off, I got back to my car and found a ticket for a bogus infraction."

Erin's jaw tightened.

"I don't know why I keep doing this." Lily's voice quavered. "Nobody cares, you know."

"That's not true. You have your group."

Lily snorted. "They were all busy tonight." She didn't say, "Including you," but Erin felt it. "And the turnouts have been getting smaller, but that's not it. Stuff like this, getting treated like dirt, usually rolls off my back. But not tonight."

"Maybe because it's McMillan Park. Your personal connection."

"Maybe. Or maybe I'm just tired of the whole fucking thing because nothing I do ever makes a difference. Nothing. I can't fight these people. It's a rigged game. Only fools keep trying to beat them."

What sounded like a sniffle made Erin want to bang her fist against her desk. She wanted to reach through the phone and comfort Lily, tell her she should be proud of herself for standing behind what she believed in. If not for her phony plans, she'd go see Lily right now. And say what, exactly? If Lily knew who she was . . .

Lily cleared her throat. "I'm sorry I'm dumping this on you. Christ, you hardly know me and I'm crying my eyes out to you."

Why had Lily called her? Sandy must have been unavailable. "It's okay. I'm glad you called me. I'm so sorry it didn't go well. If I wasn't busy, we could go for a drink and you could vent all you want."

"I stay away from alcohol when I'm feeling like this, but thanks for the thought."

"Let me take you to lunch tomorrow," Erin blurted. "Are you free?"

Lily hesitated a beat. "You don't have to."

"I want to. If you're still feeling down, we can talk it out. If you're not, you can tell me your next move. I'm sure it'll be brilliant."

"I don't feel brilliant right now, but you almost made me smile, so I think seeing you for lunch would be good for me."

"Great!"

They arranged to meet at a restaurant near Lily's, one she liked.

"Will you be okay?" Erin asked.

"Don't worry. I'm not going to off myself over this. I just needed to, I don't know. I needed someone to cry with, I guess. You probably think I'm a flake now."

"I don't. I can understand how disappointing it is, not even having a chance to watch the meeting. And the ticket's just unfair." Tomorrow at lunch, she'd suggest Lily fight it.

They said their goodbyes. Erin tossed the phone onto her desk in disgust and wandered around her apartment, her fingers laced behind her head. Had Dad been behind Lily's abrupt ejection from the council chambers? Was that how he'd handled it? By being petty.

She plopped into a chair, then stood again and went to the recreation room, needing to blow off steam. She was still there a couple of hours later, playing a vintage arcade game, when Mom peeked into the room.

"There you are. Come with me to the bar."

Erin glanced over her shoulder. "Why?"

"Just come with me."

She inwardly groaned and let the game beat her, then walked through the archway to the bar. Dad was there, triumph written all over his face. A bottle of champagne stood open. Mom had already poured three glasses.

"The council meeting went well," Dad boomed. "The purchase will quickly go through, and we can get to work." He gestured at the bar. "Well, come on, grab a glass," he said, taking one himself.

Erin accepted the one Mom handed to her and dutifully raised her glass when her parents raised theirs. "To the McMillan Park project." He gazed at Erin. "And to my daughter, who has finally agreed to come work with me. It's been a superb week. Cheers."

"Cheers," she and Mom murmured.

Erin sipped her champagne, a bundle of mixed emotions: anger, worry, pride, guilt. She felt sick. It wasn't the drink.

"We should go to the country club tomorrow for lunch," Dad said.

Mom laid her hand on his arm. "That's a great idea."

Erin quickly set her glass on the bar. "I've love to, but I can't. I have plans, and I don't want to cancel them so late."

"What are you doing?" Mom asked.

She moistened her lips. "Having lunch with a friend from university I haven't seen in a while."

Mom made a disappointed face. "We'll miss you sweetie, but you enjoy yourself."

"We'll be having a lot more lunches," Dad added. "I can't wait until we celebrate your first successful project."

Erin forced a grin and downed the rest of her champagne.

$\sim$

THE BUZZ OF CONVERSATION drowned out the muzak the not-quite-a-fast-food joint was playing. Erin finished off her hamburger about the same time Lily finished hers. So far, they'd discussed the weather, local sports—even though they admitted they didn't follow any teams too closely—online videos they'd enjoyed. Erin sensed Lily was building up her courage for something, and it came after the server whisked their empty plates away.

"I'm really sorry about last night," Lily said. "I had a moment of weakness. I shouldn't have called you like that. There wasn't anything you could do. Normally I just suck it up and move on. It's not as if I haven't been shafted before by people who look down their nose at me."

"I'm glad you called. Not that you were upset, but that you called me. Otherwise we wouldn't be having lunch." Even though it was true, she wouldn't have expressed the sentiment so bluntly if she wasn't distracted because she was working up her own courage.

"That's true," Lily said cheerfully. "I just hope you don't think I'm some delicate flower that weeps at the slightest provocation."

"I don't. I can understand how disappointed you must have been. You should have been able to express your point of view." Sorry, Dad. "Do they usually kick out peaceful protestors?"

"No." Lily paused. "Aaron Hunt was there, the Hunt part of Hunt and Bishop."

Erin glanced around for the server. Shouldn't he be asking them what they wanted for dessert?

"He looked pretty chummy with the mayor. Probably pointed me out and had me removed."

Erin wanted to disagree, but she couldn't.

"If he thinks he's won, he can think again."

Apprehension raised Erin's voice. "What are you going to do?"

"They still have to agree on what exactly will be built. How many storeys, where parking will go, etcetera."

"You think more protests will help?"

"Probably not, unless the proposed build is completely unacceptable to everyone. The developers are too smart for that." Lily frowned. "I'll come up with something."

Erin was afraid of that. She wanted to warn Lily off, but she was supposed to be on her side, and she knew how personal McMillan Park was to her.

Finally the server showed up. They ordered their desserts: chocolate cake for Erin and a banana split for Lily. After the server had bustled off, Lily pushed back her chair. "Washroom," she said. Erin watched her weave her way around tables, then rallied herself. Just ask her. Ask her. The worst she could say was no. She probably would say no. And that would be fine. Absolutely fine.

She stared at the table, at Lily's empty chair, at Lily's phone sitting near her napkin. Her phone . . . it was unlocked. Erin could easily reach across the table, grab it, and look for the emails from White Knight. She could forward the first one Lily had received to herself. But that would be wrong, and an invasion of privacy. Still, the phone called to her like a siren, pulled at her as if she were iron and it was a magnet. She clenched her hands on her lap, bit her lip.

"Here you go."

She jumped when the server set her cake in front of her, but the spell, the phone's pull, was broken. She waited until Lily returned, bit into her cake, and promised herself she'd ask the question she really, really wanted to ask before she finished the rather generous piece. Her subconscious mind must have decided that saying anything would be less reckless than asking the question, because she blurted, "Can you forward me the other email you got from White Knight?" She tried not to groan aloud.

Lily blinked at her. "I sent you the one with the documents."

"I know, but . . ." Think. Think! "Something smells off to me. Why remain anonymous? Why not make more direct contact and really help you?"

"The documents they sent were genuine."

"We think they're genuine."

"He was right, though. In his first email, he told me Hunt and Bishop had made an offer on the land to the city. And why send me fake documents?"

"I don't know," Erin mumbled.

"If it'll make you feel better, I'll forward you the first email. It should still be in my trash." Lily tapped at her phone. Her face brightened. "Here it is. Sent." She set her phone down.

Great. She had all of White Knight's emails. All two of them. If it led Dad to White Knight, her undercover operation would be over and she'd be showing up for work at Hunt and Bishop. No more seeing Lily.

At least she was only lying to Lily, and not to herself, because this lunch proved she wanted to see more of Lily, even though it was a bad idea. A really bad idea. Nothing could ever happen between them, especially when she was Erin Bartlett. She wasn't *that* dishonest that she'd start a relationship with Lily without revealing her true identity. Plus, she already had a girlfriend. A sort of girlfriend. An assumed girlfriend. She should stick to uncovering the identity of the traitor, then cut off her undercover phone and move on with her life by showing up for her first day at Dad's side.

She lifted her fork. Her piece of cake shrank. She had maybe three mouthfuls left when she laid down her fork and steeled herself. "Do you have the same days off every week?"

Lily nodded. "Mondays and Thursdays. I like it that way. Work a few days, have one off, work another few, have one off. It works for me."

So far, so good. "Are you busy this Thursday night?"

"No. Don't think so."

"I'm going to an astrophotography exhibit, and uh, I was wondering if you wanted to come along."

The few seconds Lily took to lick some ice cream off her spoon were excruciating. "What's astrophotography? Well, I can guess, but . . ."

"It's taking photos of astronomical bodies," Erin said. "Planets, stars, galaxies, the moon."

Lily grunted.

"A few local photographers are displaying their photos, along with a big name from out of town," she said, her heart sinking.

"It sounds cool. Okay. I'm in."

Erin kept her tone level, not wanting to show her surprise or appear too elated. "Great. It's at the Ferguson Gallery, so I'm going to borrow my dad's car." She'd checked, and the buses only ran every hour in that area during the evenings. "I can pick you up."

"Sure."

"Do you want to do dinner beforehand?"

"Okay, but at Chez Lily's. Eating out is fun because it's nice to be waited on for a change, but once a week is enough."

"You don't have to cook for me again."

"I love cooking. Italian again, or something else?"

"I do love Italian food."

"Say no more."

Wanting to dance a jig, Erin finished off her cake. A shadow hovered in her peripheral vision, one that reminded her of Dad, but she ignored it. For once in her life, she ignored that damn shadow.

~

THURSDAY ARRIVED QUICKLY. ERIN left her apartment, ready to pick Lily up. "Your father wants to see you," Mom said, when Erin ran into her on the ground floor. "He's in the exercise room."

Hoping it wouldn't take too long, she hurried into the western wing. Dad had just finished his daily stroke target on his rowing machine and was patting away his sweat with a towel. "You did good," he said to Erin. "We have a few possible suspects for the traitor. Three, to be exact. Ryan Fothering, Vanessa Goldstein, and Yvonne Smith."

"That was quick."

"The additional email helped. It was also sent from the library, and only three people were seen entering or leaving around the time both emails were sent."

"How did you get their names?"

"I called in a favour from someone who has image matching software and, uh, other resources. The problem is, none of the three suspects work for us, and my contacts at the city have no clue who they are."

"So how did they get their hands on confidential documents? And is it even one of them?"

"It might not be. IT told me the person who sent the emails could have been sitting outside in their car riding on the library's Wi-Fi, or it could be someone who works there and is inside from 9 to 5."

"Then it could be anybody. How are we going to find out who it is?"

Dad wagged his finger at her. "That, my girl, is for you to figure out. You didn't blow off Altree yet, did you?"

Erin scratched her cheek. "Not yet."

"Good. Find out if she knows who any of these people are."

"If she knows the person, why wouldn't they just talk to her?"

"Just do it, Erin." He flung the damp towel into the nearby hamper. "If she doesn't know any of them, I'll figure out our next move."

The image of hit squads screeching up to a curb in a dark van and throwing hoods over the suspects' heads flashed through Erin's mind. She bit back a chuckle. Dad wasn't that bad. But he'd figure something out. He always did. "I'll make contact with Altree again."

"That's my girl."

Ryan Fothering, Vanessa Goldstein, and Yvonne Smith. Repeating the names to herself, Erin left him to continue his exercise routine. Yep, she'd make contact with Altree in approximately half an hour and hopefully maintain contact throughout the evening.

9

ERIN POINTED TO A blown-up photo of the constellation Orion taken by a local photographer. "The three stars really close together make up his belt," she said, tracing the length of the belt through the air.

Lily leaned in closer. "I see it. Cool."

"He's upside down on the other side of the world." Erin wasn't sure Lily, who was still focused on the belt, had heard her. Unless she was doing a really good job of faking interest, Lily appeared to be enjoying herself. She wasn't rushing Erin along or checking her phone every five seconds. Erin was certainly enjoying herself. They'd enjoyed a delicious dinner together with no awkward silences, then Erin had driven Lily here in her own damn car.

Since arriving, Lily had taken her time, studied photos, asked intelligent questions. But the time was still passing too quickly. Erin would suggest coffee afterwards. She wished she didn't have to try to bring up Dad's suspect list in a way that didn't sound weird. She was having a physical reaction at the thought, almost like someone was inside her, thumping on her sternum. Every lie, every half truth, felt heavier. She wanted to kill Erin Bartlett and let Lily see Erin Hunt, but what would happen if she blurted out the truth? Would Lily say it was okay that she'd lied all this time, or would she rush from the gallery and never speak to her again, a possibility that made Erin's hands clammy.

"What's this?" Lily asked, making Erin jump. She hadn't noticed Lily had moved on to another photo.

"Andromeda Galaxy. You can see it without a telescope."

"That's really something," Lily murmured.

Half an hour later, they left the gallery, discussing the last couple of photos. Erin stopped in the parking lot and turned to Lily. "I have some photos on my phone."

"Photos of stars?"

Wishing she hadn't said anything, Erin nodded.

"Show me."

Damn, they weren't on her undercover phone. They were on her real personal phone. But that wasn't why she wished she hadn't said anything, and it was too late now to backtrack. She pulled out her phone, hoping Lily wouldn't notice it wasn't her undercover phone, and swiped to a photo. "Here."

Lily took the phone and peered at the display. "That's colourful. Who took it?"

"Me."

Lily jerked her head up. "You?"

"Don't sound so surprised. It's a hobby. I spend a lot of time looking through a telescope."

"Seriously?"

"Yeah."

"Can I swipe?"

"Go ahead," Erin said, planning to stop her after three or four. There were photos of Dad there. Lily would ask why Erin Bartlett was standing in a kitchen with Aaron Hunt, or in a reception room at the country club, or with him and the mayor, smiling, drinks in hand.

"These are good. They're as good as some of the ones we just saw."

"To the untrained eye, maybe." Erin lifted her hands. "Not that I mean to suggest—"

Lily chuckled. "I am an untrained eye."

After Lily had swiped another couple of times, Erin held out her hand, hoping she'd get the message.

"You'll have to show me more." Lily handed Erin her phone.

"Sure." *Show me more.* Tonight? Or another time? Meaning Lily expected them to hang out together again. Dad's face flashed across her mind. Shit. "Do you want to go for a coffee?" she asked, wanting her mind to stop reminding her that she was constantly lying to someone she was growing to care quite a lot about, that her mere presence here, breathing, was a lie.

"That sounds—"

"Lily?" a woman yelled.

They both turned in the direction of the shout.

"Oh my god, it is you." A black woman strode over to them and threw her arms around Lily. After giving her a quick hug, she stepped back. "Even in this light, I caught a flash of your hair. Every time I see red hair, I think of you. It's been a while."

Erin was dying to ask.

Lily quickly satisfied her curiosity. "Erin, this is Alisha. We were at university together."

"Spent many hours cramming together for exams," Alisha said with a laugh. "Pleased to meet you, Erin."

They shook hands.

Alisha turned to a woman Erin hadn't noticed. She must have crept up on them. "This is Christy. Do you remember Christy?" she asked Lily. "She was at university at the same time, but in biology."

"I don't." Lily flashed Christy a smile. "Nice to meet you."

"She's in med school now," Alisha said.

"Allie," Christy barked. "Don't embarrass me."

Alisha gave her an indulgent look. "You were just at the exhibit, I presume," she said to Lily.

"Yeah. Pretty cool. Didn't know you were into, uh, astrophotography."

"I'm thinking of getting into it. Took a couple of photography courses last year and want to expand my knowledge."

"Erin takes pictures of the sky."

"Really?" Alisha looked at Erin. "I should pick your brain." Her gaze moved back to Lily. "We're going to that club on Croft. It's ladies night tonight. Why don't you come with us?"

"Oh, uh . . ." Lily turned to Erin. "Do you want to . . ."

Erin tried to read Lily's face, but she couldn't. Agree, disagree? She threw it back at Lily. "Whatever you want to do."

Alisha gave Lily's arm a playful tap. "Come with us. It'll be fun." She turned to Erin. "We can talk about what I'll need to take photos of the stars."

Lily smiled. To Erin, it looked forced. "Sounds good," she said.

"Great. We'll meet you there." Alisha tipped her head in the Mercedes' direction. "Is that your car?"

"It's Erin's father's."

"Cool wheels. See you in a bit."

Alisha and Christy strolled away. When they were out of earshot, Lily grimaced. "Sorry. I didn't know what to say. It's not that I don't want to catch up with Alisha. We had a lot of great times at university."

"But you lost touch."

"You know how it is. You have every intention of staying in touch but then life gets busy. Alisha was never into any causes. We were study buddies. Different majors, but kept running into each other at the library. I didn't even know she was gay until just before we graduated."

"You can catch up with her at the club."

"Yeah." Lily scratched her head. "I'm not really a club person. I should have said, hey, why don't we go for coffee instead. I'm not sure why I didn't."

Erin wasn't big on clubs either. "It's okay."

"We'll have one drink, I'll do a bit of catching up, and then we'll go."

"Sounds good."

As they drove out of the parking lot, Erin felt deflated. She would have preferred a quiet conversation with Lily over coffee. Now they'd have to shout to hear each other, and that was if they even spoke. Lily would chat with Alisha, Erin would give Alisha a few tips about how to get started with astrophotography. Hopefully Christy wouldn't get bored.

On the other hand, Lily wouldn't ask her any questions that required lies for answers. Oh shit. Erin waited until they were stopped at a red light. "Hey, weird question, but do you know Ryan Fothering, Vanessa Goldstein, or Yvonne Smith?"

"Nope. Why?"

"Remember you forwarded White Knight's emails to me. I asked a tech whiz I know to see if he could figure out who sent them. He narrowed it down to a triplex. Those three people live there." Lame, but good enough. "You sure you don't know any of them?"

"Yes, and I really wish you hadn't done that."

"Why? Don't you want to know who it is?"

"Am I curious? Yes. But they want to stay anonymous, and they might have a damn good reason for that. Maybe they'd lose their job if someone finds out they're leaking information."

Erin was quite certain they would.

"Maybe they're afraid for some reason, and I certainly don't want to scare them off."

"You should suggest meeting them in person next time they have documents for you."

"Didn't you hear what I just said? No."

Her eyes on the road, Erin didn't have to see Lily to know she was irritated. "Sorry. I'm just worried that someone's trying to set you up."

"You're being paranoid. So far, the documents, the information, has all checked out." Lily's voice softened. "I appreciate that you're looking out for me. I really do. But let me deal with White Knight."

"Okay." Her hands tightened around the steering wheel. More lies told, but mission accomplished. The price was becoming too high, though. In the beginning, the big lie, the Erin Bartlett lie, hadn't touched Erin. Now every time she told even a tiny lie that didn't matter much, she felt as if a piece of her soul was clawed away. She could feel it fighting, straining, tearing away from her, leaving behind a ragged edge that bled every time she deceived the woman next to her.

~

WHEN THEY ARRIVED AT the club, Lily spotted Alisha and Christy right away. She and Erin joined them in the lineup. The *thump-thump-thump* of the base emanating from inside meant they had to raise their voices to hear each other. After shouting over the music once, they waited in silence until the bouncer waved them inside. Every chair at a table was occupied, and so were the bar stools, but Alisha spotted a small round table where they could set their drinks.

"Let me get the first round," Christy said.

"We'll probably only stay for one drink," Lily said, wanting to get that out up front. For the twentieth time, she wished she'd suggested they meet another time for a catch-up session. Even if she loved clubbing, and she didn't, this wasn't the ideal place to fill each other in about what they'd done in the seven years since they'd graduated.

"One round at a time," Christy said.

Lily gave up. "I'll have a beer. Budweiser."

"I'll have a Coke," Erin said. "I'm driving."

Lily wanted to hug her.

"One beer, one Coke, and I'll get our usual," Christy said to Alisha. She headed for the bar.

"I need to go to the washroom," Erin said. "Be back in a minute."

Lily watched her walk away, then turned to Alisha. "I can't believe we ran into each other."

"I know. I couldn't believe it when I saw you standing there. I thought, holy crap, it's Lily." Alisha smiled. "You're looking great. So tell me everything. What are you up to?"

Lily hated this question. She was content waiting tables but always felt like a failure when she ran into old classmates. "I'm a waitress at the Golden Goose."

Alisha frowned at her. "What happened to teaching?"

"I'm cool with waiting tables right now." Alisha's expression turned dubious. "What about you?" Lily said, wanting to change the subject.

"I'm using the degree, baby. Working with children. Enjoying every minute of it, even though it can be frustrating as hell and I have my days when I want to rage quit. Bureaucrats. The scourge of society. Oh, and I met Christy just after graduation. We got married three years ago." She waved her wedding band and engagement ring at Lily.

"Wow, congratulations."

"How about you and Erin? How long have you been together?"

Blood rushed to Lily's face. "We're not together. We're just friends."

"Oh, okay. Sorry, I shouldn't have assumed."

"No worries."

"She does seem a little too buttoned up for you."

"Buttoned up?"

"You know, proper." Alisha straightened and mimed buttoning up a shirt right up to her chin. "Just so."

Lily hadn't noticed. Well, she'd noticed the blazers, the pressed jeans, Erin's ultra politeness when she spoke to servers, something Lily approved of. She'd served too many jerks who treated her like their personal servant. She hadn't given much thought to Erin's stuffiness—was that the right word for it—because she'd never felt uncomfortable with her, not in a bad way. "I don't really see her clothes," she said.

Alisha burst into laughter.

"Okay, that came out wrong," Lily said, chuckling along with her.

Christy arrived with their drinks, and Erin returned a minute later. "Where are you living now?" Alisha asked Lily.

As they caught up with each other's lives, Lily kept an eye on Erin. She felt responsible for her, given that it was a chance encounter with her friend that had changed their plans. She'd suggest they go for coffee another time. She could see them going for a lot of coffees, actually, but she didn't know how Erin felt. When Alisha asked how long they'd been together, an honest answer would have been, "We're not together, but I'm starting to hope we could be."

Sandy would be pleased.

~

AFTER CHATTING WITH CHRISTY for a few minutes, the usual small talk about the weather, what do you do, wasn't that a great exhibit, Erin sipped her drink and listened to Lily and Alisha, not learning much new about Lily except that she'd had a dog while in university that had passed away a couple of years ago. She'd almost patted Lily's arm in sympathy, but stopped herself just in time.

A popular dance song blared. People surged toward the dance floor. Christy glanced at Alisha and off they went. Lily turned to Erin. "Sorry, I know how it is when you're the odd one out because you're with people who've known each other for a while and are talking about old times."

"Don't worry about it."

"Do you dance?"

"Of course," Erin said, without thinking.

"Come on, then, let's go. I like this song."

So did Erin, and she enjoyed dancing. She wasn't great at it, but she enjoyed it. She followed Lily onto the dance floor and was soon stomping to the beat and moving her arms around, hoping she didn't look too silly. A few feet in front of her, Lily bopped around, moving her hips in a way that Erin had tried but failed to do. Her hips just didn't have any rhythm.

Lily raised her arms and turned in a circle and smiled at Erin when she was facing her again. Erin couldn't help but smile back and realized she didn't care what Lily thought about her dancing. She'd only ever been this carefree on the dance floor with Christina, and that was because they'd grown up together. There was no point worrying about whether you looked like an idiot on the dance floor when the other person had seen you at your worst, been there when your mom or dad yelled at you, watched you puke when you were ill, seen you balling until your face turned red and your eyes grew so puffy they were slits.

Lily was a different story. It wasn't that Erin didn't care what she thought. She did, a bit too much for her taste. She felt safe with Lily. If Lily teased her about her dancing, it would be harmless fun. Lily wouldn't put her down or think any less of her because she couldn't move her hips like the woman Erin could see out of the corner of her eye, whose hips must not be attached to the rest of her body. Great moves. Mesmerizing moves. But Erin would rather watch Lily, in her jeans that fit just right and a checked blouse with the sleeves rolled up to just below her elbows, the lights making her red hair appear as if it were actually on fire, her flushed cheeks, the smile in her eyes, the warmth that enveloped Erin and made her want to close the distance between them and take Lily into her arms.

Cut!

Lily Altree, remember? Who thought she was out with Erin Bartlett, who was between jobs, trying to figure out what to do with her life. Only one detail of what Erin had just thought about her fake identity was true. But damn, she wished she really was Erin Bartlett with anonymous middle-class parents, not Erin

Hunt, daughter of wealthy parents, and someone Lily would hate, if she knew. At one time, Erin would have assumed that Lily would still smile at her, and fawn over her, and climb into that red convertible. But not anymore.

There were people who didn't care about how much money someone had. Lily was one of those people. She cared more about character. Someone who'd lied about her identity, someone who'd shown up at a protest to use her to get information, someone who sat and listened to her talk about a greedy development company, knowing her father was one of the partners in that company. Lily would not simper and smile when she found out because she wanted to be on Erin's arm at the country club.

The song trailed off and the DJ shouted something unintelligible, then the beat slowed as the next song took over. People naturally gravitated toward each other and paired off. Erin met Lily's eyes, and they did the awkward "should we or shouldn't we dance" thing. Lily stepped toward her. Erin surrendered.

The instant her arms were around Lily, she knew. Knew that whatever connection she felt for Lily was on an entirely different planet than the assumed bond between her and Christina. Slow dancing with Christina felt like she was slow dancing at a wedding with Dad. Comfortable. Familiar. But no heat.

With Lily . . . Erin wanted to melt into her. Lily felt so soft, and warm, and had ignited a fire within Erin that made the music sound distorted. She was hyper aware of her own breathing, felt the thump-thump-thump of her heart, or was it Lily's? Lily's hair brushed Erin's cheek, her hands caressed her back. Erin closed her eyes, focused on the beat, on swaying, on holding the woman who'd made all her doubts about her feelings disappear. It was just the two of them. No protests. No Hunt and Bishop. No undercover operation.

When the song ended and the beginning of another slow song played, Lily drew back but didn't let Erin go. "I hate this song."

Disappointment stabbed through Erin. "You want to stop?"

Lily's mouth turned up at the corners. "No." She rested her head on Erin's shoulder.

Erin held Lily tighter, ignoring the little voice calling her a liar. A huge, fat, fucking liar who couldn't possibly care about the woman in her arms because people didn't lie to those they cared about, not constantly. Not about the important stuff. She should let Lily go, tell her she wanted to go back to the table, avoid dancing with her until she could suggest they leave, then drive her home and never contact her again. Dad would have to find another way to figure out who was shafting him.

But she wouldn't. She wanted to stop lying to Lily. She didn't want to disappoint Dad. She couldn't see a way to do both. Either she continued to see Lily until they figured out the identity of White Knight, or she'd start at Hunt and Bishop with a cloud over her head: namely Dad. Why couldn't Lily have turned out to be straight? Why did she have to be a lesbian, and fiery, and interesting, and understanding, and cute as hell? Worse, Erin knew she'd be settling with Christina now. Sure, there was love between them, friendly love. Maybe it could grow into something more, in time. She wasn't saying she loved Lily, at least she didn't think she did, but Lily stirred something inside her that Christina never had.

Erin focused on the music, on the woman in her arms. When the song finished and the beat picked up, she opened her eyes and blinked into the strangeness, as if she'd just awoken from a dream. She reluctantly let Lily go, noticing Lily didn't seem to be in a hurry either.

They smiled at each other. Erin's eyes went to Lily's lips. A shred of sense, of decency, forced her to tear her gaze away. Not like this. Not as Erin Bartlett. Her lies were already bad enough without compounding them with anything physical, but she didn't know how long she'd be able to resist.

She stepped back, tried to appear and sound casual. "I'll go get another round of drinks. What were Alina and Christy drinking?"

Lily stared at her. The confusion in her eyes twisted Erin's stomach. "A Cosmopolitan and Bloody Mary," Lily said, her face a polite mask.

Erin turned and fled to the bar. She wanted to kill Erin Bartlett and tell Lily the truth, but doing so would also kill whatever was between them.

10

Lily leaned back on Sandy's couch and wondered how to answer her question. "No, it wasn't a date." It had sure felt like one a couple of times, though. They'd almost kissed on the dance floor. And when she and Alisha were saying goodbye, after they'd exchanged contact details, Alisha had leaned in and said, "By the way, you and Erin are together, Lily. You just haven't figured it out yet."

After the almost kiss, Lily had wondered if she'd imagined it. She was pretty sure she hadn't, though.

Sandy's forehead puckered. "I hate those types of nights."

"What type?"

"The 'was it or wasn't it a date' type."

"Yeah. We're seeing each other again, but I'm not sure that's a date, either."

"Jesus, you two need to get your act together. Where are you going?"

"Did you get your parcel yet?"

"What parcel?"

"Give me a break. The one you've been trying to get for two weeks."

"If you think I don't know what you're doing, I do. Fine, one little detour. But then I'm asking again." Sandy set her glass on the coffee table. "The courier company says I have to deal with the store. The store says it's the courier company. Tracking says it's still in transit. Last time I spoke to the courier, I said I could have walked over, picked up the parcel, and walked it home, and that would have been faster. Of course, every time I call either place, I'm on hold forever with rock music and ads blasting away. Last time I was disconnected after waiting for fifteen minutes. I'm thinking I should send them an invoice for my wasted time. But you know what they'd do with it."

Lily mimed crumpling up a paper and tossing it into a trash can. "So what's next?"

"Because it hasn't been delivered, I'm going to push the store for a refund."

"Good luck with that."

"Yeah. I'll let you know how it turns out." Sandy picked up her glass. "So where are you going with Erin?"

Lily sighed. "She's having supper at my place."

"Again?" Sandy studied Lily over the rim of her glass. "How many times will this be now?"

"Three."

"Have you ever been to her place?"

"No."

"Do you even know where she lives?"

"Somewhere in the Treeview Valley area."

Sandy's brows shot up. "That's upper middle class."

"Her father's an investor."

"You should hint at going to her place next time."

Lily shifted position on the sofa. "I like to cook. And we're going out after dinner. Erin's taking me to some lookout point so we can stargaze."

"Oh. Okay, if you don't get a kiss out of stargazing, something's seriously wrong. I mean it. One of you has to make the first move." Sandy waggled her eyebrows at Lily. "You're not usually this shy."

Wanting to appear cool, Lily shrugged. "I'm trying to take things at her speed."

Sandy barked a laugh. "Bullshit. You don't usually lie to yourself."

"What?"

"You're really into her, I mean really into her, that's why you don't want to push. You're afraid you'll scare her away."

"I hardly know her," Lily said, even though Sandy had nailed it. If she made a move and Erin rejected her, she'd be crushed. Time for a change of subject. "I've got an idea. About McMillan Park."

Sandy gave her a long look. "Okay, I'll play. I thought you were thinking of taking a step back from worrying about city planning."

"I'm seriously thinking about it." She was tired of banging her head against a brick wall. She wouldn't give up, but a change of tactics was required. Protests, petitions, showing up for city council meetings—when they'd let her—none of it worked. "But this is McMillan Park, Sandy."

"I know," Sandy said quietly.

"I have to do everything, okay? Everything." She told Sandy her idea, watched Sandy's eyes grow wide.

"Are you sure?" Sandy said.

"Yeah."

"Then I'm in."

"You don't have to."

"You're not doing it alone, and I'm betting there will be others in the group who'll stand with you. I'm pretty sure Patrick and Maria will."

Lily wondered about Erin. She wouldn't bring it up during their next . . . outing? Date? She didn't want Erin to feel obligated. No, Monday would be just for them. She didn't want any thoughts about developments. It would be a Hunt-and-Bishop-free night.

~

ERIN SANK THE EIGHT ball in a side pocket and shot Christina a triumphant smile. "That's two out of three for me."

Christina pouted. "You're really on your game today." She returned her pool cue to the rack and sank into one of the comfy chairs in the Hunts' recreation room. "So how goes the undercover operation."

Erin sank into the chair next to her. "It's going. I got some emails."

"You did?"

"Yeah, and that led to three possible suspects."

"Who?"

"Uh, Yvonne Smith, Ryan something or other. I think it begins with an *F*. And Natasha Goldstein. No, Vanessa Goldstein."

Christina picked up the glass of iced tea she'd previously set on the round drinks table and drained it all in one go. "So what's the plan? Is your dad going to send in a swat team to take them down?"

Erin chuckled. "There's no connection between any of them and the company or the city. IT suggested someone could have been outside the library using its Wi-Fi."

"I read something about how most people use lame passwords, like 'password' and '12345.'"

"Pete told Dad some people don't even set a password. But who knows? Dad has another plan."

"What is it?"

"He's going to send different versions of the construction schedule to different people and see if Lily gets one of them. If she does, we'll be able to tell from the version she gets who's leaking the information."

"Devious. But if you send a bogus version to city planning or legal or some other important department, won't that backfire? They'll be working with something that's not real."

"The changes will be small, like saying 'We intend to,' instead of, 'We will.' The schedule itself won't be changed."

Christina rubbed her chin with her right forefinger. "Well, I'll hand it to your dad, it just might work."

Erin wanted it to work. She wanted to tell Lily the truth, but she couldn't do that until they knew the identity of White Knight or Dad told her to stop seeing Lily because they didn't need her anymore. Lily would freak, but hopefully she'd be able to move past Erin's last name without too much bloodshed.

Christina glanced at her watch. "Oh, shit, I have to go. I'm meeting Tanya for dinner." She rose and glanced at Erin. "I didn't ask you if you wanted to go because I know how you feel about her."

"Thanks." Tanya was only capable of holding a conversation about one topic: Tanya. "I'll walk you to your car."

They didn't speak until they'd stepped out the front door and onto the wide brick path. "Oh, I keep meaning to ask you, how was the movie?" Erin asked.

"Movie?"

"With Julia."

"Oh, right. It was okay. Good to catch up with Julia. We're going to do it again soon."

"I'm glad you enjoyed yourself. We should see a movie soon." Guilt stirred, this time because of her plans with Lily on Monday. And the almost kiss. And the longing to see Lily again. And the minimizing of the importance of her connection with Lily to her parents. She was lying to everyone she cared about and hoped she could keep all the plates in motion until she could finally tell everyone the truth.

Christina turned when she reached her Jaguar. "I'll call you tomorrow."

Erin opened her mouth to reply, but Christina grabbed her shoulders and suddenly they were kissing. Or rather, Christina had her lips pressed against Erin's, for a second, three seconds, five seconds. She finally drew back.

Erin tried not to gape.

"I wanted to see what that felt like." Christina climbed into her car and waved as she pulled away.

Erin stared after her. She hadn't felt anything but shock. If she hadn't been ambushed, would she have felt something? Or would kissing Christina have still felt like the longest five seconds of her life? It had felt like an eternity because the kiss hadn't kindled a single ember within her, not because it had been a terrible experience she'd need therapy to get over. Why now? This was the worst time for Christina to decide it was time for them to be a couple. Her parents would be over the moon. Mom would be calling a wedding planner.

Dad's plan had better work, because Erin needed to come clean with everyone ASAP and hope that everyone she cared about would still be there when the dust settled.

~

THE NEXT DAY, ERIN stood in Dad's home office, leaning over his shoulder as she read the document open on his laptop. "That's everyone?"

Dad nodded. "They're confidential documents, Erin. We don't send them to hundreds of people, not until they're finalized."

She read the names and the modifications:

Dan in legal: We intend to
Audrey in planning: We will
Mike at the mayor's office: We are going to
Dave in construction: Our plan is to
Valerie in procurement: We will go ahead with
Melissa at the city council clerk's office: We will proceed with
Laura at the city's planning office: Our intention is to

"What did the original say?"

"We will begin construction on blah, blah, blah." Dad turned to her and smiled. "I've sent the emails. All we have to do is wait until Altree gets an email, and bam, someone's head is on a pike, and no more hanging out with Altree. Good riddance to both."

Erin's chest tightened. She rounded the desk so she could face him. "Lily's not a bad person. She's standing up for what she believes. Most people just complain. They whine. They never do anything to change whatever it is they're upset about."

Dad leaned back in his chair and folded his arms. "Do you want me to have our swag contractor make her a medal?"

"No, Dad. I want you to see her as a person, not a . . ." Erin searched for the right words.

"Yappy dog? Nuisance?"

"An inanimate obstacle that needs to be crushed."

"I'm not interested in crushing her, though giving her a bruise or two wouldn't hurt." He jabbed his finger on his desk. "I want to know who's betraying me. And once we know who that is, you'll be working with me. Your opinion of people like Altree will change when you're having to perform acrobatics at a city council meeting because people who'll never accomplish anything insist on making life hard for the adults."

Erin's hands clenched. A witty retort eluded her, and she didn't want to antagonize him.

"You've been hanging out with people you normally wouldn't hang out with. It's unfortunate it's taking so long to figure out who's betraying me. The longer you hang out with these people, the more you're seeing only their side."

"I'm not—"

Dad raised his hand, cutting her off. "Which is why I'm very happy you'll be working with me as soon as this little investigation of yours is over. If you'd already been where you belong, you wouldn't be trying to convince me that Altree's some kind of saint."

"I'm not saying she's a saint. I'm saying she's a real person with . . ." Real feelings. "A point of view that differs from yours. That doesn't make her evil, just like you aren't evil."

"I'm glad to hear you say that."

"Of course I don't think you're evil. Jeez, Dad."

His eyes met hers. "You've been taking time away from Christina and your other friends for this. Once it's over and done with, you can get back to your regular life."

He meant she'd get back to socializing with the right people.

"You'll forget about Altree and her group."

Could she turn her back on Lily like that? Forward Dad the email that revealed White Knight's identity, smile at Lily, tell her they'd hang out soon, then disconnect her undercover phone and go on with her life without a backward glance?

The ache in her chest, the burst of panic at the prospect of never seeing Lily again, answered the question. But just as lying to Lily was making her bleed, lying to her parents was hurting too. Maybe a solution, a way forward, would become obvious. Right now, Erin felt like she was trapped in an airless room with the walls closing in on her. There were no doors or windows. None that she could see. What was that pithy saying? The truth will set you free. But from what? The guilt? The pain? Or the woman she'd fallen for?

11

A couple of days later, Lily laid down her knife and fork and gazed across the table at Erin. The steak had turned out perfectly. She'd texted Erin to find out how she liked it cooked, had spent more than she usually would, and at the butchers to boot, not the grocery store, and had prepared the garlic mashed potatoes and the cheese bread just right.

Erin met her eyes. "Delicious, as usual. Seriously. Have you ever considered working on the other side of the restaurant, in the kitchen, as a chef?"

To hide her shock, she grabbed her napkin and made a show of wiping her mouth. "I've thought about it." For several years. Lain awake in bed working out how much macaroni and cheese she'd have to eat to afford to pay off her student loan (almost there), not have to live with a roommate (been there, done that, did not want to do it again), pay for the cooking program at the local college, and put gas in the car. She hadn't even told Sandy about her dream, her fantasy of herself in one of those silly chef hats and a crisp white apron, deftly juggling several skillets and pots and pans and presenting her masterpiece to a table of master chefs who'd take a bite of her perfect creation and close their eyes in ecstasy. Because it would never happen.

She'd fallen into some type of mental rut, not been able to cheerlead herself into the sacrifices she'd have to make, even though during just about every shift at the restaurant, she thought about it whenever she walked through the kitchen. Cooking for Erin had given the fantasy new life. For the first time in a while, she wanted to do more than wait tables.

"You should do it," Erin said.

If only it were that easy. "I don't know. I, uh . . ." She'd tell her the truth, see if it chased her away. "I'd like to, I really would. I just can't afford it unless I get a roommate, and I don't want one. So I'd probably have to sell my car and go back to taking the bus, which wouldn't be the end of the world, but I'd want to move closer to the college."

"You've looked into it."

"Yeah, I've checked. I mean, if I really, really wanted it, I could do it." She forced out the words she'd whispered to herself but refused to own. "So maybe I don't really want it."

Erin dabbed at her mouth with her napkin. "It's pretty clear to me you'd be brilliant at it."

Lily felt herself smile.

"And you clearly enjoy cooking."

"I do."

"What do you think's really stopping you, then?"

"I already said. Having to get a roommate, having to . . ." She trailed off when Erin shook her head.

"No, what's underneath all that? There has to be something stopping you. You're telling me excuses, not reasons. I know that because I'm the champion of excuses when it comes to figuring out what I want to do." Erin grinned sheepishly. "You said yourself you could do it if you really wanted to. So you must not want to."

Lily stiffened. "No! I do want to." She said it louder than she'd intended, but the firmness, the certainty, in her voice didn't surprise her. "I do want to, damn it. I do."

Erin's mouth turned up at the corners. "What's stopping you, then?"

Fear. That she'd upend her life and then fail the course. That she'd bite off more than she could chew—no pun intended—financially. That her parents would wonder again why she'd bothered to get a degree she wasn't going to use. They wouldn't say it out loud; their faces would say it for them. That she wouldn't be able to find a job when she completed the program. That the first meal she cooked for a paying customer would be returned to the kitchen with a note that the chef should be fired.

She swallowed but didn't avert her gaze. "I'm afraid." And pretty much never admitted that to anyone, ever.

"Of what?" Erin asked gently.

She chuckled. "How much time do we have? I have a list."

Now Erin was chuckling, making her eyes shine and her cheeks redden.

"It feels too risky, I guess."

"You don't strike me as the sort of person who shies away from risk."

"I'm not, most of the time." Only when something really mattered to her. The reason she always talked herself out of cooking school after revelling in her silly fantasy, and the reason she hadn't told the woman she'd just admitted her fear to that she liked her, in that way. The more than a friend way. And she wanted to know if Erin felt the same. And if she did, what they were going to do about it, because she wanted them to date, not just hang out. And if Erin only wanted them to hang out, she wasn't sure she could do that anymore, because she wanted more.

She squared her shoulders, gathered her courage, focused on Erin.

Damn.

She slowly exhaled. She couldn't, not here, not now, when there was such warmth and openness between them. The evening wasn't over yet. Maybe, hopefully, she wouldn't have to bare her soul even further, because what exactly they were doing would become clearer before they said good night.

"I'll give some more thought to cooking school." She rose to gather the dishes. "You might have to give me a pep talk every once in a while." She held her breath, curious about what Erin would say, then wondered how to interpret silence.

After dessert, they'd head out to some lookout point to gaze at the stars. If nothing happened, if they spent the entire evening at a polite distance, she'd have to decide whether to interpret that as "we're just friends hanging out and that's all I want" and accept it and move on, or force the issue by asking Erin outright if she was interested in being more than friends. Spending time with Erin without knowing was starting to make her crazy.

~

ERIN LOCATED THE CONSTELLATION using only her eyes and pointed in its general direction. She and Lily had arrived at the lookout point about twenty minutes ago and claimed a spot a respectable distance away from others who were taking in the stars or on a date. The lookout was popular and the sky was clear. A couple of people had set up telescopes. Erin had left hers at home. She hadn't wanted to spend a lot of time peering through it when Lily was with her. Her cameras were at home too. She'd only brought her binoculars, a piece of equipment they could share without having to leave the blanket they were now lying on, the sky spread out above them.

"The top of the cross is there," she said, gazing down her finger and feeling as if she were touching the stars.

Lily peered in that direction. "Uh, where?"

"There." Erin jabbed her finger at the sky.

Lily was silent for a moment, then she tutted. She offered her right hand to Erin. "Help me out."

Erin hesitated, then took Lily's hand and lifted it in the direction of the Northern Cross. "There." She curled her fingers a little tighter around Lily's warm hand, her heart thumping. "Look right where our hands are, where the knuckle on my forefinger is."

Lily's grip tightened around Erin's hand. "I see it."

Erin slowly pulled their hands down. "Now I'm moving down toward the intersection."

"Neat. I looked up a bunch of constellations earlier today, to remind myself of what they look like. Found a bunch of pics."

She'd looked up constellations? Erin wanted to kiss Lily's hand, the hand she still held and didn't want to let go. Lily wasn't letting go either. "The Northern Cross is part of Cygnus, the swan." Erin moved their hands in the direction of the swan's tail. "The tail."

"Cool."

She moved their hands again. "The beak." She wished Cygnus had hundreds of stars, so she could hold Lily's hand all night. Well, Lily wasn't yanking her hand away, so . . . Erin scanned for another constellation.

"Do you know why the stars are different colours?" Lily asked. "Does it depend on how far away they are?"

Reluctantly letting go of Lily's hand, Erin rolled toward her. "It's more about how hot the star is. Bluish stars are hotter than reddish ones." Despite the risk of boring Lily to tears, she couldn't help but continue on. "Every star is assigned a letter that indicates how hot they are. The possible letters are O, B, A, F, G, K, M, with O being the hottest and M being the coolest."

Lily flipped from her back to her side and propped herself up on her elbow. "Wow, you just reeled those off. Did you take astronomy classes?"

"Just one, as an elective. But don't be too impressed. There's a handy memory aid to remember the letters in order. It goes—" Blood rushed to her face.

Lily raised her brows. "It goes?"

Shit. "Um, it goes 'Oh Be A Fine Girl, Kiss Me,'" she whispered.

Their eyes met. Lily's gaze slid down to Erin's lips. Erin felt herself leaning in. Their lips touched, and Erin forgot about stars and heat scales and the other stargazers at the lookout.

When they parted, Erin figured the heat scorching through her would definitely be rated O. Their lips met again. Erin's surroundings faded away.

Someone clearing his throat brought her rudely back to the lookout. She jerked away from Lily and glanced over her shoulder.

The guy standing closest to them wasn't looking through his telescope anymore. He grinned, his teeth white in the unpolluted darkness. "Hey, live and let live and all that, but there are kids over there, and you might be better off getting a room. And I'd say that if you were a guy and a girl too. Honest."

"Sorry," Erin mumbled. She could feel Lily's laughter.

"Okay, no more kissing." Lily caressed Erin's cheek. "For now."

They rolled onto their backs, but lay pressed against each other. Erin forced herself to refocus on the sky. "Let me find Venus." She smiled when she felt Lily's hand take hers, then lifted both their hands. "There. Right there. Oh, I forgot to mention, our sun is rated G on the heat scale. Well, G2, to be more accurate. Each letter is broken down further. It blows my mind that the sun is low on the scale. Imagine how hot stars rated O, B, A, and F must be."

Lily squeezed Erin's hand.

"I'm boring you."

"No, keep talking. I am perfectly fine lying here listening to you talk."

This time Erin brought Lily's hand to her lips and kissed it.

~

ERIN'S MIND RACED AS they walked hand-in-hand back to where they'd parked. She'd promised herself that she would not move beyond friendship with Lily as Erin Bartlett. That had now gone out the window, but they'd only kissed. Just kissed. She would definitely not sleep with Lily as Erin Bartlett. That would be crossing the line for sure.

Lily squeezed Erin's hand. "This is nice."

"Yeah."

"I'm glad we know what this is. I've been wondering."

"Me too." And now would be the perfect time, before things got serious, to say, "I have something to tell you. My name's not Erin Bartlett. It's Erin Hunt. My dad's that guy you hate at Hunt and Bishop." But what if Lily freaked? They still had to drive home together, and she couldn't bear to think about what she'd see in Lily's eyes. She hoped it would be forgiveness, but what if it was hate or contempt?

If she wasn't terrified of Lily's reaction, she'd be terrified of Dad's. Until they knew the identity of White Knight, he expected her to remain in Lily's good graces. She imagined his anger, his disappointment, if she went home and told him she couldn't help him anymore because she'd fallen for Lily Altree and revealed her true identity to her. He'd see it as a betrayal. She couldn't do that to him, not when someone else was already betraying him, but now that her friendship with Lily had turned into something else, she wanted to tell Lily the truth. And Christina too. Until now, she hadn't thought about her at all, and now she knew for sure they wouldn't be the power couple everyone expected. The kiss with Lily had rated an O. The kiss with Christina had been off the scale, in a bad way.

It would be better for everyone if this baby relationship with Lily quickly fizzled, ideally right around the time Erin discovered the identity of White Knight. But she didn't want it to die. She was already thinking about when they'd see each other next.

They reached the car and shared a tender kiss before they got in.

As they were pulling onto the dirt road that would lead them to a county road, Lily said, "I didn't want to discuss business tonight, but I got another email from White Knight."

Erin kept her eyes on the road her high beams were illuminating. "What did it say?"

"It's the construction schedule for the apartment going up in McMillan Park."

That was the document Dad had slightly altered for everyone. They had White Knight! Part of Erin was excited for Dad. The other part dreaded telling Lily the truth about herself. "Can you forward it to me?" Her voice sounded a little strained, but Lily didn't seem to notice. "I'd like to take a look at the schedule."

"Sure." Lily pulled out her phone and tapped at it. "Done."

If Erin were alone, she'd pull over and check it right away. Fortunately, it wasn't difficult to chat with Lily until they pulled up to the curb outside her apartment. Their tastes in entertainment were so alike she believed they'd never have to try to fill an awkward silence. There would only be comfortable ones.

"I had a great time," Lily said.

"Me too."

Lily undid her seatbelt. "I'd kiss you, but I'd be here all night." She blew a kiss at Erin instead. "Until next time."

Erin smiled and waited until Lily was safely inside her apartment building, relieved Lily hadn't invited her upstairs. Because Lily's apartment faced the street, Erin drove around the corner and parked again. She couldn't wait to look at that email.

She opened it, examined the document Dad had doctored, and . . . She didn't understand. She read the sentence again.

"We will begin construction on . . ." That was the original wording. How could it be the original wording?

Then it hit her, making her lean back against the headrest and close her eyes. She knew the identity of White Knight, but unless she had more proof, she didn't dare reveal it to Dad. The fallout could be bad. Really bad. So bad that she might not ever tell him.

12

THE NEXT AFTERNOON, ERIN strode through the Hunt and Bishop lobby and rode the executive elevator up to the 50th floor, but rather than turning toward Dad's office, she turned right and entered Royce Bishop's reception area. Erin returned his administrative assistant's smile with a sickly one. She was not looking forward to this conversation, but she had no choice.

When she stepped into his office, Royce rose and gestured to one of the guest chairs. "I was so pleased when Rita told me you'd called and wanted to see me."

"Do you mind if I close the door?"

"Of course not."

Erin did so, then lowered herself stiffly into one of the chairs. Royce sat down again, rested his elbows on his desk, and peered at her, curiosity evident on his face. He wore a pale gray suit he'd had fitted at a tailor's, a white pressed shirt, and a pink tie. Always dapper, just like his daughter, who Erin had tried not to think about since last night.

"What did you want to see me about?" Royce said.

She clenched her hands in her lap. "Do you know someone's leaking documents, confidential documents, to The Citizens for Responsible Housing group?"

"Your father mentioned it to me."

"We've been trying to figure out who's leaking them."

Royce nodded. "You've been a mole, I've heard."

"Dad came up with a plan. A few days ago, he sent out the construction schedule for the McMillan Park project to all the appropriate people, but there was a catch. He'd changed one tiny part of each copy in a unique way."

Royce's expression and body language didn't change. He merely appeared interested. Erin plunged on. "Lily Altree, the head of the citizens group, received the schedule last night from her anonymous informant. When I looked at it, it was the original version of the document. It didn't contain any of Dad's changes."

She waited, but Royce didn't say anything. "You and Dad are the only two people who would have the original version."

A second passed, two seconds, then Royce's brow furrowed. "Wait a second. Are you suggesting *I'm* the one leaking documents to Lily Altree?"

"I don't see who else it could be."

He shook his head. "Erin, your father and I don't always see eye to eye, but we founded Hunt and Bishop together, have poured our hearts and blood and sweat and tears into this company. I would never do anything that could hurt it, or him, in any way."

She believed him, and not just because she wanted to. There was nothing in his manner or voice or expression that suggested he was lying. "I don't know who else it could be, then. I thought it must be you. I'm so sorry."

"No need to apologize. I would have jumped to the same conclusion." He leaned back in his chair. "Is it possible your father made a mistake, perhaps sent the original to someone, or maybe didn't alter the documents at all?"

Anything was possible. Maybe he'd forgotten to alter one, or maybe when he said he'd altered them, he'd meant his assistant Katie. Erin had seen the list of modifications, but not the documents themselves, and she hadn't been there when he, or someone else, had emailed them.

"I'm pleased to see you taking an interest in the company," Royce said.

"So's Dad."

"What do you think about the Citizens for Responsible Housing group? Have you learned anything from them?"

Erin quickly gave it some thought. "I hadn't really considered how what we build, and where, could affect the community. I always assumed our builds were an improvement, that our intention was always to make things better."

"You don't think we do that anymore?"

"I'm not saying that. I just hadn't given it any thought. Take McMillan Park. It's in a poor neighbourhood. It's the only green space for blocks and blocks. The proposed apartment rent will be too expensive for residents to afford, meaning people with more money will move in, and that could change the whole community, displacing people who are already there." Lily had talked about this over one of their dinners. "Gentrification. I'd read about it before, glossed over it. Frankly, I hadn't thought about it much."

"I think it's great you're thinking about these issues. I wanted to build affordable housing on that site."

"Christina told me."

"Your father said you'll be working for us soon."

"I'll be starting in planning and seeing an entire project through."

"Your father focuses on luxury condos now. The McMillan Park project is an exception, but I think he knew luxury would be too far out of reach. I've been trying to diversify us a little, get us back to the reason we founded the company."

"Get back to?"

Royce leaned forward. "When we started, we were determined to do exactly what you described. Make the world, and the community, a better place. Over time, our focus has shifted. I didn't mind at first because we were still building for a range of price points, but the last few years have been challenging. I've gone along with your father, but I don't think I can do that anymore."

"You're going to leave?"

"No. I love this place, and it's my company as much as his. I've already told him I'm going to build an affordable project next. He doesn't have to participate, and I doubt he will. It's caused some friction, but we'll get past it. We always do. We're like an old married couple that way."

Erin smiled. "Dad's not greedy." She'd heard him, or rather Hunt and Bishop, described as pigs quite often while hanging out with Lily and her group.

"I didn't say he was. I think he's afraid to do affordable housing."

"Dad, afraid? That doesn't sound like him."

Royce pressed the palms of his hands together, as if he were praying, and tapped his fingertips against each other. "Keep this to yourself, but our last affordable housing project failed. It's the only project we've lost money on. We sold the development and weren't in danger of folding, but it hit your father hard. He doesn't like failure."

Understatement of the year.

"He insisted we sell all our affordable builds, and he's stayed away from similar projects since then. Won't even entertain them. I've been patient, but I want to get back to projects that will give me the greatest satisfaction. I was wondering if you'd like to join me."

For a second, Erin wasn't sure she'd heard him correctly. "Join you?"

"Come work with me, instead of working with your father. Daniel is in med school, and Chrissy," he said, using Christina's childhood nickname she'd asked everyone to stop using when she'd turned twelve. Royce had ignored her. "Chrissy wants to get her real estate licence, and I'm proud of her for that. As for you." Royce paused. "I've gotten the impression you think coming to work here will be as exciting as watching paint dry."

Erin opened her mouth to protest, then decided to be honest, for a change.

"Your father is right. You should get a taste of everything, but ultimately you'll be a project lead, and ultimately, you'll sit in one of these offices and oversee the entire company. You'll choose the projects everyone working for you will work towards building." Royce kept his eyes locked on her. "Ask yourself what projects would excite you, because that's the key to being on fire here. Not planning, not legal, not persuading city council, not construction, architecture, none of that. It's putting the first shovel in the ground at a site you know will make a tiny piece of this planet a better place. Ask yourself if luxury condos or affordable housing will make you feel that way."

He slowly exhaled, then cleared his throat. "You're my goddaughter. Working with me on the affordable housing project I'll kick off soon will make it a true Hunt and Bishop project, except it will be Erin Hunt, not Aaron Hunt."

Erin stared at him, blown away by his proposal but not entirely surprised by his passion. Royce had always been the quiet one except when it came to things he really cared about. She felt for him, having his projects pushed aside, labouring on stuff he didn't really enjoy with the hope Dad would eventually relent and see what Royce really wanted. She could relate.

But Dad wouldn't see her working with Royce as anything but disloyal, a slap in the face from his ungrateful daughter. She stood and gazed at the photos hanging on the west wall of the office. Family photos. Royce, his wife Margot, Christina, Daniel, Royce's parents, when his father was still alive, wedding photos, the Hunts. One of Erin and Christina when they were five, in matching bathing suits.

"I'll take you under my wing," Royce said, making Erin turn toward him. "You'll sit in on every meeting, see every document, understand my reasoning whenever I make a decision. You'll be my right-hand woman on the project, so you'll still get a taste of every step in the process. But from a different vantage point. After all, you'll never work in planning or legal or construction. You'll work with them, and eventually, not even that. Your staff will handle most things." He slapped his hands on his desk. "So that's it. My proposal. If you think building affordable housing is something you'd be interested in doing, something that will fulfill you, say you'll work with me."

She certainly wasn't going to dismiss his proposal out of hand, especially since something inside her had stirred when he'd made it. But there was Dad to think about, and another potential issue. Would Royce still be enthusiastic about taking her under his wing when he found out she and Christina would never be a married power couple? Erin had no idea what would happen with her and Lily, especially once Lily knew the truth, assuming they didn't break up before then. But even if they did, being with Lily had scuttled any possibility of a relationship with Christina. Erin loved Christina dearly as a friend. She'd always be there for her and hoped they'd remain friends forever. But trying to be in a relationship with her, marrying her . . . it would be settling, maybe worse than settling, for both of them. She could at least be honest about that now.

"Does Dad know about this?" she asked Royce.

"I mentioned it to him. I didn't want to go behind his back."

Dad hadn't said anything to her about it. Was he confident she'd turn Royce down, or was he standing back and giving her room to choose? "I need time to think about it."

"Of course. But I'm serious about this."

"I know you are. Once I've figured out who's leaking documents, I'll make a decision. When will you start work on your project?"

"I'm looking for potential sites right now. It's an important decision, one you would definitely want to be involved in so you can learn how to choose your own projects."

Choose her own projects. She liked the sound of that, but only because it gave her a sense of control.

"But even if you can't be on board for that, there will be other projects. I'd love to have you work with me, but if you decide you'd rather stick with your father, I'll completely understand."

"Thanks. For that and the offer."

After making small talk about family, she left his office, her mind in a whirl. Part of her must want to accept his proposal, because she hadn't immediately shot it down, even though Dad's potential reaction to her accepting it made her want to run back into Royce's office and decline. Maybe Lily was rubbing off on her.

She'd reached the elevator and was looking at her phone when a familiar voice rang out. "Erin!" Dad towered over her. "You didn't mention you'd be coming to see me today."

"Uh, aren't you heading somewhere? We can talk another time." She realized it was dumb the moment she said it, but bursts of panic always froze her brain. She didn't have to tell Dad she'd seen Royce because she'd suspected him of being White Knight. Dad knew about the offer Royce had made her.

He waved away her question. "Let's go to my office. What were you doing standing there, anyway?"

"I just wanted to check something on my phone."

Inside his office, he got right to the point. "You met with Altree's group last night."

Altree's group . . . "Yeah." Another lie to add to the pile.

"Well. Which version of the email did she get?"

Erin wandered over to Dad's photos and looked at them for the thousandth time, the ones with celebrities and city officials, and breaking ground. Behind him hung his degree and the certificates he'd earned since graduating from university. Awards cluttered the small display case on the other wall.

She focused on Dad. "She didn't get an email from White Knight."

Dad frowned at her. "No? But I sent it days ago. And it's a juicy document."

"I asked her, and she said she didn't get one."

"Maybe she was lying."

"I don't think so."

Dad picked up the pen on his desk and twirled it in his fingers. "Keep asking. What's she planning now? What was the meeting about?"

"Just a general catch-up meeting about what's going on in the city regarding new builds. McMillan Park didn't come up." Lily had said she didn't want to discuss McMillan Park, Hunt and Bishop, or anything else related to real estate developments. Erin had been happy to oblige.

"I want you to wrap this up already. If there's no progress in a couple of weeks, you're coming to work with me. I don't want you hanging out with these people for much longer."

"Maybe I should stop now." And come clean with Lily, a thought that terrified her and made her want to take back what she'd just said to Dad.

"What, you mean give up? Jesus." He threw the pen down on his desk. "Sometimes I wonder how you're my fucking daughter. Can't you manage to do one simple thing?"

She shifted her focus to the photos again, tears welling in her eyes.

"I'm sorry," Dad said. "I shouldn't have said that. I know you're trying. But that's why I want you to come work with me. You need guidance, Erin. You need someone to help you get on track."

Erin took a moment to brush away her tears, then perched on the edge of one of the guest chairs. "I just saw Royce. He asked me if I wanted to work with him on affordable housing. He said you know about it."

Dad picked up the pen again, focused on it. "It's your decision."

"Really?"

"I want you with me, but at least you'd still be here, where you should be. Maybe your first project could be with Royce. Your next project could be with me." He briefly met her eyes.

Erin glimpsed the vulnerability in them. All right, it was her decision. But if she went with Royce, she'd deeply hurt Dad. Right now, she was so occupied with keeping the plates spinning that she couldn't cut through the noise, quiet the conflicting voices that grew ever louder, and figure out what she wanted. The only desire coming through loud and clear was to see Lily again.

~

BREATHING IN THE WARMER, natural air, Lily stood in her usual spot in the alley behind the restaurant and called Sandy.

"I left you two messages today, and texted," Sandy said. "I was about to come to the restaurant to make sure Erin hadn't murdered you last night and dumped you out in the bush somewhere."

She snorted. "I've been busy." Not true. She hadn't wanted to call Sandy and breathlessly recount her wonderful time with Erin, not wanting to come across as lame.

"So?"

"We're an item."

"Ha! So she doesn't belong to some weird religious group that forbids physical contact or something."

"Come on. She wanted to be sure, I guess."

"When do you see her next?"

"I don't know."

"You haven't talked to her today?"

"We did, but she said she needs to make an important appointment and once she knows when it is, we'll arrange to go for coffee somewhere."

Sandy must have heard the sigh in her voice. "What's wrong?"

"Nothing."

"Spit it out."

Lily wished Sandy couldn't read her like a book. "We're going out for coffee again."

"Okay. And?"

"It's always my place—"

"Or somewhere else. Right." Sandy paused. "You don't think she's got another woman stashed somewhere, or maybe she's a tourist."

"She's not a tourist. I'm pretty sure she's a lesbian. And I'd be really surprised if she's already involved with someone." Erin was pretty much always available when Lily called her. She'd have to be telling a hell of a lot of lies to keep another girlfriend happy. "I know she lives with her parents. Maybe she's not ready to introduce me yet."

"She could still, you know, drive you by her place to show you, or arrange a time when they won't be there. We all lived at home once. We all managed to bring our boyfriends and girlfriends home, even if we had to sneak them in."

"I don't want to push it."

"Better to find out if there's something fishy there before you get too involved."

Too late. "I'll think about it." Time to move on. "I'm going to call a meeting soon, tell everyone our next play regarding McMillan Park."

"You think your plan will work?"

"It will certainly get their attention." Maybe only Sandy, and hopefully Erin, would agree to do it, because everyone else seemed to have given up on saving the park. But Lily couldn't let it go, not McMillan Park. It was time to be bolder, to do something Hunt and Bishop couldn't ignore.

13

Erin rubbed her eyes and got up from her desk to stretch her legs. She'd gone back to the only solid lead they had to White Knight's identity: the three names Dad had given her. She'd pored over all the public information she could find about them online but couldn't find a connection between any of them and Hunt and Bishop or city hall. IT's suggestion that it could have been someone else using the library's Wi-Fi was plausible, but those three names were the only clue she had.

Maybe Dad had forgotten to alter the documents, or maybe he'd accidentally sent one of the recipients the original version. She didn't want to ask him. He'd blow up at her, and he'd want to know why she was checking his work. She didn't want to tell him yet.

Even if Dad had screwed up, Erin wanted to do more than wait for Lily to get more emails. In fact, she didn't want to talk to Lily about White Knight ever again because she wanted as few reminders as possible that she was a Hunt who'd initially inserted herself into Lily's life to use her. She couldn't tell Lily who she was, not until Dad made it clear he didn't want to use her anymore. But she could at least stop using Lily herself.

If she uncovered White Knight's identity, that would be it. Dad would be happy. She could tell Lily the truth and ask, beg, plead for her forgiveness. That was why she'd spent the last hour researching private investigators. If she read another review, she'd go cross-eyed.

She called the one at the top of her list and arranged to meet with him the next afternoon at 3 p.m. Then she almost called Lily on her real phone. She remembered to switch to her undercover phone when she realized the phone she held didn't have Lily's contact information.

"I can make it on Friday afternoon," she said to Lily, after they'd exchanged greetings and raised the subject of coffee again. "At two?"

"Sure." Lily paused. "Instead of going somewhere, I wouldn't mind seeing where you live."

Oh, shit. Erin furiously thought of something to say. "Friday's not a good time. My dad often works from home on Fridays, and my mom's home most of the time."

"She's a housewife."

"Yeah." True. For once. Though Mom would not appreciate being called a housewife.

"Am I ever going to see where you live?" Lily's voice was a little higher than usual.

"Yes." Erin sincerely hoped so. "Can I be honest?"

"Please."

"I'm not ready to introduce you to my parents yet, and I'll feel funny sneaking you in as if we're doing something wrong." Truth again. See, she wasn't lying all that much. Not really. Just about her last name. "If I lived alone, it wouldn't be a problem. But I respect my parents." Yes, she was on a truth roll.

"I'm just curious about you, that's all. I want to know everything."

A desire that warmed and terrified Erin. "Me too," she squeaked. "So we're okay for coffee on Friday somewhere other than my place?"

"As long as you won't keep me hidden from your parents forever."

Erin wished she'd put it another way. "I won't."

"Let's meet at the usual coffee shop near McMillan Park. I wouldn't mind visiting the park again."

But Dad had won. Why did Lily want to torture herself? Erin understood the significance of the park to her. At the same time, she would hate to see Lily wallowing in it. "Sure."

"Great. I'm looking forward to seeing you."

"Me too."

They said their goodbyes. After Erin disconnected, she tossed the undercover phone onto her desk and flopped onto the bed. Okay, so tomorrow she'd meet with a private investigator who would hopefully find out something that would get her out of this mess so she could finally be honest with Lily.

Tomorrow night she was having dinner with Christina, which she dreaded. There was no way she could tell her that she and Lily were involved. If Christina flipped, she could go straight to either of their dads, or both of them. That wasn't the way Erin wanted her parents to find out. But what would she do if Christina wanted to find out what kissing her felt like again? Now it would feel like cheating, because it would be. Lily would not be happy to find out she was kissing other women. And yes, she'd see Lily for coffee on Friday and continue to lie through her teeth about certain aspects of her life.

She could handle it. Those plates were still spinning. None of them were wobbling. Yet.

~

ERIN ENTERED THE COFFEE shop where she'd arranged to meet one Douglas Wong, PI, and spotted the blue wind breaker he said he'd be wearing. Dad had said he wanted to keep their little document leak problem within the family, but she just wanted it to be over. She was about to go to the counter to order her coffee, when she noticed Wong point to the cup sitting across from him. He'd chosen a table in a quiet corner.

"Your favourite latte," he said to her as she pulled out the chair across from him.

She sipped it. Vanilla. Damn, he was right. "How did you know?"

"I did my research."

"My social profiles are pretty locked down."

"True, but not everyone close to you is as careful. A photo on Christina Bishop's profile of you is public. According to what Ms. Bishop wrote, you're holding your favourite vanilla latte."

Impressive.

"Let's get down to business. On the phone, you said you want me to find out if there's a connection between," he glanced down at his phone, "one of Vanessa Goldstein, Ryan Fothering, and Yvonne Smith, and either Hunt and Bishop or city council."

She nodded. "Someone is leaking confidential documents. We—my father and I—used the emails to narrow down the point of origin to a library. Those three people were at the library both times an email was sent. But it's possible someone else was on the library's Wi-Fi."

Wong raised his hand. "One thing at a time. Let me dig into this list first, and if they don't pan out, we'll figure out our next move."

"My father can't know about this."

"You're the client."

She gulped down some latte. "We haven't been able to find a connection between any of them and the company or city hall. I checked online too."

"I'll do it again." Wong tapped something into his phone. "I'd like to do surveillance."

"You mean watch them?"

"If they're connected to someone you know, they could be making an effort to keep their connection offline. But to keep an eye on them 24/7 will require more manpower."

"Whatever you need is fine." Erin wanted to unmask White Knight ASAP. "This is a long shot, but can you also see if there's a connection between any of them and Lily Altree. I don't want Lily under surveillance," she quickly added, not because she cared if Wong found out about their relationship, but because she wouldn't invade Lily's privacy like that. "But she's the one who received the leaked documents through email."

When Wong opened his mouth, Erin continued. "I know it wouldn't make sense. Why wouldn't they just hand the documents to her? But maybe someone doesn't want her to know they're the source for some reason."

"I'll check into it."

"I'll tell you up front you'll find out she's, uh, protested against Hunt and Bishop projects."

"Which is why someone chose her to send the documents to."

"Yes." She'd told him so he wouldn't call her up and say, "Guess what I found out? Lily Altree hates Hunt and Bishop and everything connected to it." She didn't need the reminder. "That's how we knew she was getting the documents. She protested against a project that wasn't public knowledge yet."

"You wouldn't by any chance have any of the emails?" Wong asked.

"I do." She forwarded them to him.

"Do you mind if I ask how you got them?"

"She—Lily—forwarded them to me."

Wong's brow furrowed. She could see his wheels turning. Why would someone who opposed Hunt and Bishop projects tell the company she was receiving confidential company documents?

He added two and two together and got five. "When you, meaning Hunt and Bishop, realized there was a leak and she was the recipient, did you approach her and pay her to help you?"

"No! Lily Altree is totally on the up and up. She'd never work with us, no matter how much money we offered her." She clutched her cup, consciously reminded herself not to crush it because it wasn't empty. "She willingly forwarded them to me, and that's all I'm saying."

"We all have our secrets," Wong said levelly. He stared down at his phone. "White Knight. Interesting." His head came up. "I think I have enough to get started."

They reviewed the payment details they'd discussed on the phone. Erin sent him the agreed upon deposit.

Satisfied, Wong drained his remaining coffee and stood. "I'll contact you in a few days or when I have something concrete to tell you, whichever is earlier."

After he'd left, Erin sat alone and finished her latte, wondering what Lily was doing. She was about to leave when her phone vibrated. Christina. Erin had tried to forget about their dinner that evening.

"I have to cancel tonight," Christina said after saying hello. "Something's come up."

"Is anything wrong?"

"No, just something I need to do today."

"You sure everything's okay?"

Christina blew out a sigh. "It's to do with my real estate licence, or rather, my application for the courses. I forgot something and now I'm feeling flustered. Let me deal with it and we'll get together another time."

Erin had no idea what was involved in applying for a real estate licence and didn't want to think about Christina's reason too hard. She was glad their dinner was being postponed, but also sad she felt that way. Christina was her closest friend, someone she felt completely comfortable with and could share anything with—almost anything. She hoped it would stay that way when Christina found out about Lily.

"Okay, no worries," she said to her. "We can reschedule."

"You're a dear. I'll call you soon." The connection went dead.

Erin pocketed her phone. Christina didn't usually rush off the phone like that, flustered or not. She hadn't sounded angry, but Erin wondered if she'd found out about her brief meeting with Royce. No, if she was mad because Erin had pretty much accused her father of leaking confidential company documents, she'd just say. Christina wasn't one to beat around the bush. She'd had her mind on other things, as Erin did.

She hoped Wong would contact her in a few days with news she could take to Dad, even though the thought of telling Lily her true identity filled her with so much dread that she could hardly breathe.

14

Erin strolled with Lily toward McMillan Park, wishing she was brave enough to take her hand. They'd met for coffee about ten minutes ago and decided to drink them on the way to the park, which was only a five-minute walk away.

"So you said your mom's a housewife?" Lily said.

As usual, questions about her family made Erin tense and wary. "Yeah."

"What does she do all day?"

Golf, tennis, horseback riding, driving caterers crazy, mixing mean drinks in their cozy basement bar, volunteering with her two favourite charities. Oh, and she liked tinkering with electronics, something that drove Dad crazy. "We can pay someone to fix it!" was one of his favourite shouts whenever Mom wanted to take something apart. She blamed her fascination with electronics on being the only girl with four brothers, all of whom were tinkerers.

"She has a lot of interests, enough to fill her days," Erin said.

"Like?"

She chose something safe and true. "Volunteer work."

"What does she do?"

"She volunteers at the humane society." Dad was allergic to just about everything so Mom had to be content with being an official cat stroker and dog walker. Erin had always wanted a pet.

When she finally moved out, she'd be dreaming about which cat to adopt, not what furniture to buy.

"That's so cool. I want to get a cat, but I'd prefer to have two and I don't think my apartment's big enough."

Erin grinned. "I want a cat too! My dad has allergies, so I've never had a pet."

"That sucks."

She shouldn't have mentioned Dad. "When we were at the club, I overheard you say you had a dog until a few years ago."

Lily enthusiastically launched into a dog story, much to Erin's relief. Keeping the lies to a minimum was an iffy proposition when Lily was asking questions about family. Every time she lied to her, even if it was only a tiny fib, she could almost feel her being, her inner core, kicking back at her, the decent, kind person she'd always seen herself to be yelling to be let out so she could tell the truth, stop lying, stop disrespecting the woman next to her who also wanted a cat and made her want to stop worrying about what people on the crowded sidewalk thought.

"Oh, yeah." Lily stopped walking and pulled out her phone. "I saw this ad online and thought of you right away," she said, swiping and tapping a few times. She offered Erin her phone.

Erin took it from her and read the information about an astrophotography course being offered at a local community college, one that would then lead to more advanced courses and, if she completed the program, a certificate and help finding a placement.

Lily patted Erin's arm. "That course sounds right up your alley."

"Yeah, but I'm not sure I want to take a course." Help finding a placement. She tried, but failed, to clamp down on the excitement shooting through her. Imagine being paid to take photos of the sky! But she was only an amateur. The application process mentioned sending a portfolio. And then there was Dad.

"I'm going to be working with my dad," she said to Lily.

"Do you want to work with your dad?"

Erin could feel Lily's eyes on her. She wanted to say yes, but her mouth wouldn't open.

"Tell him the truth," Lily said gently.

I can't believe you're my fucking daughter.

"I wasn't sucking up when I said some of your photos were as good as the ones in the exhibit. You'd be great at this."

"I'm not sure I want to turn a hobby into a job." Liar.

"Think about it, okay? Not that I'm one to talk about not pursuing a dream, but that's probably why I wouldn't like to see you doing the same thing."

"I'll think about it." But she felt depressed. She'd think about it and go work with Dad. And wonder. And regret. And wish she'd had the courage.

She gave Lily her phone back. They continued walking and turned a corner. Lily's pace quickened. Erin had to almost jog to keep up with her.

"They just couldn't wait." Lily thrust her free hand toward the sign that hadn't been there when they'd last held a protest at the park.

Erin stopped in front of the large, rectangular sign attached to the iron fence.

Hunt and Bishop Newcastle Development
Family Apartments Coming Soon

Private Property
No Trespassing

"They locked the damn gate." Lily shook it, making the metal ring against the chain and padlock. "They don't waste any time, do they?" Her eyes grew distant for a second. "I bet the north entrance is locked too, but there's a side entrance that doesn't have a gate. Come on." She took off, blowing past Erin, who hurried after her.

"Lily," she called. "It says no trespassing."

Lily turned into the adjacent apartment complex and strode up the wide asphalt path. Erin veered around the people on the path walking toward her. She caught up with Lily and grabbed her arm. "It says no trespassing."

"It's a city park," Lily snapped. She tossed her empty coffee cup into an almost overflowing trash can off the side of the path.

Erin threw her own cup in and tried to reason with her. "The city sold it."

"Fuck the city. If we had councillors who actually cared about the community, it would still be McMillan Park." She shook Erin's hand away. "Here." She pointed, then moved the metal barrier blocking a narrow entrance into the park.

Erin followed her in, feeling like she was committing a crime, even though technically she herself wasn't trespassing. By extension, she supposed Lily wasn't either. "Okay, okay, we'll have a quick look around and then leave."

Lily made a beeline to the sandbox they'd chatted by before and plunked herself onto the grass next to it. "Jay-Jay and I loved building stuff here. Even though I sucked at it and ended up knocking over everything I built, Jay-Jay helped me. It's one of the few vivid memories I have of her, and sometimes I wonder how much is actually memory now, and how much is me filling in the gaps. And over there." She pointed to the nearby bench she'd spoken about before, where she sat on Jay-Jay's birthday. "I won't be able to sit there anymore. I guess I'll gaze at a fucking apartment building now from the sidewalk. Wouldn't want to trespass."

Erin didn't know how to console her. What could she possibly say? It was true. At the same time, things couldn't remain the same forever. Cities changed. Buildings came and went. The same applied to parks. Though she had to admit, this park was a shame. It was the only greenspace in the area, and quite a large one. If the city hadn't neglected it, would Dad have moved in and bought it?

She went to sit next to Lily—

"Hey!"

Erin jumped and glanced behind her. Great. A security guard was hustling over to them. Then her heart thumped when he got closer. She knew him. He knew her! "Let me deal with him," she said, then sprinted toward him to head him off, adrenaline coursing through her.

His stern expression morphed into a smile when he recognized her. "Ms. Hunt. I didn't know it was you."

Dad made a point of inviting everyone to the annual Christmas party, from the cleaners to city councillors to the security they hired to keep the riff raff away from sites like this one. "Hello, Mike."

His smile broadened.

"I'm here with a friend who just wanted to see the park one last time. We won't cause any trouble."

He grinned. "I couldn't do much if you did."

"We'd just like a little privacy."

He looked past her, at Lily. Erin held her breath, hoping security hadn't been sent a photo of Lily with a warning to keep an eye out for her. Then he focused on Erin again. "Sure, sure, no problem. I'll let the other guard know you're here and to stay away. Shout if you need anything." He mock saluted her and strolled away.

Erin turned her attention back to Lily and wondered if she'd even noticed the security guard and heard his shout. She hadn't moved a muscle. In contrast, Erin's hands were shaking. If he hadn't shouted, if he'd walked over to them and said, "Good afternoon, Ms. Hunt." She did not want Lily finding out that way. She wanted Lily to hear it from her, in private.

She tucked her hands into her pockets, waited until they were still, then went back to Lily. She lowered herself down next to her. "I told him we won't cause any trouble."

Lily grunted.

Still not sure what to do, Erin slipped her arm around Lily's shoulders and took her hand. Lily's fingers tightened around hers.

"This place means something to the people around here, not just me," Lily murmured. "But they just let it go. They didn't give a shit about the people around here, the kids who need a place to play or blow off steam. The moms who sit on the benches, take a break, chat to their friends. That fucking rezoning proposal talked about how the park wasn't extensively used. What the hell did they expect when everything's falling apart? If they'd put just a little bit of money into this place every year, the park would be filled with people. Kids wouldn't be warned to stay off the equipment because they might get hurt. The stupidity of it, the total lack of, I don't know, common sense. I just . . . it makes me so angry."

Erin kept her mouth closed. Let her get it all out. She knew what the park meant to her.

"It's a self-fulfilling prophecy. They reduce the money they put into the park, which runs it down, which means fewer people come, which they use as justification to put even less money into it, and it spirals like that until hardly anyone comes and they say the community isn't using the park anymore. And then a company like Hunt and Bishop comes along and they sell it. And on the subject of Hunt and Bishop, why don't developers put money into places like this, rather than ruining them?"

"You mean invest in parks?"

"And other types of public spaces."

"They invest in real estate developments. It's the city's responsibility to maintain its spaces."

"I just wonder why these developers don't give something back to the communities every once in a while. I know they give to charity, but writing a cheque is easy. They could give back in a more meaningful way than another hundred-thousand-dollar cheque to whatever the mayor's pet charity is. When it comes to parks and land and neighbourhood spaces, all they do is take."

"I've never thought about it," Erin said sincerely. Maybe she'd ask Dad. When he was in a good mood. A really good mood.

Lily squeezed Erin's hand. "I shouldn't yell at you. You're not the one responsible."

Not yet. She might be the next time Hunt and Bishop planted a sign announcing a new development.

"I have one more Hail Mary in mind for saving this place," Lily said.

Erin gaped at her. "What can you do? Everything's settled."

"Until the plans for the apartment building are approved and the construction crew shows up, there's time. I usually stop at this point, but I have to keep going. For the park." Her voice dipped. "For Jay-Jay."

"But what can you do?"

"I'm still settling on the exact details. When I'm sure, I'll call a meeting."

Erin wanted to press her for details now, but restrained herself. She'd find out soon enough, and Lily had fallen silent again and was gazing pensively at the dirty sand in the box.

"Is there anywhere like McMillan Park for you?" she asked Erin. "Anywhere that brings up memories about someone you wish you could talk to?"

Her integrity, her morality, those parts of her she was repressing so much lately, made her blurt out the answer. Because she would not dishonour Nan by keeping this truth to herself. "My grandmother's house."

Her grief surfaced before she could beat it back down. She still couldn't think about Nan without her throat thickening and her eyes moistening and the pain almost making her double over. More than three years, and it still felt like yesterday.

"What about it?" Lily asked softly.

The defence mechanism she'd quickly developed, the one that kicked in every time she and Lily touched on family, rang an alarm bell in her head. But Lily had shared about Jay-Jay, and Erin wanted to tell her about Nan. She could do it without giving away her identity.

"I told you I'm an only child." When Lily nodded, Erin continued. "Well, my father is an only child too, so I was her only grandchild. My grandfather died when I was quite young so I don't remember much about him, but my nan was almost like a second mom. I spent a lot of time at her place." Erin blinked away her tears. "We laughed at the same things, and when I was younger, she didn't mind watching the same cartoon a billion times and tossing around a ball and letting me screw up another pie when I was," she made air quotes, "helping her bake. She gave me my first telescope, showed me how to use it." She sucked down air. "She died a few years ago. Cancer."

"I'm sorry."

Erin cleared her throat. "Anyway, I know every inch of that house, hid in every cupboard, braved the spooky attic." She wouldn't mention the guest house out back. Nan's house wasn't huge, but it sat on ten acres of land. "We played hide and seek a lot. When I was younger. We weren't still playing by the time she passed away." When Lily chuckled, so did Erin. "I miss her. I miss being in that house with her, eating gooey spaghetti and running around outside and curled up watching movies."

"What happened to it? The house?"

Even though Erin had expected this question, she still wasn't prepared for it. She wished Nan was alive, so she could talk to her about the mess she was in regarding Lily and all the lies. And she would not lie, not this time, not about Nan and her house and how she felt about it. She wanted the list of lies she told Lily, the important ones, to be short. Lying about the house would betray everyone, including herself. She wouldn't do it, wouldn't say, "Oh, I don't know, my father dealt with it," or, "Oh, we sold it," when the truth was Erin owned it. She could go over any time, visit the house her cousin lived in but would vacate soon when he graduated from university and returned to British Columbia, leaving her with yet another decision to make.

She wouldn't pretend she didn't care about its fate when the truth was that stepping across its threshold still evoked such sorrow that she'd been happy to offer it to her cousin, giving her a reason to stay away. She wouldn't sully the precious gift Nan had given her, or her shock and gratitude when the attorney had read the will and she realized she wouldn't lose one of the most joyful places she knew. She wouldn't brush away the tears in Dad's eyes, not tears of jealousy or resentment, but tears of joy for his daughter, because he knew how much she loved her nan.

"I am so sorry," she heard Lily say. "I wouldn't have asked if I'd known how much it would upset you."

A lump rose in Erin's throat when Lily gently wiped away one of her tears.

Erin furiously rubbed away the rest. She hadn't realized she was weeping. "Can you ask me that question another time?" When she could tell the truth. When Lily could step into that house with her, so she wouldn't have to do it alone or appear strong for Mom and Dad. "I mean it. Ask me again sometime."

"I will."

Erin leaned into Lily when she felt Lily's arms around her shoulders. They drew each other close and rested their heads together, lost in their memories.

~

ERIN CLUTCHED HER COFFEE cup and waited for Lily to take the floor and tell everyone what action she had planned to try to save McMillan Park. Lily's group had pretty much taken over the second floor of a coffee shop in the downtown area. Quite a few people had come out in response to Lily's intriguing email promising she had something different in mind that would make a statement. Erin didn't recognize a handful of them. Right now, Lily was talking to Sandy. Erin, not knowing if Lily wanted everyone to know they were dating, had hung back and grabbed a wingback chair away from where Lily had set her coffee.

"Okay, everyone." Lily waved her arms. "Let's talk."

The chatter died down. Lily sipped her coffee and surveyed those gathered. "McMillan Park. Hunt and Bishop now owns it. The barriers are up. Security guards are there."

Several of those gathered hissed and booed. Erin wanted to slink down in her chair.

"Petitions, protesting at the gates . . . developers don't care. They don't see the signs or engage with us. We don't exist to them. It's time to make them see that we exist."

"What do you have in mind?" Patrick asked.

"We protest somewhere they can't ignore us." Lily paused. "We protest at the Hunt and Bishop tower."

Erin felt as if someone had punched her. No, no, no. Crazy idea. Batshit crazy idea. Dad would go ballistic. He wouldn't listen. Engage? Ha! Erin wasn't sure what he'd do but hoped it wouldn't involve violence.

"There's a large courtyard in front of the building," Lily explained. "Plenty of room for us to gather and wave our signs."

Erin tried to fight it, but her hand went up anyway. She couldn't let this happen, not without trying to stop it.

Lily smiled at her. "Erin."

"Uh, I assume the Hunt and Bishop tower is on private property. You—we'd be trespassing if we were to protest there."

Maria nodded. "She has a point. They can't stop us from protesting in a public place, but if that's not a public place . . ."

Lily waved away Erin and Maria's concerns. "What's the worst that can happen? They boot us off the property. People will see that. If we're lucky, the news will pick it up. Even they'll want to come out for a protest right in the company's face."

Erin wanted to leap to her feet and say, "Don't do it! My father will not react well and I'm afraid of what he might do." But she gulped down coffee instead, her mind and heart racing. If she brought up another reason not to protest there, would Lily wonder why?

"It will be a peaceful protest," Lily said. "Well, we'll shout. We'll make our voices heard. But we won't stop anyone from going into the building or damage any property."

It wouldn't matter. Dad would see it as a personal attack, which it would be. As for Royce, he wouldn't blow a gasket, but he would not be pleased. How far would they take their anger? Would they limit themselves to having the protestors removed?

She raised her hand again. "It's not only Hunt and Bishop in that building. The company only occupies a few floors. The rest are occupied by other businesses. You could disrupt their services. Some are medical offices."

Lily's face tightened. "It'll only be for a few hours."

"And we won't block access to the building," Sandy added.

So Lily had discussed all this with Sandy. Erin felt a bit jealous, even though she knew she had no right.

"It'll have to be a weekday," Lily said. "I know that'll be difficult for some of you, but think about all the projects that have gone ahead regardless of community concerns. It's time to make a stand. Who's with me?"

"I'm in," Patrick said.

Maria punched her fist into the air. "Me too."

A chorus of "Let's do it" and "I'll be there" rose. Erin hoped Lily hadn't noticed her voice wasn't among them. Now she scrambled for some excuse for why she couldn't attend.

"We have a plan," Lily declared.

An excited charge ran through the air. While everyone else discussed what date and time to hold the protest, which signs to bring, whether they should hand out leaflets to people entering and leaving the building, and where they should all stand, Erin sat in silence, fraught with worry.

"Hey."

She jerked her head up. Lily plunked into the chair next to her. "I get the sense you're not thrilled with our plan."

Erin swallowed. She could lie, say she was busy, but Lily would wonder why she hadn't spoken up when they were choosing the date. "I'm not. I'm sorry."

Lily's face fell, but she laid her hand on Erin's arm. "It's okay. You don't have to agree with me about everything. But what's the problem?"

"I think it'll have the opposite effect of what you're hoping for." What Lily wanted was already a vain hope. Unless something bizarre happened, like Dad having some religious experience and becoming a monk, he wouldn't drop the McMillan Park project. "You'll only anger the company."

"Maybe that'll be enough. Maybe I just want to stick it to them for once, be the reason they're having a bad day." She smiled sheepishly. "I know, childish. But I need to feel like I did everything possible."

Erin reached for her hand, squeezed it. How could she want the project to succeed and fail at the same time? How could she be loyal to two people on the opposite sides of a conflict? "I won't be there."

Lily's shoulders sagged.

"I can't. I think this is a bad tactic that will do more harm than good."

"You have to do what you think is right, and so do I. Would have been nice to have your support, though, even though you think I'm being dumb."

"I don't—"

"Lily!" someone called.

Lily pulled her hand from Erin's, but patted her shoulder.

Erin watched her walk over to one of the people she didn't recognize. She'd let her down, on top of lying to her. But even if Lily knew the truth, Erin would still be saying she couldn't go. Who was she kidding? If Lily knew the truth, Erin wouldn't be sitting here listening to her plans to stick it to Dad and Royce and everyone else at Hunt and Bishop. Not that the protest would change anything. With luck, Dad would be working from home that day, which raised an interesting dilemma. Should she warn him?

If she did, Lily would wonder how the company had known and might turn in Erin's direction, especially since she'd made it clear that she didn't agree with the plan. If she didn't, Dad could brush the protest off, or he could go ballistic.

Right now, she was more concerned about Lily, about their connection. She hoped Lily's parting pat on the shoulder meant she wasn't about to get dumped for refusing to go along with her plan to tweak her nose at Hunt and Bishop. But what about next time?

15

ERIN LOUNGED BY THE side of the pool and listened to Christina in disbelief. She shifted her phone to her other ear. "But we haven't seen each other since . . ." Since Christina had wanted to see what kissing her felt like. "In what feels like months."

"I know, and I said we'd reschedule dinner, but this real estate course is more difficult than I expected. I really need to study."

Or she'd concluded the same thing Erin had concluded: that there was as much passion between them as there was between two dead fish and no amount of trying to be a couple would change that. She loved Christina dearly as a friend and wanted to keep her as a friend. "It feels like you're avoiding me."

Christina laughed, an obviously fake laugh. She wouldn't win any Oscars. "Why would I do that?"

Erin was about to be honest—for once—and talk about the kiss that felt flatter than a pancake, but motion in the corner of her eye caught her attention. Dad, waving at her from the patio door. "Let's pick this up another time. My dad wants me."

"I'll call you."

Seriously? "Okay. We'll talk soon." If she didn't hear from Christina in a week or two, she'd go over there and tell her it was perfectly okay, that she wouldn't be offended if Christina told her the kiss was a dud, because she felt the same way and could they please go back to being best friends without any expectations of more. Christina was important to her and she'd hate for them to grow distant.

Dad strolled onto the patio and met her halfway between the pool and the house. "You said you'd be meeting with Altree's group today."

"Uh, yeah."

"Did she get the email from White Knight?"

"No."

Dad shook his head. "I don't get it. There's tons in there for Altree to bitch about. The number of storeys, the exterior parking, the road shutdowns, the construction noise, the colour of the fucking bricks. Why send the other documents but not this one?"

"I'm working on it." PI Wong had let her know that surveillance was underway. Hopefully it was only a matter of time before a connection was found between one of the suspects and Hunt and Bishop.

"Working on what? If there isn't an email, there's nothing to work on."

She wanted to tell him about Wong, but then he'd pester her about progress or tell her off for involving an outsider. Plus, she didn't want him to know about the investigation in case she found out something she didn't want to tell him. She still wasn't completely convinced Royce wasn't somehow involved.

"I'm sticking close to Lily," she said to him. "I'm sure she'll hear from White Knight at some point."

"So what happened at this meeting? Anything I should know about?"

She hesitated. If she told him, he might freak out right now and do something to make Lily's life difficult. If she didn't tell him, there was a chance he'd be working from home, or he'd laugh at the pathetic protestors, or he'd have security hustle them off the property and leave it at that.

"No, nothing." Lying to him wasn't any easier than lying to Lily. How had she ended up here, lying to everyone she cared about? "What can they do anyway? The project is a go."

"They can still yap."

"Which is sometimes all they want to do. Say their piece. Once they've done that, they'll move on." Hopefully. "Just let them say their piece." Please.

"I'm more interested in finding out who's betraying me. A couple of more weeks, Erin. If you haven't found out anything by then, we'll call time on it and you'll start work. Have you decided whether it's me or Royce yet?"

The way his voice inflected told her he cared about the answer. "Not yet."

"Make a decision. You have to be good, and quick, at doing that. You'll be making a lot of decisions when you're working on a project." He glanced at his watch. "I have to conference with someone in five. See you at dinner."

He hurried inside. Erin trailed after him, went up to her bedroom, and flopped onto the bed. She was lying to people she cared about to keep them close, so why did it feel like they were all slipping away?

~

ERIN LIFTED HER HEAD away from the telescope she was peering through and moved on to the next demo model in the store. She really didn't need another telescope, but when she and Lily had passed by the camera store, a telescope in the window had caught her eye. She examined the eyepiece.

Lily lifted the price tag hanging from the telescope and nudged her. "It's five-hundred and ninety-nine dollars," she whispered.

"There's no harm in looking," Erin whispered back, especially since the eyepiece was solid and she could imagine adding this telescope to the several on her bedroom balcony. But dropping

$599 in front of Lily wouldn't be a good idea. She forced herself to move away and head for the exit.

"You must already have a telescope," Lily said to her on the sidewalk.

Sure, but she bought telescopes like other people bought clothes or shoes or action figures. "I like to keep up with the newest models, run my hands along them."

Lily snickered. "That would sound creepy if I didn't know how much of a nerd you are."

They strolled to the hobby store they'd intended to visit and went inside. Erin hadn't been in this one and marvelled at all the action figures, model kits, train sets . . . She could spend forever in here.

Lily stared up at an action figure in a locked display case. "Still here," she said.

Erin peered over her shoulder at the rare collectible released to commemorate a popular sci-fi show's one-hundredth episode. Only 500 had been manufactured.

"I've already seen them going for over a thousand on online auction sites," Lily said. "Which would make this an investment if I had the seven-hundred bucks to buy it. Not that I'd turn around and sell it, though. I'd put it on my shelf." She sighed. "One can dream."

Erin's eyes went back to the action figure. She'd love to buy it for Lily. She was itching to buy it for her. But how the hell would she explain a $700 gift? Not only would Lily freak, but she'd probably see it as too much, too soon. Then again, maybe she'd see it as ultra-romantic. Erin would never know, because Lily was dating Erin Bartlett, who was between jobs, and not Erin Hunt, whose investments would make back the 700 bucks in no time.

She followed Lily to the rear of the store, where row upon row of comics were on display. "I didn't know you were into comics."

"I used to be. I stupidly got rid of the ones I had when I was a kid, tossed them in the garbage. Now people are selling them online and making some good money. Oh, look." Lily moved down the nearest aisle. "Now this I can afford." She removed an action figure in a plastic container from the shelf. "Just came out last week, I think."

Erin eyed the price. $27.99. "Let me buy it for you."

Lily drew back in surprise. "Why?"

"As a gift."

"You don't have to buy me a gift. If anyone's going to buy anyone a gift, it should be me. I'm working. You're not."

"I do have money."

Lily gave her an indulgent smile. "If you really want to buy me something, wait until after you've been working for a while. But I don't need gifts. Really."

She wanted to scream. She could buy Lily the whole store right now.

Her temples pulsed. She blew out some air and reminded herself that Lily would not be impressed, not even a little, if she bought her the store, or everything in it. She'd be mortified. Just like she'd be mortified if she knew she was standing next to Erin Hunt, smiling at her and telling her she had to be careful with her money.

Now Erin wanted to cry. She'd wanted someone who was with her for her, and not for her money, right? But was Lily really with her for her? Erin would like to think so. Like one of those contradictory riddles that seemed unanswerable until you figured out the trick, Erin Bartlett was Erin Hunt, and Erin Hunt was Erin Bartlett. *I'm still the same person, Lily. The person you like. The person you'll hopefully love. It's just a name. You've been with Erin Hunt this whole time.*

But would Lily see it that way?

〜

LILY STROLLED FROM THE movie theatre with Sandy, chuckling at her opinion of the sci-fi flick they'd just watched.

"And another thing," Sandy said. "When they were paranoid about the Zarayans waiting to ambush them, their detection beam thingy worked, but then later on, when they were rescuing those people from the planet, all of a sudden it didn't work, and they said it was because of the radiation. But they had to fly through the radiation earlier, and they were able to amplify something or other and make the beam work."

Lily groaned dramatically. "What do I tell you every time we have this type of conversation?"

Sandy nodded. "I know, I know. Don't think too hard about sci-fi stories because you'll always find something. Just let yourself enjoy. No questions."

"Exactly. I'm not saying there's something like that in every story. But even when there are no plot holes, thinking too hard can ruin it. I used to hate the parts when some piece of technology suddenly won't work. 'Oh, we can't use that now. The atmosphere has radon particles,' or something like that. Like, wouldn't they know about these atmospheres and have accounted for it in their designs. But I told myself, stop thinking about stuff like that."

"It's like when cell phones suddenly can't get a signal, or oops, no battery, like the person wouldn't have checked before driving to the shack where a serial killer might be hiding."

"Exactly." She paused. "Did you at least enjoy the movie?"

"Yeah. The guy that played Marano was fun to watch."

Lily wanted to playfully punch her. "You can watch some cute guy next time." When it would be Sandy's turn to choose the movie.

They stopped at a corner to wait for a light to change. "Speaking of romance, how goes it with Erin?" Sandy asked.

She tried to smile, but it was difficult when her mouth felt so pinched.

"That bad?"

"No, actually. Good. Mostly good."

"Uh-oh. What does mostly good mean?"

"She won't be with us on Tuesday." Lily stepped back when a driver took the corner a little too closely.

"You can't be mad at her for that. At least she was honest about it."

That was what Lily kept telling herself. "I saw her yesterday. We had a great time. Popped into a camera store that sells telescopes. Thought I'd be bored, but it was pretty interesting, actually. Then we went to the hobby store on Pine where they sell action figures and spent over an hour there."

"Jesus, you're made for each other. Did you make her breakfast in bed yet?" Sandy asked.

"Not yet." She raised her hand when Sandy drew breath, and waited until they'd crossed the street to continue. "I'm hoping to do that Friday." After the protest at Hunt and Bishop was out of the way. "She's coming over for dinner on Thursday."

Sandy squealed. "Sounds to me like things are going great."

"I asked her if she'd have dinner with my parents and she dodged."

"A hard dodge or a soft dodge?"

Lily shot her a questioning look.

"Did it sound like 'not yet' or 'never'?"

"Not yet. And honestly, it was fine. I wouldn't have suggested it if I hadn't stupidly mentioned her to them. Of course, they were all, can we meet her? Not that I don't want her to meet them."

"You want breakfast in bed out of the way first."

"No, it's more that I want to see her place first."

Sandy's eyes bulged. "She still hasn't invited you over?"

Lily's silence answered the question.

Sandy slowly exhaled. "Do you even know her address, not just the neighbourhood, but an address?"

"I haven't needed it. And, come on. When you're getting to know someone and you ask where they live and they say, 'In the Iron Court area,' do you say, 'Sure, but what's your address? Street name and number please.'"

Sandy chuckled. "I see your point. But you have to admit, she's been over to your place a few times. Usually there's some reciprocation."

"Look, she explained why she hasn't invited me over. She lives with her parents. She's not ready to introduce me yet and doesn't want to sneak me in. But you know what? It's not even that."

"What the hell is it, then?"

"I can't shake the feeling she's, I don't know, there's something there that I can't see. That she's hiding something."

Sandy pulled open the door to their usual after-movie coffee shop and held it open for Lily. A blast of coffee aroma hit her in the face. She breathed it in, savoured it. They joined the line up.

"Why do you think that?" Sandy asked.

Lily folded her arms. "She chooses what she says too carefully sometimes. I'll ask what should be an easy question to answer, like, 'Where did you go to elementary school?' I haven't asked her that, but you know what I mean. And she'll think about it and then sort of dance around the answer. It's weird."

"We couldn't find much about her online, remember?"

"You couldn't find much about her online."

"Same thing." Sandy ordered a regular coffee. "You sure you want to make her breakfast in bed before you shake this feeling?"

Lily shrugged. "We wouldn't be getting married."

"You're not the casual type, though."

"I'll just have a regular coffee," Lily said to the barista. She turned back to Sandy. "It wouldn't be casual. We're dating. And I really—" She stopped herself.

"Like her." Sandy searched Lily's face. "Or more?"

Lily wasn't sure. Definitely an intense like she could see growing into more. "She's someone I wouldn't mind being with for a while."

They lapsed into silence until they'd picked up their coffees and found a table near the window.

"Not to be a downer," Sandy said, "but what if the thing she's hiding is another woman. A wife, even? Or worse, a husband."

Lily had considered that. "That would explain why she hasn't invited me over, but not why a simple question about her background or life sometimes ties her in knots."

"What the hell could she be hiding, then? Maybe she went to prison or something."

They both laughed at the notion.

"Yeah, I know. Totally wouldn't fit." Sandy sipped her coffee. "Okay, um, maybe she grew up in some religious cult and thinks you'll think she's weird if she tells you."

"Maybe. I could see that."

"Or maybe her father's the one in prison. Or her mother."

"Same as the hiding a woman possibility."

"She could have grown up in the foster system."

"I don't think so."

Sandy jabbed her finger on the table. "If you can't shake the feeling, there's got to be something. You could always ask her."

Lily snorted. "What? Say, 'Erin, what are you hiding?' I don't even know if she's hiding anything, not for sure."

"Push her about going to her place. It might force it out."

"I don't want to do that." She played with the stir stick she'd picked up along with her coffee. "The truth is, I don't want to risk ruining things. I want to see where it goes."

"You do like her. A lot." Sandy plunged ahead when Lily didn't contradict her. "All the more reason to find out what she's hiding."

"I don't want to push her. I've thought about it, and the only thing I wouldn't be able to handle is if she *is* with someone else. That would be the end for me. But I don't think it's that. I honestly don't."

Sandy reached across the table and took Lily's free hand. "I don't want to see you hurt."

"I don't, either." She squeezed Sandy's fingers and let her hand go. "See, if there was one thing I could put my finger on, maybe I'd broach it. Erin, every time we talk about high school, you dodge my questions, or Erin, every time I ask you about the scar on your arm, you deflect. But there isn't. It's random questions here and there. Okay, always personal questions about her, but she doesn't always dodge them or take her time." She dropped the stick to the table. "Maybe I'm being paranoid."

"Because you like her a lot, you're looking for things. It can't be this good, so there must be something. She'll end up hurting me, so I'll poke holes in it now. That way I won't feel so let down. I'll be prepared. Do you think that's what's going on?"

"Maybe," Lily admitted.

Sandy eyed her pensively. "It's your relationship. You have to handle it the way you think is best."

"If she doesn't invite me to her place soon, I'll talk to her about it."

"But you want breakfast in bed first."

"Yeah."

"As long as you're okay with her dropping some bombshell after that, something you can't handle."

"I'd be okay."

Probably.

Maybe.

The truth, if she was being honest with herself, was that she really could see herself with Erin for a while and didn't want to rock the boat in any way, shape, or form right now. She didn't want to burst their cozy bubble. Sandy would laugh at her, would say, "Seriously, Lily? You scoff at all the romance movies and think Valentine's Day is more for merchants than anyone else." She did. But then she'd met Erin and her feelings were soaring in a way they never had before. She'd still scoff at Sandy's beloved romances and romcoms, still grumble about why Valentine's Day, and all the other Days, were invented. And then she'd go out and buy Erin chocolate and flowers.

~

ERIN PEERED AT THE moon through her new telescope, the one she'd returned to the store to buy because she hadn't wanted Lily to see her drop hundreds of bucks on it. She was supposed to be between jobs, after all. She was tiring of the charade, the lies, the number of times she had to stop herself from saying something. She could hardly stand to look at Lily's interesting face sometimes, because of how it condemned her. Worse, her feelings for Lily were growing, to the point that she could see herself bringing Lily over, introducing her to Mom and Dad—definitely a fantasy because Dad smiled and shook her hand—taking her over to Nan's house and showing her around, whisking her off for a holiday. Another fantasy because Lily wouldn't be impressed with grand gestures. So fine. Just taking a day trip with her would be wonderful.

Those jagged edges of her soul that bled, the dishonesty permeating everything Erin said, even when it was true, meant she wasn't walking on the clouds, wasn't punching her fist into the air, wasn't telling everyone she spoke to about what a wonderful woman she was dating. The wonderful woman she was lying to. Hiding from.

She had to tell Lily the truth. Soon.

Her phone rang. She went into her bedroom, picked it up from the desk, then shook her head. The other phone. She plucked it from her nightside table and smiled, even though blood dripped from one of those ragged edges.

"I thought I'd give you a quick call while I'm on break," Lily said.

"I'm glad you did." It was now or never. "Don't hate me, but are you sure you should go ahead with the protest tomorrow?"

Lily was silent for a moment. "Look, I know you don't think it's a good idea, but everyone else is pumped up for it, and so am I. What's the worst that can happen?"

Hopefully security would boot them from the property and that would be that.

"We won't be blocking access to the building, and we won't be hoisting some of our ruder signs."

Yeah, the ones about greedy developers and pigs weren't going to change any minds at that location.

"I need to do something. McMillan Park isn't just any park."

"I know." Erin paused. "I'm just worried, that's all."

Lily's voice softened. "And I like that you're worried. How do you like your eggs?"

The sudden change of topic threw Erin. "What?"

"Your eggs. How do you like them?"

"Uh, sunny side up. Over easy. Scrambled."

"Choose one."

"Sunny side up."

"Good."

"Why?"

"You told me you're not busy on Friday."

"Right." But they were seeing each other Thursday night, so why would—oh, shit. Erin searched for something to say that wouldn't come across as rejecting her. Nothing came to mind, perhaps because she didn't want to reject her. But she wouldn't cross that line as Erin Bartlett. Absolutely not.

"You still there?"

She shook herself. "Still here."

"Still coming over on Thursday?"

The strain in Lily's voice made Erin wince. Enough was enough. She would not hurt this woman because she was a coward. "Yes. Looking forward to it."

"Great. Me too. Okay, well, my break is almost over. I'll call you tomorrow, let you know how it went."

"Please do." Though Erin would already know how it went. She'd already staked out where she'd park and watch the protest.

They said their goodbyes and disconnected. Well, she'd driven a stake into the ground. Friday night was when Erin Bartlett would become Erin Hunt. If Dad needed her to be undercover with Lily after that, tough. She was done. No more lies, not big ones, anyway. She wanted to be with Lily, for real. She wanted Lily to truly know her.

Her phone, still in her hand, rang again. She lifted it to swipe and answer. Not this phone. She snatched her real phone from her desk. "Hello."

"It's Douglas Wong."

The PI.

"I wanted to update you on the investigation. We think we've found the connection between one of the people on your list and Hunt and Bishop."

"That's great!"

"I'd like a sense of the larger picture before I send you what we have, but I wanted to let you know that you should have something within a few days. But . . ."

Erin's hand clenched around her phone. "But?"

"Sometimes when you undertake an investigation like this, you can find out something you'd rather not know. I always bring this up about now. You can't unsee or unread anything."

She sank onto her bed. "I know you said you want more before you tell me, but answer one question for me. Is it someone attached to Hunt and Bishop?"

"Yes."

Damn. She needed to know. "I'll look forward to your report."

"All right, then. I'll be in touch."

After they'd disconnected, she remained on her bed and stared into space. Was it Royce, then? Had he gazed right at her and lied? Or was it one of his or Dad's administrative assistants, women who'd worked for them for years and were compensated extremely generously for their loyalty? Dan in legal, with the company for over ten years. Audrey down in planning, who'd turned down at least two offers from rival developers because she "enjoyed her work at Hunt and Bishop and had a good working relationship with everyone." The gigantic bonuses Dad threw at her probably helped.

Was it someone who didn't have direct access to the documents but had sneaked into an office and made copies, someone with a petty grievance against the company who wanted to cause trouble?

As much as she was curious, White Knight was the least of her concerns right now. Thursday was only a few days away. She couldn't back out of telling Lily, no matter how much the thought terrified her. Lily clearly wanted her to stay the night, and Erin wanted that too. Turning her down, coming up with some pathetic excuse as to why she couldn't stay . . . she already hated herself enough for not having the guts to tell Lily earlier and face up to Dad's anger. She wanted—needed—to tell her, and explain herself, and beg for her forgiveness, and hope there would be a relationship afterwards, because she just might be falling in love with her.

16

A T THE CORNER OF Third and Duncan, Lily squared her
shoulders and waved to the group trailing behind her. They'd
met at a coffee shop a block away, bolstered each other's courage,
and marched their way here. Now it was time to take the protest to
Hunt and Bishop.

She hoisted her sign in the air. "Save McMillan Park. Save our
green spaces," she chanted, her courage growing along with the
voices of the others.

Passersby in suits and stilettos and coiffed haircuts slowed to
gape, or stare, or record with their phones.

They crossed from city sidewalk to private property.
Fortunately the Hunt and Bishop tower was set back quite a ways
from the street, at the north end of a cement courtyard, so there
was plenty of room to form a line to the entrance. Anyone who
entered or left the building would have to walk past the line of
signs and listen to the chants.

"Save McMillan Park. Save our green spaces."

There was a constant stream of traffic into the building. The
reactions of those hurrying by them didn't surprise Lily. Some
people hunched their shoulders and bowed their heads and
pretended the protestors weren't there. Others stole glances at
them. A few fuck off's and get a job's were thrown their way. A

couple of people who must have been entering the building for appointments with other businesses stopped to chat and said they agreed with them and asked for more information. Fortunately Lily had remembered to give everyone a few cards with the group's website address, and Maria had a bunch of leaflets she was offering to people. Most would go straight into the trash, but a few people would actually read them later on, when they were alone.

Sandy, who'd taken the day off, elbowed her in the ribs. "Looks like they've noticed." She jutted her chin toward the entrance.

Lily looked that way, saw the three security guards huddled near the entrance, one talking into his 2-way radio. "That didn't take long." They'd only been here about fifteen minutes.

A minute later, two of the guards lumbered their way toward them. "Move along," one of them shouted. He swung his arms toward the sidewalk. "Come on, people. This is private property. It's time to leave."

"I'm tired," Lily said. "I think I'll sit." She lowered herself onto the cement. Fortunately the weather had cooperated today. "Sit!"

Sandy sat cross-legged next to her and raised her sign. Lily looked down the line and smiled. Everyone except Maria had followed suit.

"Green over greed. Save McMillan Park."

The guards glanced at each other. One stepped toward Lily and reached for her.

"Touch me and I'll sue the fucking pants off you," she shouted.

He jerked his hands back and went inside with his buddy, to figure out what to do, she suspected.

"That was easy," Sandy said.

"They'll try again. With more guards. And after they've consulted legal."

"They'll have to drag us," Patrick yelled from the other side of Sandy.

"That's the spirit." Lily shouted as loud as she could. "Green over greed. Save McMillan Park."

~

Across the street, Erin peered out the driver side window of her Mercedes, trying not to hyperventilate. She'd arrived here over an hour ago, early enough to grab the parking spot. Lily had planned the protest to start at 8:30 so they'd catch people going into work. Dad usually showed up at the office around 7:00. He was an early to the office, early to leave type of guy, though he never really left. He always did more work at home and took calls at all hours. "I can answer a phone on the golf course," he always said, "or at a restaurant, or during intermission at the theatre." Only vacation times were sacred. When they were away, he dealt with work at designated times only.

So, he wouldn't have to walk past Lily's line, and Royce likely wouldn't either. But that wouldn't matter. Screaming protestors right on their doorstep? Erin had watched the security guards approach the line, seen everyone sit down and the guards retreating. It would be a temporary reprieve. Would reinforcements arrive and swarm the protestors? Erin didn't know what was legally permitted. Lily and her group were on private property. If they were asked to leave and didn't, they'd definitely be trespassing. Would that mean the guards could manhandle them?

Half an hour passed, with nothing happening. Erin felt herself relaxing. Maybe the best-case scenario was playing out. Legal, or maybe even Dad and Royce themselves, had decided to let the group have their say. They weren't preventing anyone from entering or leaving the building. Let them shout their slogans and go home feeling as if they'd accomplished something.

Feeling peckish, she grabbed a granola bar from the glove compartment. As she munched on it, the faint sound of a siren reached her ears. If she were driving, she'd glance in her rearview mirror and scan the road ahead, to see if she needed to pull over. Parked, she didn't think anything of it until the wailing of the sirens grew louder. Much louder.

A cop car screeched to a halt across the street. Another one quickly arrived. Four cops spilled out and rushed toward those seated and waving signs.

Erin's mouth fell open. Seriously? The cop cars were obscuring her view. She craned her neck, glimpsed one of the uniforms talking to Maria. Another cop was gesturing to a woman Erin didn't recognize, seated just behind her. The woman stood and handed the cop her sign.

Pedestrians slowed to gawk at what was going on, making it even more difficult to see, but Erin got the general gist when Maria emerged from the crowd and walked away. Then the woman Erin didn't recognize. Shawna. Patrick. They all left, their signs confiscated. But no Lily. Where was Lily?

Erin had to restrain herself from leaving her car and darting across the street. Maybe the crowd would hide her. Maybe not.

Sandy suddenly appeared, talking to the cop next to her. Then Erin saw her. Lily. Oh, shit.

Lily was arguing with a cop, her hands furiously moving and her voice carrying over to Erin.

". . . peaceful protest," she was saying. "We weren't blocking access to the building."

The cop said something, too low for Erin to hear.

"What damage? We were sitting the whole time."

The cop's mouth moved again.

"I already told you I lead the group."

Now the cop was pointing to the cop car. No way. Erin slid her phone from her blazer pocket and called Dad.

"You have reached Aaron Hunt. I am not available—"

She disconnected.

The cop grasped Lily's arm and steered her toward the car. Erin thumped the steering wheel. She didn't know what she'd say. *Dad, please stop the cops from arresting my girlfriend for protesting at our building?* But she tried again anyway.

"You have reached Aaron Hunt. I am not available—"

She tossed the phone onto the passenger seat and pummeled the steering wheel with her fists. "Fuck. Fuck!"

The cop car drove off with Lily in the back seat. The two remaining cops dumped the group's signs into their car's trunk and left. Those who'd stopped to gawk or record the spectacle trickled away.

Erin stared across the street. It was as if the protest had never happened. But it had, and Lily had been taken away by the cops. Erin could go to the police station, but what would that accomplish? Instead, she pulled away from the curb and headed for home.

As soon as she was up in her apartment, she called Lily.

No answer.

17

Five hours and three unanswered calls later, Erin was climbing the walls. Even the latest edition of her favourite astronomy magazine couldn't hold her attention. She was descending the stairs, hoping a walk around the flower garden would calm her nerves, when a shout made her jump.

"Erin!"

Dad did not sound pleased. He was standing in the living room, his phone in his hand. "There you are. We had protestors at the office this morning, on our fucking property. How did you not know they were going to do it right under our fucking noses?" He stabbed his finger at her. "I thought you were hanging out with these people."

She scrambled for something to say, but she wasn't used to lying to Dad.

"Well?"

"I, uh, didn't know."

"What, they don't talk to you? They had to plan the thing. You were the only one left out?"

"I—"

His phone rang. He answered it.

Mom, who'd silently watched from the sofa, met Erin's eyes. She shot her a questioning look. Erin shrugged her shoulders and thought about what she'd say when Dad hung up.

". . . works for me," he was saying. "And I think I'm being extremely generous by letting it go at that. Thank you."

He hung up. "That was Bill Brody."

The police chief. Of course.

"He'll go ahead with what we discussed earlier, after those," Dad's mouth twisted, "people were removed from our property."

Erin clasped her hands behind her back. "What's going to happen to Lily? Altree."

"She'll be let off with a fine." He raised his finger. "But if she doesn't pay it, we'll pursue charges."

That didn't sound so bad.

"How much is the fine?" Mom asked.

"Five-thousand dollars."

"Five-thousand dollars!" Erin blurted. "Are you serious?"

"I could have had her arrested. Trespassing on private property, damaging private property."

"What was damaged?"

"The sign about where smoking is permitted was knocked off its post."

Erin barked a laugh. "That sign has been threatening to fall off for months."

"Well, it happened this morning."

"Don't you think that fine is a bit high?" Mom said evenly. "Five-thousand dollars is a lot of money for some people."

"It serves her right. It'll make her think twice about pulling a stunt like that again." His attention shifted to Erin. "Obviously you seeing these people isn't helping at all. You claim you didn't know about it. You think I'm being too harsh on them. You've been useless in finding out who's fucking with me by leaking documents. And this White Knight idiot seems to have stopped emailing the other idiot anyway. What day is it today?"

"Tuesday," Mom said.

"I expect you at work next Monday," Dad said to Erin. "Not this Monday. Next Monday. Enjoy your remaining time off." He pocketed his phone. "Have you decided who you want to work with yet?"

"Not yet," Erin mumbled.

"Figure it the fuck out." Dad stormed past her.

The silence he left behind was deafening. When Mom sighed, it sounded like a plane taking off. "Did you know about the protest?" she asked quietly.

Erin hesitated. "Yes."

Mom blinked at her. "Why didn't you warn him?"

For a moment, she thought about coming up with some story about how she might have lost their trust if she'd told Dad, but it would have been a lame story that didn't make much sense, and she was tired of the lies. All the lies. She sank onto the soft next to Mom and gazed at the cold fireplace.

"I'm seeing Lily Altree."

Silence, then, "Seeing her?" Mom asked, her slightly higher voice the only indication she was surprised—or alarmed. "You mean, you're in a relationship with her?"

"Yes." Erin turned to her. Mom was staring at her, but she wasn't freaking out. "I know you thought me and Christina were going to be a power couple."

Mom shook her head. "Margot and I discussed it and knew it wasn't going to happen. Your fathers are the ones who saw you as a power couple, taking over the reigns from them."

"I think Christina and I recently figured out we weren't going to be a power couple. Now she's avoiding me."

"Does she know about Lily?"

"No."

"Are you sure seeing Lily is a good idea?"

"You don't approve."

Mom ran a manicured nail across her lower lip. "It doesn't matter whether I approve or not. You'll see her either way. I'd rather you be honest with me, with us. Having said that, you're from different backgrounds. That can matter."

"Just because she's not wealthy doesn't mean we can't get along."

"It's more than that. But I'll keep an open mind."

Erin moistened her lips. "She doesn't know who I am."

Now Mom's eyes widened. "You haven't told her?"

"She still thinks I'm Erin Bartlett."

"Erin," Mom breathed. "You have to tell her."

"I'm going to." She drew a deep breath and slowly exhaled. "I really like her, Mom. I'm afraid of what'll happen when she finds out."

"All the more reason to tell her. You don't want to string her along, or yourself. You need to know whether she'll still be interested when she finds out."

Erin wanted to ask if Mom was hoping Lily would break up with her. At the same time, she didn't want to know. "Are you going to tell Dad?"

"No. You're going to tell him. But I'd leave him out of it for now."

"Why?"

"I'd wait until after you've told her who you are."

Her heart sinking, Erin nodded. Mom was probably hoping Lily would dump her, making what could turn out to be an inconvenient problem go away.

"Now, go upstairs and apologize to your father." Mom raised her hand when Erin opened her mouth to protest. "You don't have to tell him you knew. Apologize for not knowing. You owe him something. Apologize."

"Okay."

Mom smiled but couldn't mask her concern. "See, these are the sorts of situations that arise when people are from different backgrounds."

Erin could see her point but didn't entirely agree. People from different backgrounds got together all the time. Some even stayed together. Also, it wasn't so much that their backgrounds differed, but that they were on opposite sides of an issue, or rather, Dad and Lily were. But most of all, this situation, as Mom had put it, had arisen because Erin had lied to everyone.

At least she could stop lying to Mom. And soon, she could stop lying to Lily. If Lily was still talking to her.

~

AFTER TELLING DAD SHE was sorry she hadn't been able to stop the protest—she was getting good at not lying, but leaving out enough that it felt like she was lying—she went out to the flower garden, where she'd intended to go before Dad had bellowed her name. She'd barely had the time to breathe in the scent of a peony when her phone rang, the one in her right back pocket, making her heart race. Her undercover phone. She'd taken to making sure she always had it.

"I haven't been picking up because I was stuck at the police station for the last, feels like, three days," Lily said.

"I was worried. You could probably tell from the number of messages I left."

"It was nice, getting my phone back and finding out you were thinking of me." Lily chuckled. "You even beat out Sandy for the number of calls."

"So what happened," Erin said, knowing most of it but wanting to hear it from her.

Lily described the protest, the cops arriving, how she'd been taken to the police station and confined to what she figured was an interview room for almost four hours, though they had brought her water and a snack, and she had to admit the cops had been nice and treated her well.

"Then around 1:30, one of the cops comes in and says Hunt and Bishop has decided not to press any charges. I said, for what? Trespassing? And he said, damaging property. I had no idea what he was talking about."

Erin wasn't surprised. The sign that had apparently been dislodged from its place, probably by accident, or even by the security guards or cops, was smaller than a stop sign.

"He told me we damaged some sign, and since I'm the head of the group, I was fined."

"How much?"

"Five grand."

She whistled. "That's a lot of money."

"I have to pay it because if I don't, not only will the cops come after me, but Hunt and Bishop will too. The cops made it clear the company intends to get me one way or another. Fuckers."

Erin agreed. She was not happy with Dad about this. "Do you have the money?"

"Yeah, in my private Swiss bank account." Lily huffed a sigh. "I might have enough room on my credit card, but I'll have to check."

She wanted to say, "Try to avoid that. The interest rates will kill you. You'll just fall further behind every month." But Lily had told Erin about her thoughts regarding chef's school, that she could only afford it if she got a roommate and lived like a monk for the entire time. What would this bogus fine do to those plans?

Erin didn't say anything. Nothing she said would make this situation better. Lily didn't deserve trite crap.

"I'll figure it out." Lily fell silent.

"Are you glad you protested anyway?"

"Yeah. I wanted them to notice, and they did."

But it wouldn't change anything. Erin wandered over to a bed of roses and inhaled one of the flower's scent. "I'm sorry this happened to you."

"It's not your fault."

It felt like it was.

"Nobody else was fined or anything. The cops asked who was leading the protest, I said it was me, and I took the fall." Lily snickered. "I wouldn't be much good if I was interrogated for real."

"You protected your people. That's what leaders do, right?"

"I suppose."

"If nobody had stepped forward, you might all be facing fines."

"That would suck. At least half of the people there were students."

Erin almost said, "I know," but stopped herself in time.

"Anyway, enough about what happened. I can't wait to see you on Thursday."

"I can't wait to see you, either."

Lily's voice softened. "I bought eggs."

"Good."

"Yeah?"

"No, great." Erin hoped.

Thursday Lily would find out she was actually dating Erin Hunt. Erin hoped to eat the eggs on Friday morning, not wipe them off her face.

They chatted a few more minutes, then Lily said she had to eat and go to work. After they'd hung up, Erin wandered around the garden, wondering what she could do to help. Well, it was pretty obvious what she could do. The question was whether to do it. Given the fine was due to trumped up property damage, it would grate to see Lily in debt for months, maybe years, and potentially give up on her dream.

She pulled the phone she had in her left back pocket, looked up the family's attorney, and called him.

"Are you sure?" he asked her, after she'd explained what she'd like him to do.

"Yes."

"It's not the money, it's, um, who it's for."

"This conversation is confidential, right?" She'd already asked him, but felt compelled to ask him again. "You can't tell my father about it."

"Of course not. For this, you're my client."

Which was why he couldn't tell her Dad had spoken to him that morning about legal options regarding the protest. Otherwise she doubted the name Lily Altree would be at the top of his mind.

"If you're sure you'd like me to proceed, I'll take care of it immediately," he said.

"Yes, please go ahead."

After hanging up, she transferred the money to him. Maybe she'd tell Lily. Maybe not. All that mattered was Lily wouldn't be saddled with a debt she didn't deserve, or worse, not pay it at all and end up facing charges. Erin hoped Dad wouldn't go that far when the protest was a distant memory, but she wasn't sure he'd drop it.

Now all she had to worry about was telling Lily about her real last name.

18

Feeling despondent, Lily sank onto her sofa, sipped her morning coffee, and thought about the unreasonable fine the cops had slapped her with, on behalf of Hunt and Bishop. She had enough room on her card, the card that currently only had a couple of hundred dollars on it that she'd pay off at the end of the month, like she always did. Other than a few recurring charges, it was supposed to be for emergencies. Did this qualify as an emergency? What would happen if she didn't pay? She wouldn't put it past Hunt and Bishop to come after her. And it was moot, anyway. She'd pay. She wasn't one of those people who grabbed a parking ticket off their windshield, crumpled it up, and threw it down the nearest sewer.

She could ask Mom and Dad, but they weren't rolling in cash. They'd take it from their retirement funds, which wouldn't be fair. She'd made the decision to protest on Hunt and Bishop property. The damaged property thing was a crock, but there wasn't anything she could do about it.

Tears threatened, but she fought them off. She squeezed her eyes shut and lowered her head. She would not cry over this. Okay, with Erin's encouragement, she'd been thinking about taking concrete steps toward chef's school. She'd even drawn up a tentative plan in her mind, had figured out that if she sold her car to a junkyard, and if Erin was willing to spend cozy days and nights in, to keep expenses down, she could manage to keep her apartment. Moving in with a roommate was the last thing she wanted to do when her relationship with Erin was growing. She was willing to take buses and avoid coffee shops and stay away from hobby stores for that. With her classes and homework, their time together would be more limited. She didn't want someone else in her space when Erin was there. She wanted it to be just the two of them.

But this fine meant she wouldn't be going to chef's school for a while. She'd repressed her dream for so long, finally let it soar, and now it had crashed to earth. Next time it threatened to burst forth, she'd stomp on it until it stopped moving.

Her phone rang, making her jerk her head up.

"How are you feeling?" Sandy said.

"I'm trying to figure out how to pay the fine."

"That's why I'm calling. Don't pay it. Fight it."

Lily groaned. "I'll end up paying a lawyer thousands of dollars, and I might lose and still have to pay the five grand."

"No, no. Remember I've mentioned Robbie to you a few times."

She thought about their recent conversations. "The guy you met online that you might be seriously interested in?" They'd already been out a couple of times.

"Yeah, him. I'm pretty sure he's interested too, so he's keen to do me a favour."

Now it was all coming back to her. Robbie was a lawyer. A junior one, but still.

"He said he'll dig into it for you, see what your chances would be if you did nothing and went to court."

"They say they have proof we knocked some sign off the building."

"Must have been an expensive sign."

"Really, eh?" She could visualize Sandy nodding.

"Take pics of whatever documents you have and send them to me. He'll take a look and I'll get back to you. Don't do anything until then."

"Thank him. I'll take whatever help I can get."

After they hung up, Lily snapped photos of the two papers she had and sent them to Sandy. She finished off her coffee, took a shower, and was just buttoning her shirt when her phone rang. Sandy again.

"He couldn't possibly be that quick," Lily said to her.

"Yeah, well, something weird happened."

Lily tensed. "What?"

"Robbie called the police station and said he's your attorney, blah, blah, blah, and he'd like to see the report about the property damage, and after they put him on hold for a while, they came back and basically treated him like an idiot because the fine has already been paid, so what the hell is he doing calling them for information." Sandy paused. "You didn't pay it, did you?"

"No!"

"Then who did?"

"They didn't tell him?"

"They said the city would know, so he called the city, and they said it's some law firm. So I figured it wasn't you, but . . ."

"What's the name of the law firm?"

"Hold on, I wrote it down. Wright, Avery, Wang, and Associates."

Lily had never heard of them.

"Videos of you being taken away were on social media, and there was an article in the paper today too."

Yeah, a tiny column on page 12.

"Maybe a good Samaritan paid it," Sandy suggested.

"Maybe."

"Anyway, you're off the hook."

But who'd paid her damn fine? Eager to get off the phone, she thanked Sandy. The moment she disconnected, she flipped to a search engine and tapped in, "Wright, Avery, Wang, and Associates."

A typical law firm website came up, men and women in business suits, sporting wide smiles. She scanned their About page. They obviously didn't list their clients, but Lily could tell their fees would be way out of her league. Calling them would be pointless. They wouldn't divulge the identity of the client who'd dropped five grand on her behalf.

She was off the hook, but it would bug the hell out of her. She didn't like being indebted to anyone, especially without her consent.

~

After tossing and turning all night, Erin woke up feeling like hell but looking forward to her date with Lily, which would hopefully last until tomorrow. Then she reminded herself that tonight was the night, the night she'd tell Lily the truth. Dread chased away her anticipation.

She could spend her day sitting in her apartment driving herself crazy with all the ways Lily could tell her to get lost, or she could do something constructive. Do something about one of the things that had kept running through her mind while she was trying to fall asleep.

At two o'clock, she sat in one of Royce's guest chairs, hoping the PI wouldn't inform her that Royce was White Knight. She'd cross that bridge if she came to it. Today she wasn't here to accuse him of betraying Dad, but to talk to him about McMillan Park.

"Is it too late to save the park?" she asked him.

Royce's brows drew together. "What do you mean?"

"I know the site has been rezoned and there are plans to build an apartment, but the ground hasn't been broken yet." She stared at her hands. "I had an interesting conversation with Lily Altree. She asked why developers don't give back to the communities they invade. From her point of view." She looked up at Royce. "She said it's easy to write a cheque, harder to give back in a meaningful way. You have to admit, the company's reputation takes a hit every time it doesn't build affordable housing in a neighbourhood where it should."

"I agree. I've already said I'd like to build more affordable housing."

"McMillan Park is the only green space for blocks and blocks in that area. Wouldn't it be great if the company revitalized it as a park, instead of building apartments there? I know the land's been rezoned, but I doubt city council would care if you wanted to keep it as a park and be responsible for it. I'm sure we could figure out ways to make money there."

Royce leaned forward. "How?"

"I was thinking maybe we could build an outdoor theatre area there and have local groups do stuff and either pay to rent the space or give us a cut of any ticket sales, if they charge, and we could maybe have some outdoor classes there, yoga, tai-chi, stuff like that."

"Who would give the classes? What would the income stream be?"

"We could have instructors give us part of any enrollment fee."

Royce shook his head. "This is all pie in the sky stuff. It's not what we do." His voice was gentle.

"I just wish we could save the park."

"Why?"

"Because it's the only park in that area." And she wanted to do it for Lily, but honestly, she'd also come to understand that people in the area would use the park if the city hadn't neglected it. She said as much to Royce.

He leaned back in his chair and steepled his fingers. "Even if I agreed with you, it's your father's project. It's not me you need to convince." He shot her a self-deprecating smile. "I'm not sure how much weight my support would count with him. But you might be able to sway him."

"I doubt it."

"Not with words. He just might agree to keep the park as a park, and put money into it as a goodwill community gesture, if you agree to lead the project."

Her shoulders slumped. As much as she wanted to save the park, for Iron Court residents and Lily, the thought of leading the project, any project, filled her with dread. Not because she wasn't capable and couldn't learn, but because she didn't want to do it. Work at Hunt and Bishop. Learn the ropes. Become her dad. It wasn't her. She had something else in mind for her life, or at least something else she wanted to do for the next year or two. A seed Lily had planted, that Erin had initially dismissed out of hand, but hadn't been able to get out of her head.

She forced her eyes to Royce's. "I don't want to work for the company."

Her words hung between them.

"Does your father know?" Royce finally said.

"No. I don't know how to tell him. How did you feel when Danny and Christina told you they didn't want to work here?"

"A little disappointed. But not for long. I want them to be happy with whatever they're doing."

"I wish Dad felt the same way."

"I'm sure he does. Can I be completely honest with you?"

Erin nodded.

"I think your father sees you as drifting right now and he's hoping that bringing you under his wing will give you some goals to reach for."

Erin decided to be honest in return. "He's right about the drifting part, but honestly, I've been drifting because I've been avoiding coming to work here. I didn't know what I wanted to do instead."

"But now you do?"

"Maybe. Probably."

Royce's mouth turned up at the corners. "Does it have anything to do with telescopes and cameras?"

Erin couldn't believe it. "Why am I always the last one to know anything?"

"It's best you figure some things out for yourself."

"I'm not sure I want to make a career out of it, but I'm willing to give it a try to see how it feels." She focused on her hands again. "There's a new program at one of the community colleges. I'm thinking of applying for the fall. The deadline's pretty soon though, so I need to make up my mind real quick. I probably won't get in, but if I don't try, I'll always wonder."

"You might get in, Erin. I hope you do."

"I can't work here and do the program."

"You don't want to work here anyway. My advice, as someone who knows you well and cares about you, is this. Even if you don't get in, don't come to work here. I wouldn't hire someone who wasn't enthusiastic, that's for sure. Your dad wouldn't either." Royce's voice dropped. "You need to tell him."

"I know." But one thing at a time. She already had a terrifying conversation happening in a few hours' time. "What about the park? Is there nothing we can do? And the park wouldn't be a one-off. Maybe Hunt and Bishop could do a goodwill project every few years. I don't pay attention to this stuff, but I have the impression the company could afford it, and who knows what opportunities it could bring. People like to do business with companies they like. Maybe people with land to sell will call you first. Maybe if you're in competition with another developer for something, your goodwill credit will earn you an edge in the competition. Or maybe I'm talking pie in the sky again."

"Let me think about it and look into whether the city would be open to rezoning it back."

"Really?"

"Really. I do like the idea of giving back beyond writing cheques. And I'm sure we'd figure out how to get a tax break out of it somehow."

"Thank you." She grimaced at him. "Would you hate me if I wanted you to be there when I tell my father about not wanting to work here?"

"I don't think it will help, but if it'll make you feel better, sure. Just let me know when you want to talk to him."

She thanked him and left, not sure how she felt. She'd said it, to Royce. Told him the truth. The world hadn't ended, but he wasn't Dad. He wasn't in a position to say, "I can't believe you're my fucking daughter. You want to take pictures of the fucking moon or whatever? Go ahead. Waste your life away." Or maybe she was being unkind to Dad when she practiced how she'd tell him in her head and gave him those lines.

Telling Royce the truth hadn't lightened her spirit or bolstered her confidence. But at least she had his support, and she'd tried to save the park. Maybe Royce would look into it, or maybe he'd told her what he thought she wanted to hear and had already forgotten about it.

Either way, Erin had to forget about the park and talking to Dad about her future for now. One of her other three billion worries had to take centre stage. In a few hours, she'd arrive at Lily's and tell her the truth. This time tomorrow, she could be walking on air and imagining herself and Lily and their great life together, or crying her eyes out, alone, wishing Lily didn't hate her.

19

ERIN REHEARSED WHAT SHE'D say one more time as she drove to Lily's for their dinner-and- hopefully-more date. To other drivers, she probably looked as if she were speaking to someone hands-free. "I didn't think I'd develop feelings for you." Earlier that had sounded okay; now it sounded too stilted. "Fall in love with you." While she thought that might be happening, she didn't want to say the word "love" for the first time while telling Lily she'd been lying to her about something important. "I'd fall for you." Better. But would Lily care? Once the word "Hunt" came out of Erin's mouth, Lily might stop listening, so she'd get the "my feelings are real" part out of the way first.

She was soon riding the elevator up to Lily's floor, trying to remember driving over here, but drawing a blank. Walking into Lily's apartment felt surreal, as if she were moving in slow motion. Erin drew Lily into her arms, kissed her, held her warm body close, and didn't want to let go.

Over Lily's shoulder, she took in the flowers on the table, the candles burning. Oh, god. Maybe today wasn't the best day to tell her, but no, Lily had bought eggs. If she didn't tell her over dinner, she'd have to reject her, come up with some flimsy excuse as to why she wouldn't stay the night. If only she were Erin Bartlett with middle-class parents, between jobs, trying to figure out what to do with her life, rather than Erin Hunt, ridiculously wealthy, daughter of Aaron Hunt of Hunt and Bishop, the company Lily hated.

~

LILY SWALLOWED A MOUTHFUL of garlic bread and searched for something to say. This was not how she'd visualized the evening when she'd spread her only white tablecloth over the table, brought out her great-grandmother's candlesticks and lit the scented candles, set the folded red cloth napkins next to each place setting, and arranged the daffodils she'd picked up from the corner store. She'd thought about roses, but hadn't wanted to scare Erin away. As she'd worked in her small kitchen, she'd seen them talking, laughing, and gazing into each other's eyes, the candles' flames flickering between them.

Instead, Erin seemed distracted. Going through the motions. She'd hardly said two words since arriving. She hadn't removed her blazer and draped it over the back of the chair, like she normally did, as if she wasn't expecting to stay. If not for her warm kiss and the way she'd clung to Lily when she arrived, Lily would be worried she was about to be on the receiving end of an, "I like you, but . . ." conversation.

"I've been meaning to tell you about something weird that happened," she said, saying something she figured was bound to elicit some type of reaction. "Someone paid my fine. Dropped five grand anonymously."

Erin didn't say anything. She forked more pasta into her mouth, as if she hadn't heard what Lily had said.

"The five-thousand dollar fine I got for allegedly damaging property." She would have chuckled, if Erin hadn't been sitting there like a zombie. "Don't you think that's weird, someone paying it?"

Erin laid down her fork. She drew a deep breath, rested her elbows on the table, met Lily's eyes.

The set of Erin's shoulders, her tight face, made Lily set her fork down too. She clasped her hands on her lap.

"I paid your fine," Erin said.

Huh? "You paid my fine?" Lily wanted to make sure she wasn't imagining things or making up Erin's side of the conversation because she wasn't saying anything.

"I paid it."

Lily stared at her. "Why would you do that? Five-thousand dollars? What the hell? Why didn't you tell me, or talk to me about it? You can't just do something like that. I'll pay you back."

"No."

"Erin. Come on. You can't—I can't." Lily wanted to scream in frustration. "I'll pay you back."

"You're not paying me back. The alleged property damage was bogus, and you know it."

"Of course it was bogus, but that's not your fault."

Erin picked up her napkin and started playing with it. "Not directly, but I'm partially to blame."

"How are you partially to blame?" Lily almost gasped when she understood. "Oh, okay. Look, I know you weren't there, and sure, I wasn't totally pleased about that, but you wouldn't have been able to stop what happened. Even if you'd been there, I would still have been the leader. They still would have come up with some bogus reason to fine me."

"That's not what I meant." Erin balled the napkin in her fist. "I . . . withheld information from you. If I'd been honest with you, told you everything, I think I could have stopped you from protesting, maybe helped you come up with something else. Maybe not. I know how determined you are." Her small smile didn't reach her eyes. "But maybe things would have turned out differently. And that's not the only reason I see myself as partially responsible, or maybe indirectly responsible would be a better way of putting it."

The thought their dinners were going to get cold popped into Lily's mind. Funny how insignificant thoughts like that popped into one's head when something serious was going down. Because this was going to head in a direction she didn't like. She could sense it. "Why would you be responsible?" she asked, her voice hushed.

"Okay, let me say up front that I really like you."

Lily wanted to crawl under the table and die.

"I like you a lot. I want to spend a lot more time with you, and bring you into my life in a way I haven't yet."

Wait. This wasn't so bad. "You mean, invite me over to your place?"

"That's exactly what I mean." The napkin she still held in her fist dropped to the table. She picked it up again, played with it. "Everything I've said about the way I feel about you is true. I'm falling for you. I want to be with you." She swallowed. "But I haven't been honest with you about something important."

If she said she was married or lived with someone, Lily would upend this table without a second thought. Erin could shove any thoughts they'd ever be together.

"When I showed up for that protest at McMillan Park, the first one I went to, I wasn't there because I cared about the park."

"You already told me that."

"I wasn't completely honest about why I showed up. I was there because you knew Hunt and Bishop were going to buy the park and build on the site, but that information wasn't public yet. So the question was, how did your group know? I came because I was hoping to find that out."

Lily felt her shoulders relax. "Are you saying you're some type of investigator? A PI?" That would sort of explain why she'd been a bit wary about letting Lily completely into her life.

"No, that's not what I'm saying. I was there because my father asked me to go and see what I could find out. I was doing him a favour." Erin shrugged, but it looked unnatural, maybe because she was wound so tightly that lifting her shoulders threatened to make her body snap. "And that's why I've continued to show up for your group activities. You told me about White Knight, and so the question became, who is White Knight? That's why I kept coming to the group stuff. And it's separate from what developed between us. I didn't expect us to hit it off the way we did. My feelings . . . Us . . . it's all real and true and I haven't lied about any of it."

So far, Erin hadn't said anything so terrible that they were broken. Lily did not like being lied to, being used, but she could deal with it. They could deal with it, talk about it, see where it left them. It wasn't upending-a-table worthy.

"So now the part I should have told you about already and I really wanted to, but my father still wanted me to figure out who White Knight is, and the stronger my feelings were for you, the harder it felt to tell you the truth. Sort of like when you come out. Telling the people you care about the most scares you to death, which is why you keep putting it off." Her voice dipped so low, Lily had to strain to hear it. "You don't want to lose them."

She went back to putting her hands on her lap and clenching them tightly. Erin had already admitted to not being completely honest. She'd already admitted to not really giving a shit about McMillan Park and greedy developers. What else could there possibly be? "You said you were doing a favour for your father."

"Yes."

"Why? What's your father got to do with the park?"

Erin grabbed her glass with her free hand but didn't drink from it. Her pale face made her eyes appear unusually dark. "That's what I want to tell you. My father is Aaron Hunt, of Hunt and Bishop. My name's not Erin Bartlett. It's Erin Hunt."

Time stood still. The words seemed to echo in Lily's brain. Aaron Hunt, of Hunt and Bishop. Erin Hunt. Erin fucking Hunt. At her protests. In her apartment. Sitting across from her, with candles burning and clean sheets on the bed.

She leaped to her feet. "Are you fucking kidding me? Are you kidding me right now? Get the fuck out of my apartment!" Her body shook. She gripped the back of the chair.

Erin scrambled to stand up and stretched her hands toward Lily. "I didn't mean for this to happen. Everything I feel for you is real. I've never lied about anything to do with us. I wanted to tell you."

"You've sat at our meetings, pretended to give a shit, used me." Now she understood why Erin had wanted the emails. "Gone home to fucking daddy and told him everything, and you expect me to believe your feelings are real?"

"They are. I'm still Erin. I'm the same person I was two minutes ago."

"I don't even know you!" Lily roared. She pointed at the door. "Get out!"

"Lily, please."

"Get the fuck—" Her knees buckled and her vision narrowed, like she was looking down a tunnel.

20

ERIN FROZE WHEN THE blood drained from Lily's face and she stumbled backwards. Oh, shit. She rushed to Lily's side, grabbed her elbow, steered her toward the sofa and lowered her onto it. "Lie down and raise your legs," she said, recalling what she'd learned during the first aid refresher she'd taken last year. When Lily sort of fell back onto the sofa, Erin swung Lily's legs onto it and slipped a cushion under her feet. "I'll get you some water."

"Just leave," Lily whispered.

"I'm not leaving until I know you're okay."

She went into the kitchen, found a glass, didn't fill it all the way because her hands were trembling, and carried it over to Lily. She realized there was nowhere to put it, so she held on to the glass and crouched next to the sofa. "Don't sit up until you feel you won't faint."

"Leave," Lily said, her voice stronger.

"When you can stand, I'll leave." Erin looked at Lily and cringed. She ached to hold her and had to stop herself from taking her hand. "I'm so sorry. I know I should have told you earlier, but . . . there's no excuse, okay? I meant everything I said about us, about how I feel about you. I care about you a lot. Really a lot. You *do* know me. I hope we can work this out."

Colour had returned to Lily's face. She sat up. When Erin pressed the glass of water into her hand, she didn't protest, but she didn't take a sip. "Listen to me, Erin. Oh, wait. Is that your name? Or was it just your last name you lied about?" She didn't wait for Erin to respond. "If you're being honest about your feelings, if there's one shred of you that does actually care about me, you'll leave my apartment right now. Right now."

"But we need to—"

"Now!"

Erin wanted to stay, to plead her case, to get down on her knees and beg, if that was what it would take. But right now, it didn't matter what she wanted, and more than a shred of her cared about Lily.

She gazed at her for what she hoped wouldn't be the last time, then forced herself to turn on her heel and leave. As she walked down the corridor she felt as if she were walking through quicksand. Not wanting to hang around, she took the stairs, burst out of the lobby into the warm evening air, strode to her car feeling like a robot. It wasn't until she was safely in the driver's seat that she let herself feel, and then it rushed at her, like a spring river, the sobs wracking her body, and the memory of Lily's stricken face and shocked eyes taunting her over and over again.

~

ERIN RARELY USED THE private entrance to her apartment. It wasn't conveniently located relative to the driveway, and she rarely had a reason to avoid her parents. But she wasn't in the mood for talking. She wanted to go upstairs and hide in her room. She didn't have a roadmap for how to escape this depth of pain, of bleakness.

Safely inside her bedroom, she collapsed onto her bed. She'd sniffled all the way home. Now she felt numb. Tears lurked, but her body wanted a break.

She pulled her undercover phone from her blazer pocket and wondered whether to call. Maybe Lily had calmed down. Maybe she'd pick up. Or maybe she'd already blocked Erin's number.

Someone knocked at her door. Shit. Erin pushed herself into a sitting position. "Who is it?"

"It's Mom."

Oh, no. "I'm tired. Can we—"

The door opened. Erin quickly lay down and rolled over. Seconds later, Mom strode into her bedroom. "I wasn't expecting you home this early." A pause. "What's wrong?"

Erin silently cursed herself. Yeah, pretending to be dozing off while fully clothed on top of her bed had been a wonderful plan. She rolled over to face Mom, whose face fell at the sight of her.

"What happened?" Mom asked.

"I told Lily who I am."

"It didn't go well."

"No."

Mom's forehead creased with sympathy. "I'm sorry, sweetie, but maybe it's for the best."

"Why?"

"She obviously has a problem with our family. It's good you found that out now, when you're not too involved."

Erin swung her legs off the bed and sat up. "But I am involved. I've never felt this way about anyone. Not that it matters now. She wants nothing to do with me. The moment 'Hunt' left my lips, she wouldn't even talk to me." She pressed her hand against her heart. "I feel like crap. I've never felt this bad before. It feels like nothing matters now. Nothing."

"Everyone feels that way after a breakup. You'll feel better eventually."

"I'm not going to kill myself, and I'm sure I'll smile again at some point. But dating? Anyone else will feel like I'm settling."

Mom folded her arms and studied her. "Call her."

Erin shook her head. "I doubt she'll pick up."

"You won't know if you don't try."

"What's the point? Let's say she does pick up and agrees to see me, and through some miracle, forgives me. You and Dad won't be happy about it."

Mom's mouth pressed into a thin line. "Don't use your father and me as an excuse. I can't speak for him, but all I care about is that she's right for you."

Mom's words cut deeper than she'd intended. If Erin was honest with herself, she'd used Dad as an excuse to not tell Lily, because she was afraid of what would happen when Lily knew who she really was.

"She's broke, Mom."

"That's not what I meant."

"It's what everyone will think."

Mom looked down her nose at her. "If you're that concerned about what everyone will think of her, it's probably best she not date you. I certainly wouldn't want to be with someone who was always worried about whether everyone thought I was good enough. If that's how you feel, dry your eyes and get on with your life. It's not love." She turned to leave.

"Mom!"

Mom whirled to face her again.

"That's not what I meant. I mean, I'd worry for her. I'd worry that some people would treat her badly, make her feel like she isn't good enough, when she is. More than good enough." Her voice dipped. "Better than me. She's honest, for one thing."

"You're worried about how she'd feel. That's promising," Mom said, her face softening. "Call her, and if she doesn't pick up, keep trying. Don't be a stalker. But do try. If she never picks up, then you'll know and move on. But at least you'll have tried. You don't want to go through life wishing you'd tried." She sat next to Erin and wrapped her arms around her. "I hope she picks up, though. I really do. If you like her so much, she must be a, uh, wonderful woman. Someone I'd like to meet."

"Do you really mean that? Dad will freak."

"We'll work on Dad. I know he doesn't always show it, but he wants you to be happy. If Lily will make you happy, he'll eventually accept it."

Eventually accept it. She didn't like the sound of that, and how open would Dad be to her dating Lily when she also told him she didn't want to work at his side, at his company?

Mom let her go. "Do you want to go down to the bar and have a drink?"

"I just want to be alone right now."

"All right." Mom rose. "If you change your mind, you know where I'll be. I'll leave a note for Michael to make your favourite pancakes tomorrow."

Erin wasn't sure she'd feel like breakfast, but she nodded. "Thanks."

Alone again after Mom had left, Erin flopped back onto her bed. *If that's how you feel, dry your eyes and get on with your life. It's not love.* But it was. When Mom had used the word love, nothing within Erin had protested. Great time to realize it.

She pulled out her undercover phone and called Lily. Seven rings later, it went through to voicemail.

"Uh, hi, it's Erin. I know you're upset with me right now and you have every right to be, but could we talk? I'd really like to talk to you. Please call me. I hope you're okay. I know I screwed up really badly, and I'm sorry. I really am." She disconnected, feeling like a complete jerk, and inadequate, and lost.

Lily hated her. Lily would never see or speak to her again. Erin thought she'd been in love already, but now she realized she hadn't, because she'd been dumped before, and it had never hurt like this. Right now, she didn't believe her despair would ever go away. No matter what she did and who she met, she'd know, know Lily was out there. And it would hurt. Damn, it would hurt.

Her heart soared when her phone rang, until she realized it was her other phone. She sat up and fished it from her pocket. Douglas Wong. Her voice had sounded okay with Mom, so she answered the call.

"I wanted to let you know we've completed our investigation," Wong said. "I'll courier you a full report tomorrow, but I just sent you an email with the essentials."

"You're sure you've uncovered a connection between one of the people on the list and Hunt and Bishop."

"Yes. Take a look at the material. I'd say you'll be pleased, but I'm not sure you will be."

She couldn't feel any lower than she already did. "I'll take a look. Thank you."

They hung up. Erin went to her laptop, where she preferred to read emails when she was home. Rather than reading his email, she went straight to the photos he'd attached to it, clicking on the first one and . . .

No. No way. She gaped at the crystal clear image of Vanessa Goldstein in the arms of a woman whose face Erin knew so well, a woman she loved, a woman she'd thought she could always count on.

Christina.

21

LILY EXAMINED HERSELF IN the bathroom mirror and winced. Who were the morons who said a good cry made people feel better? Had they ever looked at themselves in the mirror afterwards? Maybe one crying session wouldn't have made her look so awful. Maybe if the tears were purely sorrowful, were devoid of rage, her skin wouldn't be so blotchy. Calling in sick had been the right call. Carlos would have taken one look at her and told her to go home anyway, not wanting her to frighten the customers away.

Her phone dinged from the living room. If it was Sandy, Lily would throw it out the window. Sandy had texted her numerous times, called, even emailed. Didn't she understand that sometimes a person just wanted to be left alone?

She went into the living room to see what Sandy had to say this time. Someone banged on her apartment door, making her jump.

"Who is it?" she shouted.

"It's me."

Sandy.

"Let me in, or I'll have the super open the door."

Lily unlocked the door and yanked it open. "Jesus, Sandy, what's the matter with you?"

"What's the matter with me?" Sandy barged in and slammed the door behind her. "I've been worried about you. I had images of you lying in here in a coma or something."

Any other time, Lily would have chuckled. "I'm fine. As you can see."

Sandy studied her. "Like hell you are. What's wrong? You look like you've been through the wringer. It's not like you to be weepy."

Weepy. Is that what she called it? "Want a coffee?"

"Sure, but I won't be that easily distracted. What's wrong? I tried calling you earlier and left a message, but you never got back to me. I tried calling you again this afternoon, and texting you.

Yeah, Lily was aware.

"Then I called the restaurant, and Carlos told me you'd called in sick today." She paused. "He didn't sound too happy about it. Said you hadn't given him much notice."

She'd make it up to him. Carlos was a good guy. Usually Lily could drag herself into work no matter what was going on. But Erin . . . she busied herself with getting the coffee brewing.

"What's wrong?"

Lily sighed and wandered into the living room. She'd have to tell her. It would be humiliating, embarrassing, excruciating, all of the above and everything else. "It's Erin."

"I was wondering. I know you had dinner with her last night and you were expecting to make her eggs today. I thought maybe that's why you weren't answering anything. But when I called the restaurant—" Sandy's eyes widened. "Oh, no. It didn't work out? I'm surprised. I was pretty sure she wanted to be closer to you."

"She does. She wants to, how did she put it, bring me into her life in a way she hasn't already. Show me her place. Spend more time with me." She sank into the chair Erin had occupied when she'd dropped her bombshell.

Sandy frowned down at her. "Now I'm confused. You're behaving like you had a blow up."

"We did."

"You didn't tell her you don't feel the same way, did you? Jesus, Lil. Why would you do that?"

Lily shot to her feet. "I didn't tell her anything. I didn't get the chance, because she dropped a fucking anvil on my head."

"Don't tell me she's with someone else."

That would have been less humiliating. Lily would have told Erin to get lost. She wasn't a cheat. And nobody would fault her for unwittingly falling for one. "Nope, not that." She spread out her arms. "It turns out that Erin is, and always has been, one big fat fucking lie."

"What do you mean?"

"She's been lying to everyone about who she is."

"How?" Sandy gasped. "She's not a nun, is she?"

Lily chuckled. "I'll give you a point because you made me smile, which I would have thought was impossible right now. No, not a nun. But on the big fat lie scale of 1 to 10, if a nun would be a 10, Erin's lie would be a 9.5."

"That serious, eh?" Sandy's face scrunched up. "Not a nun, not a cheater. Tell me."

"What name did she use when she introduced herself? Erin Bartlett?"

Sandy nodded.

"That's not her name. It's Erin Hunt."

Sandy didn't flinch. "Okay. Not seeing the problem."

"Erin Hunt. Hunt. As in Hunt and Bishop."

"Oh, shit."

"Yeah, oh shit is right. Erin fucking Hunt. Here, in my fucking apartment, listening to my fucking plans and pretending she gives a shit."

"So she's who, exactly, in the Hunt family?"

"Aaron Hunt's daughter."

"Wow," Sandy breathed.

"Yeah, wow."

"You've been dating Aaron Hunt's daughter?" Sandy barked a laugh.

Lily wanted to throttle her. "It's not funny."

Sandy pulled out a chair and sat at the table. "How did it come out? What did you say? Details, details."

Lily sat across from her. Coffee aroma wafted into the room. She'd make the coffees after she'd purged her soul. "She was trying to find out who White Knight is. That's the whole reason she came out to the protest that first time. Then she found out he was emailing me and latched onto me."

"She's been faking a relationship with you this whole time?"

Lily scratched her cheek. "I don't know. I don't think so." This morning, when she'd finally calmed down enough that her brain had engaged, she'd gone over their conversation and concluded that Erin's feelings for her were genuine, that their relationship was real to her. Erin hadn't said, "I'm Erin Hunt. Fuck you, I'm outta here." She'd said, "I want to bring you into my life, so you need to know who I am."

"I don't think so, either," Sandy said. "I've seen the two of you together. If she's been faking it, she deserves an Oscar."

"It doesn't matter now anyway. I told her to get the hell out of my apartment. And she left. The end."

Sandy's brows shot up. "That's it? No discussion, no why did you lie to me, let's talk about what it means for us, nothing? You just threw her out?"

"What the hell did you expect me to do?" Lily said, even though she wished she'd handled it differently.

"Talked. Okay, she lied. You have every right to be pissed off with her for that. But are you sure you want to just dump her? She wants to be with you." Sandy's voice softened. "And I think you want to be with her."

"I don't even know who she is."

"Bullshit. You didn't know her real name or her true motivation for coming out to our protests. But you've spent a lot of time with her that has nothing to do with any of that. Or were all your conversations about real estate and White Knight?"

"No," Lily mumbled. She wouldn't add that when they'd first started hanging out, White Knight had come up quite a lot, but not lately. Not for a while, actually.

"It doesn't matter, though," she said to Sandy. "She's a Hunt."

"That's too easy and you know it. I know you're angry because you're hurting. I'd be angry too. I'd hurt too. It's a shitty thing to find out—that she's been lying to you, not her last name. But I'm sure she didn't know she'd develop feelings for you when she showed up that first time."

Erin had said as much. Obviously she couldn't have known.

"And you're not only angry at her right now. You're angry at yourself."

"For being gullible? Hell, yeah, I'm angry at myself."

"That's not what I meant."

"Spit it out. I know you're dying to."

"Dig deep, Lil. You know what I'm going to say."

"Say it!"

"You're angry at yourself because you fell for a Hunt. One of the evil people."

Lily wanted to deny it. She wanted to tell Sandy she was crazy. But she wouldn't. She couldn't. Because it was true. And humiliating, embarrassing, maddening. How the hell could she fall for a Hunt? Really fall. Thinking about a future together fall. How could she feel that way about someone who shared Aaron Hunt's genes?

"You're really going to let her name get in the way of what could be? You're going to give it that much power over your life?"

The rage she'd felt since Erin's bombshell threatened to boil over and lash out at Sandy. But she wouldn't drive another person from her life, especially when Sandy was right. "How can I still feel that way, though? How, knowing who she is?"

Sandy smiled. "She's the woman you fell for. That's who she is."

"I should pour the coffees." She escaped to the kitchen, wanting a break before Sandy asked her what she was going to do about it all. She hadn't told her about Erin paying her fine, which she intended to keep to herself, because she was still thinking about how to handle that too.

With a sigh, she carried the coffees into the living room and set them on the table.

Sandy blew on her coffee. "Has she tried to talk to you?"

"She's left me a few messages."

"Are you going to call her back?"

Lily cupped her hands around her mug. "Maybe. I don't want to leave things where they are, but I need more time to make sure I won't blow up at her again."

"What if she stops calling?"

"Then that'll be it." Lily had sounded casual, but if Erin stopped trying, she'd be crushed. It would mean everything she'd said during their last conversation had been a lie. "I'll talk to her. I just need another day or two to calm down."

"What are you going to say?"

"What is this, an interrogation?" She shrugged and shook her head. "I'm not sure. But I have questions."

"I bet. I'm glad you're willing to talk to her, though."

"It doesn't mean we'll . . ." Get back together? Had throwing Erin out of her apartment meant they'd broken up, or had it been the way they'd ended a furious argument? "I'm not sure what I want."

"She came clean. And before you made her eggs."

Lily had wondered about that. When she'd gone over the evening in her head, she'd understood why Erin hadn't been herself from the moment she'd arrived. She'd intended to tell the truth about her identity. "I'm glad I heard it from her. If I'd heard it from anyone else, I think I would have ended it. I would have wondered if she'd ever intended to tell me, or if she was just going to drop me at some point and let me think she was Erin Bartlett for the rest of my life."

"The reason she came clean is important too. She wants to bring you into her life."

Yeah, which scared the shit out of her. Not only could she see them together for a while, but Erin was not from this neighbourhood, hell, not from this planet, as far as Lily was concerned. If they managed to get past this mess, what would happen when the honeymoon phase was over, when the hormones stopped raging and thoughts of each other weren't all consuming, when Erin didn't long to see her when she wasn't there? Would Erin wonder why she was with a waitress who had less than four figures in her bank account?

Lily did not believe her worth depended on crap like bank account balances, where she lived, and who she rubbed elbows with. But she was also a realist. The last thing she wanted to do was jump off the cliff, only to find out Erin wouldn't be there to catch her when the madness evolved into maturity.

~

AT THE BISHOP RESIDENCE, Erin drove a golf cart to the pool area, where Christina was apparently sunbathing. She was not looking forward to this conversation, but anything was better than willing her undercover phone to ring. Every minute felt like an hour. Not being able to stand it anymore, and knowing she had to confront Christina at some point, here she was. The fact that she was already agitated would help. Erin was usually a wuss about this sort of thing.

She parked the cart and strolled to the pool. Christina was lounging poolside in a bikini. She shielded her eyes with her hand when Erin stopped and stared down at her. "I didn't know you were coming over today."

"If I'd warned you, you probably wouldn't be here right now. You've been avoiding me, and now I know why." Erin pulled out her phone and swiped to one of the photos Wong had sent her.

Christina frowned. "What are you going on about?"

"This." She thrust the phone in Christina's face.

"Oh."

"Oh? That's all you have to say? Oh? You've been lying to me. From the very beginning, when I told you my dad had asked me to go to Lily's protest and find out who's leaking company documents, you've lied through your teeth."

Christina swung her legs off the chaise and sat up. Her calm demeanor irritated Erin.

"Your dad looked me right in the eye and said he wasn't the one leaking documents. But here it is, in colour. Your girlfriend, who I didn't even know existed, sent the emails."

Now on her feet, Christina slipped into a hooded terrycloth robe and flip flops. "Let's stroll." Not waiting for Erin to agree, she walked away from the pool.

Erin fell into step with her. "I can't believe your dad would stab mine in the back like that."

"He didn't. He had nothing to do with it. He doesn't know about it."

Erin stopped walking. "You did it yourself. Why?"

Christina grabbed her arm, pulled her back to her side. She looped her arm through Erin's, making Erin walk again. "I know you don't pay all that much attention to the company, at least not until lately. But I do. Or at least I pay attention to how it's affecting Dad. It hasn't been great for a while. Your dad treats him like garbage."

"Your dad told me they're like an old married couple."

"One that's perhaps careening toward a divorce. He's given up on trying to get your dad to listen to him. He says it doesn't matter, but it does. He doesn't smile as much as he used to. Sometimes he has a drink when he comes home. I don't like seeing him that way."

"Okay, let's say I accept that my dad hasn't been the best business partner lately. How does leaking documents help?"

"It doesn't. I just wanted to do something to upset your dad."

They'd reached one of the garden gazebos. When Christina let go of her arm and sank onto the cushioned bench the gazebo shaded, Erin followed suit.

"You did this just to piss off my dad?"

"Yes."

Erin took a moment to digest the information. "And then you watched me bumble around and asked me how the investigation was going, to stay one step ahead."

"Not really. We, Van and I, we didn't really plan much. When I found out you were going to try to figure out who the leak was, I thought about stopping, but I wanted to see if you'd figure it out." She patted Erin's knee. "You did great."

"Oh, well, thank you. Thank you very much. I have one question for you, though. When you found out about the plan to send different versions of a document to different people, why did you send the original?"

Christina adjusted the cushion behind her and leaned back. "I thought about not sending anything, but it bothered me that you were starting to suspect everyone. I knew they were all loyal. I sent the original so you'd stop suspecting them."

"I thought it was your dad."

Christina nodded. "When he told me you'd talked to him, I decided to stop altogether. Van never quite felt comfortable with it, but she did it anyway." A smile crossed Christina's face. "For me."

"Yeah, let's move on to you and Van. How long have you been together?"

"Like in the photo? Not very long. We were friends first. I met her in my spin class. I probably mentioned it to you, but you usually tune out when I'm talking about spin."

True.

"When I kissed you . . ." Christina laid her hand on Erin's leg. "I wanted to see how it felt because I'd been holding Van off. Because of you. Because of what everyone was expecting. If fireworks had gone off, I wouldn't have pursued anything with Van. It would be me and you." She grimaced. "But they didn't. I'm sorry."

"No need to be sorry. Nothing happened for me, either."

Christina's other hand went to her chest. "Oh, thank god. We can be best friends again and hang out. I was so afraid you'd want us to do it again. Because we're best friends. I'd say even more. We're the sisters neither one of us have."

The reason the kiss had felt all wrong. It had felt incestuous, like she was kissing her damn sister. She laid her hand over Christina's. "We are. And I've missed you."

The air lightened, as if they'd been sitting inside a pressure cooker and someone had opened the valve.

"I won't tell Dad," Erin said. "About you being White Knight."

"You'll have to tell him."

"Why?"

"Because I want to introduce Van to everyone. The moment he meets her, he'll know, and there's no way I'm letting her take the blame. It was all me. And it'll be a win for you too."

"I don't need the win."

"Sure you do. You look like you've been run over by a truck."

Erin barked a surprised laugh.

"What's going on? You haven't been sleeping and you've been crying. I hope it's not because of me."

Erin wanted to hug her. "I'm so glad we've cleared the air. I thought I'd lost you."

"Never. You couldn't get rid of me if you tried. Now out with it."

"It's Lily."

"Lily Altree?"

Erin nodded. "You're not the only one who's been secretly seeing someone."

Christina's brows lifted ever so slightly. "I wondered. You relished your assignment a little too much. Also, when I was over at yours once, your mom asked me how our dinner was the night before. I think I covered for you well enough."

"Sorry."

"No need. Back to Lily. Obviously something's happened."

"I told her my last name is Hunt."

"It didn't go over well, I'm guessing. Have you tried talking to her?"

"She's not returning my calls. I'm starting to feel like a stalker."

"Has she served you with a restraining order?"

"No."

"Then keep trying, unless she tells you to stop. And if she does tell you to stop, you'll know you did everything. That's how you'll go on with your life and be able to love someone else—if she doesn't melt. But let's hope she melts. I'm curious about her now. I'd like to meet her."

Erin knew instinctively that Christina was right about time lessening the pain. But right now, it was difficult to believe the ache, the longing, would ever go away. And she wasn't giving up. Unless Lily explicitly told her to stop, she'd keep trying.

Christina pursed her lips. "Maybe you can do something she can't ignore, some grand gesture, like hiring a quartet to serenade her or . . . what does she do?"

"She's a waitress at the Golden Goose."

"Reserve the entire restaurant when she's working and tell her you did it so you can have a quiet dinner with her."

Erin shook her head. "Something like that won't matter to Lily." Quite the opposite. Lily would be horrified.

"Pity. It would be so much easier."

She agreed but wouldn't have Lily any other way. Funny how Erin had pitied that guy in the red convertible and worried that women would like her because of her money. Maybe the guy wasn't so gullible after all. Maybe the woman next to him sincerely loved him.

"I really like her," she said to Christina. "I might even love her."

"Oh, dear. Not that it's a bad thing, but I'd be happier for you if you were still speaking to each other."

"I can't blame her for being angry. I used her." She gave Christina a pointed look. "So did you."

"Sorry." Christina had the decency to look contrite. "I don't know what else to suggest."

"That's okay. Just knowing I can talk to you about it has helped."

"Of course you can. I hope you work it out, I really do."

"Do you really mean that? We're talking about Lily, who is an incredible person, but also the leader of the Citizens for Responsible Housing group."

Christina waved away Erin's concern. "She has convictions. I can respect that. And we both know our dads always get their way in the end."

True again. She had something else she wanted to talk to Christina about, something she'd clung to since Royce had called her that morning, so she wouldn't be thinking about Lily and figuratively biting her fingernails 24/7. "When I tell my dad about you being White Knight, how about you come with me and we tell both our dads together? Because I have something else I want to talk to them about, and I'd appreciate your support."

"Tell me." Christina gazed at Erin, her eyes alight with interest.

"Okay, so you know I'm going to work at the company soon, right?"

"Yes."

"And your dad has asked me to work with him, and they're waiting for a decision?"

"Uh huh."

"I've decided not to work for either one of them."

Christina squealed.

"But only your dad knows, because I talked to him about maybe doing something different with McMillan Park. He called me this morning and told me he supports my proposed change to the project."

Erin told Christina about what she and Royce had discussed and the possibility that Dad would agree to it, which they figured was about 25/75, odds not in their favour. Dad would probably throw a fit and tell them they were crazy.

"But you think we should try," she said to Christina.

"Absolutely." Christina clapped her hands together. "First we tell them about White Knight, because that'll earn you points with your dad. Then you and Dad can talk about your idea. I'll call Dad, set something up with them for . . . tomorrow afternoon? I'm sure they'll fit us in."

"Sure. But I can call."

"You have too much on your mind already. I'll do it." She gave Erin's knee one final pat and rose. "Let's go back to the house and shoot some pool. You'll stay for dinner? You can tell me how you got that photo of me and Van."

"And you can tell me all about her. But I'll follow you in. I want to try Lily again."

"Good luck," Christina mouthed.

Erin waited until she was out of earshot, then pulled out her undercover phone—she hoped to give Lily her real phone number—and called her, ready to leave her usual pleading message.

"Hi."

"Lily, it's Erin, I'm calling again because—oh, hi." Her heart leaped from her chest. She chuckled nervously. "I wasn't expecting you to pick up."

"We should talk," Lily said, her voice flat. "Can you meet for coffee at the place just around the corner from me, the one we've been to a couple of times before?"

"Sure."

"Wednesday, two o'clock?"

"I'll be there."

"See you then. Bye." She disconnected.

Erin stared at her phone. This was a good thing, right? Lily was willing to talk, face to face, to give Erin a chance to plead her case. Or was she going to do the noble thing and dump her once and for all in person? Erin had desperately hoped Lily would pick up, but now that she had, a different scary scenario would taunt her.

22

Erin studied the two men sitting across the rectangular conference table from her and hoped she wouldn't sweat. Royce Bishop smoothed his aqua blue tie and smiled at Christina, who was sitting at Erin's left. Next to Royce, Dad wasn't scowling exactly, but he certainly wasn't giving her an encouraging smile and his arms were folded.

"So what's this about?" Dad said. "I thought perhaps you'd come to a decision, but then why would Christina be here?"

"I have come to a decision," Erin said. "But there's something else I want to discuss first."

"What?"

"I've uncovered the identity of White Knight."

Dad unfolded his arms. Now he was grinning. "That's my girl. Whose ass am I firing?"

"Nobody's."

He frowned.

"I'm White Knight," Christina said.

A shocked silence ensued. Royce gazed at Christina. "Chrissy, what are you saying?"

"I sent the information to Lily Altree."

"But why?" Royce asked.

Erin could tell Dad wanted to shout. Good plan, letting Royce do the talking.

"I did it for you."

"For me?"

"You two don't get along the way you used to," Christina said. "You used to be partners. Now you're a dictatorship." Her eyes settled on Dad. "With you as the dictator."

Dad opened his mouth, but Royce got there first. "What makes you say that?"

"He doesn't listen to you anymore. He decides everything and you go along with it. I'd call that a dictatorship."

"I do not decide everything," Dad said. "We both have to sign off on projects."

"You don't listen to him. You stick a form under his nose and tell him to sign."

A pained expression formed on Royce's face. "It's not that simple, Chrissy."

"Isn't it?"

"No. You're right, I wish we weren't so focused on luxury condos and expensive rentals. But I could have fought back if I wanted to."

"If that were true, you wouldn't come home most nights and head to the bar. You never used to do that."

Royce's cheeks grew red. "Maybe we should discuss this at home."

"You'll just tell me not to worry and to mind my own business. I won't do that anymore." Christina shifted her attention to Dad. "You need to listen to him."

Dad glowered at Christina. "Let me get this straight. You think there's a problem between us, and your solution is to leak confidential company information. I don't see a connection."

"I wasn't trying to solve the problem. I wanted you to squirm."

Dad's face froze. Erin braced herself for the explosion. He blinked, then laughed. "It worked, young lady." He slow clapped. "Well played."

Erin couldn't believe it. If it had been her, he'd be screaming at her, telling her how useless she was.

"How did you find out it was Chrissy?" Royce asked Erin.

"I hired a private investigator to see if there was a connection between the company and any of the people on our short list. The people in the library footage," she said to Dad. "I know you wanted me to keep it in the family, but I wasn't getting anywhere on my own." The truth, and Dad would believe her. After all, he thought she was useless. Maybe that was why he wasn't yelling at her about it. "One of those people was Vanessa Goldstein."

"Van did it for me," Christina said. "We're seeing each other."

The two men glanced at each other. "But what about you two?" Royce said.

"There's never been an us two," Erin said wryly.

"We're close," Christina added. "We're pretty much sisters. We're not interested in each other that way."

Dad lifted his hands and dropped them to his lap. "Your mother will be disappointed."

Mom already knew, and when Dad told her, she'd act surprised.

"I want you to meet Van," Christina said to Royce. "I'll talk to Mom about it."

Royce nodded. "Invite her for dinner."

"You did well, Erin," Dad said, making her flush. "As for you, Christina, next time you have a problem with me, talk to me. Don't pull any more of this fucking bullshit."

Christina lifted her chin. "I want you to listen to my father."

"I always listen to him."

Royce twisted toward Dad. "You haven't listened as much lately. We used to do a mix of projects. Ever since . . ." He trailed off.

Dad's eyes were hard. "Ever since . . ."

"Ever since your mother passed away, you've been less tolerant of loss."

Erin expected him to deny it, but he remained silent, his Adam's apple bobbing. She felt her eyes well up in response. It didn't help that she was prone to crying fits at the moment.

"I didn't want to make things more difficult for you. I was fine going along with what you wanted, but it's been a few years now."

Dad drummed his fingers on the table.

"Take McMillan Park. I was opposed to that project from the beginning. I still am. But you ignored me, didn't even read my proposal, and plowed ahead anyway."

"Speaking of McMillan Park, Erin said she has two things to discuss." Christina turned to Erin and shot her an encouraging smile. "Take it away."

She sat straighter and cleared her throat. "Let's talk about McMillan Park. Royce and I have an alternate proposal for the site."

Dad gave her a surprised look. "Really? Does that mean you've decided to work with him?"

"No, I'm not going to work with him."

"Ha! I knew you'd choose me."

"I'm not coming to work with you, either."

Dad went rigid. "What the fuck does that mean? What are you saying?"

"She's saying she's not going to come work at the company," Royce said.

"Thank you for the fucking translation. Jesus." Dad banged his fists on the table. "What are you going to do, then? Waste your life away?"

"I'm applying for a spot in an astrophotography program at college," Erin said.

"Are you serious?"

"Yes, I'm serious." She could feel her chin trembling. "It's what I want to do, Dad. The program includes help with placement afterwards. I can make money doing what I enjoy. Isn't that what matters?"

"You mean you can make money taking pictures of the sky?"

"Yes."

"You know Erin loves doing that," Christina said. "She's fortunate in that she can do anything she wants with her life. Don't you think it makes sense for her to do something she loves?"

He drummed his fingers on the table again.

"Daniel doesn't work here," Royce said. "Chrissy isn't going to work here. What's the point of forcing our children to work here if they're not going to like it?"

Dad blew out some air. "I suppose it's something. At least you won't be sitting around on your ass all day. You're really going to apply for this program?"

She nodded.

"All right. Let's see how it all plays out. You can always change your mind."

She wanted to groan, but at the same time, she was encouraged. He hadn't disowned her. Yet. "I might help out on the McMillan Park project. If you accept our alternate proposal."

"Which is?"

"To keep it as a park, as a public relations gesture."

"We can write off some of the expenses," Royce added. "I had accounting check into it."

"Wait, wait." Dad glared at her. "It's that fucking group, isn't it? You've swallowed it all."

"No," Erin said. "But I did listen. Not everything they say is crap."

Royce jumped in. "Aaron, I had problems with your proposal from the start. The apartment you want to build isn't a good fit for the neighbourhood. And—"

Dad motioned for Royce to stop talking. He pointed at Christina. "You don't work here." He pointed at Erin. "Neither do you. This is between me and Royce. Leave."

Erin's jaw tightened. "B-but I proposed it to—"

"I don't want Altree's influence in this discussion," Dad shouted.

Christina gave Erin a sidelong glance.

"You've discussed it with Royce, now Royce will discuss it with me. Go somewhere else." He made shooing motions with his hands.

Erin hesitated, then left with Christina. In the corridor, they both rolled their eyes.

"Hopefully my dad will be able to talk him around," Christina said.

Erin hoped so too. If anyone could do it, Royce could. She didn't believe he was as submissive and powerless in the partnership as Christina did. He was good at reading Dad and biding his time.

Christina's tone lifted. "So if Lily isn't dumping you, when are you going to tell him?"

"I don't know."

"Wish I could be there, but I know I can't be."

"You'll be there to help me pick up the pieces, though, right?"

"Of course."

Shouts from within the conference room made them both jump. They glanced at each other, then went to the elevator and rode it down to the lobby. Erin didn't know who'd tell her the outcome of the two partners' discussion: Dad or Royce. She just hoped they were still partners when they left the conference room.

~

THE REST OF THE afternoon crawled by, even though she and Christina hung out for most of it. They window shopped—Erin pretending to be interested in clothes and Christina pretending to be interested in anything nerdy—and drank coffee at a gourmet coffee shop. Both checked their phones regularly, and in Erin's case, both phones, even though she doubted very much Lily would call. They'd see each other tomorrow. Dad would be upset with her, because she was more worried about what Lily would say than about whether Hunt and Bishop survived his and Royce's argument.

By the time she pulled into the Hunts' driveway after dropping Christina off, neither of her phones had rung. The moment she stepped into the house's grand entryway, she heard voices coming from the living room. Dad and Mom, talking.

She considered slinking by them, but she needed to know. "Hey," she said, stepping into the room and glancing from one to the other.

Dad's piercing eyes focused on her. "You won."

"What do you mean?"

"I've agreed to your proposal about the park." He lifted a finger. "Mainly because I needed to throw Royce a bone to keep the peace."

"Mainly? What's left?"

"I can see the PR angle. And you said you'd help."

Her spirits rose. He wasn't foaming at the mouth. "I will! As much as I can."

He turned to Mom. "Did she tell you about this program she's applying to at college?"

Mom nodded. "She told me this morning. I think it's a great idea."

"It's good she's finally doing something with her life."

Erin wanted to wave, to remind them she was standing right here.

"Let's have a drink," Dad said.

They headed to the downstairs bar, where Mom broke open a bottle of champagne and poured three glasses.

"A toast," Dad declared, raising his glass. "To my lovely wife, for always standing by me."

Mom smiled. They all sipped their champagne.

"To my daughter," Dad said, turning to Erin. "For figuring something out, at least."

Erin grinned. They drank.

"Finally, to Royce. It just wouldn't be the same without him, even if he is a pain in the ass sometimes."

Another sip.

"That's all I got." Dad focused on Erin again. "Now that we know who White Knight is, you—"

"Who is it?" Mom asked.

"Can you believe Christina?"

Mom's eyes widened. "Why?"

"I'll fill you in. Let me finish what I was saying first. Now that we know it was Christina and it won't happen again, you can get yourself away from Altree and her group, which is absolutely fantastic. Would you have made the proposal if you hadn't spent time with them?"

"Probably not," Erin mumbled.

"Exactly. Good riddance to them."

Erin wanted to tell him, she really wanted to tell him. He seemed to be in a good mood. She opened her mouth—Mom caught her eye and gave an almost imperceptible shake of her head. Not now. Erin clamped her mouth shut. Telling him could cause a huge stir for nothing, anyway. It would depend on what Lily said tomorrow. Erin was counting the hours, minutes, seconds until she could see her again and plead her case.

23

Lɪʟʏ sᴀᴛ ᴀᴛ ᴀ window table in the coffee shop, with two coffees in front of her. She'd arrived early, not wanting Erin to arrive first and wonder whether she'd been stood up. Erin would sweat, and Lily didn't want her to sweat, something she'd have to remind herself of when they talked, because a part of her wanted to lash out at her. She'd calmed down since their blow up. She wanted a genuine conversation. But she was still angry. Not a red-hot irrational anger that made it impossible to think. A more indignant anger at the way she'd been lied to and used.

The door opened. Erin walked in. A lump formed in Lily's throat. Okay, one question answered. She still had feelings for her. Strong feelings. Wanting to be with her feelings.

She waved. Erin came over and sat down. Lily winced. She wasn't the only one who'd spent some portion of the last few days balling.

"Here." She pushed one of the coffees over to Erin.

"Thanks," Erin murmured.

Lily wanted to say, "Now I only owe you $4996.25 of the five grand you dropped on my fine," but she bit her tongue. Genuine conversation, remember?

"I'm really grateful you want to talk," Erin said. "I'm so sorry. I should have told you earlier. I—"

Lily raised her hand. "Can I just ask you some questions?"

"Sure." Erin cupped her hands around her coffee.

"I want to make sure I heard what you said the other night. Okay, so you're Erin Hunt. You came to a protest because your father wanted you to find out how I knew certain things. That's why you—" Lily formed air quotes with her fingers "—joined the group."

"Yes."

"We started hanging out together, you fell for me, I fell for you, you didn't tell me who you really are because I'm not sure, but for whatever reason, it was difficult to tell me the truth, and then you finally told me, maybe because I wanted you to stay the night. Does that about sum it up?" Oh yeah, and Erin had paid the damn fine, but that was a separate issue and a separate conversation, one that would potentially take place through third parties, depending on where they ended up with each other.

Erin moistened her lips. "I wanted to tell you for a while, but I was afraid."

"Of what?"

"That you'd dump me."

"Didn't you realize that—"

"And of how my father would react. You want honesty. Okay." Erin looked down at her coffee, then lifted her head. "I felt caught in the middle. He wanted me to find out who was leaking documents, and in his mind, you were key to that. He can be a real hard ass with me. If I'd told him I'd blown my cover, he would have freaked. When it came to you, I'm acutely aware of how you feel about him. You hate him and everything he stands for and does, so I was terrified of telling you because I was—am—terrified of losing you."

Lily sipped her coffee. "I don't hate him. I don't know him. I hate what he does. I hate that he doesn't give a damn about some people. But I'm not here to discuss your father. I'm here to discuss where we go from here. You lied about your last name. What else did you lie about?"

Erin stared at her.

"There must have been other lies." Lily pointed. "You're wearing a watch I've never seen before." Which she gave Erin a point for. She'd shown up as herself.

Erin lifted her wrist and looked at her Rolex. "I've never worn it because it's an expensive watch and I thought you, or Sandy, or someone else might wonder how someone between jobs could afford it."

"You lied about being between jobs."

Erin cocked her head. "Yes and no. I've only ever worked for Hunt and Bishop. Summer jobs. I graduated from university a little over a year ago. Dad wanted me to start work with him right away, but I wasn't sure it was what I wanted. So I stalled, told him I needed time to think about it."

"So that's what you've been doing for the past year? Thinking?"

"Not exactly. Coasting would be more like it. You'll probably play the world's smallest violin when I say this, but when you don't have to work to put food on the table, when there's no urgency, it's easy to coast. It's difficult to figure out what you really want to do."

Lily would not play the world's smallest violin. She wasn't one of those idiots who thought money solved everything, that the wealthy didn't have problems and challenges. They had different problems and challenges than the masses, but they did have them. If that wasn't true, nobody wealthy would be committing suicide or overdosing. But she wasn't here to reassure Erin that she could appreciate the lives of the rich and famous weren't all bunny rabbits and rainbows.

"I've figured it out, though. You helped."

Lily cursed her curiosity, and that she cared. "What are you going to do?"

"I'm applying for that astrophotography program you told me about."

"That's good."

"I might not get in."

"You have to believe in yourself. Yeah, I know, look who's talking."

"You'll make a brilliant chef."

Damn, she wanted to smile and hug her.

"I want to tell you everything, so I'll be doing something else too. I'll be helping out on a new project Royce Bishop is leading."

Double damn. "That's not surprising. You're the heir apparent, right?"

"No, I'm not. It's a one-off. A project I'm personally interested in."

Shit, she really was going to be her father's heir. Which neighbourhood was her personal little project going to destroy? And a one-off? Erin believed that now, but there would be others.

"You, your group. I learned a few things from you."

She wanted to groan and tell Erin she wasn't born yesterday, but what if she was telling the truth? Genuine conversation, remember? "What's the project?" she asked.

Erin grimaced. "I'm not trying to hide anything, but I just had a discussion with my dad and Royce—Royce Bishop—about this yesterday. I don't want to say anything about it just yet."

"Because it's me."

"No. We're meeting with someone from the city tomorrow. If we don't get the outcome we want, there won't be anything to tell."

"But you can't tell me anyway, like, this is what we're trying to do but the city might not agree?" Lily sighed. "See, this is how—"

Not yet. "Forget that for now. What other lies have you told?"

Erin looked down at her coffee again. "The Mercedes is mine."

She'd figured.

"You don't have my real phone number."

She hadn't figured. "What do you mean?"

"I bought a phone to use just with you and your group. The number, the email address . . . not me. Do you want my number, my actual number?"

The vulnerability in Erin's voice made Lily cringe, but she stuck to her guns. "I'm not sure yet." She wanted to look away when Erin bit her lip. "What else have you lied about?"

"I don't live in the Treeview neighbourhood. I live in Harbour Valley."

Of course she did. Multimillion-dollar homes, large estates, pools, helicopter pads. "But you live with your parents?"

"Yes. In a private apartment, though. Well, not really private in the sense that it's completely detached from the house. It has a private entrance."

Lucky her. "What else?" She could hear the terseness in her voice and wanted to reign it in, but the sinking feeling inside her wasn't helping.

"I . . . I don't think there's anything else. I said my father is in investments, which is true. Real estate investment. Uh . . . I can't think of anything else. If there is anything, it would be small. I know that wouldn't excuse it, but . . ." She finally gulped down some coffee. "I should have told you everything earlier. I'm sorry I didn't. I want you in my life. I want to be with you. I'm so sorry I hurt you."

Lily clenched her hands in her lap. "I care about you, a lot. If I was sixteen, I'd say, our feelings are all that matter. But I'm not sixteen. And I'm concerned about whether we can work."

"Why?" Erin whispered.

"We're from very different backgrounds." She'd have to bring up the fine. "You dropped five grand on my fine as if it was nothing."

"I didn't think you'd gauge someone's worth based on how much money they have—or don't have."

"I don't. I'm talking about a power imbalance. You can throw money around. I can't. I'll hold you back."

"How?"

"Wait until you want to go away for a vacation somewhere, and I say I can't go because I can't afford it."

"But if we were to do that—"

"You'd foot the bill? How do you think that would make me feel, when you have to do that over and over again? Then there's your family business. You'll be helping out with a project. You're becoming Hunt and Bishop. Hell, you *are* Hunt and Bishop. You won't even tell me what you'll be meeting about tomorrow. What will we do if you take on a project I don't agree with? What if I decide to protest against it? Would it make sense for me to hold a sign and chant, and after the protest is over, head off on a date with you? Would it make sense for you?"

"I might not be involved with any other projects, but let's say I do get involved with another one in the future. Have you considered that I'd discuss projects with you before I take them on?"

No, she hadn't considered that, because she was used to developers doing whatever they damn well pleased without consulting with the community first, and certainly without consulting with her.

"It's not that I can't discuss what's happening tomorrow. I'm holding back for a personal reason I can't tell you. I'd really, really like to tell you. But I can't, not right now. I only brought it up because I want you to know I'll be working on a project."

A personal reason? Lily's curiosity was piqued, then she reminded herself of what she'd decided before she'd shown up at the coffee shop, when Erin wasn't sitting just a table width away, and she wasn't fighting the urge to reach out and touch her.

She forced herself back to the reason for this conversation. "What will your parents think about you being with me? Do they know?"

"My mom does."

"And?"

"Whatever makes me happy."

"Your father doesn't know."

"Not yet. I don't think he'll be happy about it, but Mom says he'll come around."

That sinking feeling dropped another few floors. "What do you think will happen when we're not thinking about each other twenty-four hours a day? You know, when the honeymoon period wears off? Will our different backgrounds, our different situations, still not matter in a year or two?"

Erin thought about it for a moment. "I don't know. Nobody can know that. I'd like to think they won't. I believe they won't. But I can't give you a guarantee. Nobody would be able to do that."

Another point. She really was being honest, but her answer didn't quell the fear that had raged inside Lily since she'd found out who Erin was. Yes, relationships were a risk. Yes, there was always the possibility that once the lust subsided and the hormones returned to their normal levels and the rose-coloured glasses came off and the cute habit that used to be endearing was now irritating as all hell, that the two people in the relationship would truly see each other for the first time and decide to call it quits. But some relationships were riskier than others, and this one with Erin Hunt, of Hunt and Bishop, would feel like she'd be skydiving without a parachute, hoping against hope that something would save her before she splattered onto the ground.

"Like I said, if I was sixteen . . . But I'm not. A relationship with you doesn't make sense, for either of us."

Erin's lips trembled and her eyes moistened. She grabbed one of the napkins on the table and dabbed at them. "I think I love you," she whispered. "Can't you forget my name and my money and see me? Please try to see me."

Lily blinked away the tears that sprang to her eyes. The longing, the pull to go and wrap her arms around Erin, was palpable. "I'm sorry, but I can't be with you. Don't call me. Okay?"

"Lily . . ."

"I'm sorry, but we can't be together."

Erin nodded, then jerkily got to her feet. "I'm leaving now," she mumbled.

Lily watched her stride to the entrance and leave, suspecting Erin would run if she could. Hell, the sixteen-year-old in Lily wanted to run after her. Instead, the adult inside her sat and finished her coffee, and asked herself if she'd just broken up with her because she wanted to punish her for lying. She didn't think so.

Right now, she couldn't see how it would work between them. She wished she could. She'd wanted honesty from Erin, so she'd be honest with herself. She loved her. She wanted to be with her. It just didn't make sense, for either of them.

She'd go home, cry more tears, pick herself up, and try to move on. Though it would be difficult. Every time she saw or heard "Hunt and Bishop," she'd feel like she'd been kicked in the gut and wonder if she'd made the worst mistake of her life.

24

A week later, Lily accepted the coffee she'd ordered from the barista and joined Sandy at a window table. She twirled the stir stick in her fingers and tried not to think about Erin.

"Did you take in any of the movie?" Sandy asked. "You chose it, but I get the feeling you didn't watch it."

"I watched it. It was okay." Like everything else. Just okay. Just bearable.

"You need to call Erin and tell her you've reconsidered."

"No. We're done. The end."

"Lil, I've never seen you like this before. You love her, for crying out loud. You're letting her go because she's rich?"

"It's not that."

"Well, what is it then, because everything you've said about it makes it sound like her money intimidates the crap out of you. If she was poor, would you have broken up with her?"

"If she was poor, she wouldn't be Erin Hunt and none of this would have happened."

"Great dodge."

"I'm not dodging." Her voice rose. "Am I the only one who sees the problems? Think, Sandy. Let's say we date. Who's going to take me seriously when I'm trying to save a site and they know I'm dating Erin fucking Hunt?"

"How would they know? Do you think it'll show up in the society pages or something?"

"These things have a way of getting out."

"Okay, so the optics might look bad, for both sides, by the way. But that has nothing to do with you and her."

"It has everything to do with me and her."

"No, it's about what other people think. Nothing to do with you two personally."

"You're splitting hairs, but let's say I give you that point. She's filthy rich. I'm not."

Sandy nodded. "See? It's about the money."

"No, it's about how different our lived experiences are. She probably went to private school, spent vacations skiing in the Alps or sunning herself in the Bahamas, she drops five grand on a fine like it's a quarter, drives a car that cost more than most people make in a year. I'm not the right person for her."

Sandy folded her arms. "So you're eliminating yourself as a good match based on what? Wealth? Possessions? I didn't think you cared so much about that stuff."

"I don't!" Lily scowled. "And stop doing that thing with your eyebrows."

Sandy waggled her eyebrows even more.

Lily glared at her. "Just let it go. We're not right for each other. The end."

"If you say 'the end' one more time, I swear I'll throw something at you."

"The end."

Sandy rolled her eyes.

Lily wanted to punch her. "I don't know why you're so sure Erin and I should date."

"Because it's obvious you're crazy about her and letting all sorts of irrelevant crap get in the way. Yes, you're angry. Yes, she's rich, you're not. Yes, you and her father don't agree on where developments should be built. Is there anything in that list about her heart?" Sandy tapped her chest. "Anything that says she's a bad person, or a bad match for you? You fell for her when you didn't know about her family. That says it all."

"I don't know. Relationships are difficult enough when both people are from the same worlds. Erin and I could date. We'd even enjoy dating. But I'm not the sort of person she'll take home to mom and dad. When she's ready to settle down with someone, it'll be bye-bye Lily. She'll suddenly be busy. She'll stop returning calls. I think she'd probably let me down gently, but still let me down."

Sandy pointed in the direction of the coffee shop's exit. "Since you're suddenly a fortune teller, maybe you should buy a lottery ticket. I saw a sign saying the jackpot is thirty million this week."

"I'm being serious. I don't want to . . . Jesus, why do I have to spell it out? I'm afraid I'll let myself believe it'll work and then she'll dump me because I'm a waitress with less than a thousand bucks in my bank account and I didn't go to Harvard or whatever. Can you understand that?"

Sandy's eyes brightened. "Everyone is taking a risk when they get together with someone. Most of the time, we don't think about it. I understand why you are in this case, but don't deny yourself the chance at a decent relationship with someone you want to be with."

But could it work? Would it? The thought of finding out terrified her, so why wasn't she just shutting Sandy down and getting on with her life. Why did she keep wondering how Erin was doing? "You think I should call her?"

"You're the one who broke up with her."

"She's probably moved on."

Sandy snorted. "I doubt it, but let's say she has. Better to know than to wonder ten years down the line."

"I don't know." She sighed. "Part of me wants to call her and tell her I miss her. The other part keeps listing all the reasons it would be a really bad idea."

"I'm not saying it won't be scary. Do you trust her?"

"After she lied to me so much? I must be stupid, because I do."

Sandy's mouth turned up at the corners. "You sure you want to let her slip away?"

If she was sure, she'd be sleeping for more than four hours a night. But the thought of calling Erin petrified her. Something was stopping her. That damn fear again. It was just too strong.

"I know I'm not a lot of fun right now," she said to Sandy. "I'm glad you're my bestie."

"I'll always be your bestie. No matter what happens with Erin, you know you'll always have me."

Lily's throat tightened. She swallowed more coffee to soothe it. But it tightened again when she thought about calling Erin. Not today, that was for sure. Maybe tomorrow. Maybe next week. Maybe. Maybe not.

~

ERIN SPOONED MORE ICE cream into her mouth, even though everything tasted like cardboard. She didn't have much of an appetite, and she hadn't really wanted to have lunch with Christina and Van at the country club, but it was important to Christina, and it was better than moping at home, going over her last conversation with Lily and wondering if there was anything she could have said that would have made a difference.

"Sorry I have to run, but I told my manager I'd only be an extra half hour." Van rose.

Christina followed suit. "Don't forget our nail appointment."

"As if I would."

The two women embraced and shared a chaste kiss. They were in the country club's main dining room, after all. Anyone sharing more than a quick peck on the lips would be frowned upon.

"I'm glad I finally got to meet you, Erin." Van's face scrunched up. "Sorry about the emails."

"Don't worry about it." Once Dad had known it was Christina, he'd taken it on the chin, though Erin suspected he'd silently fumed. Christina was his goddaughter, so she got a pass. More passes than his daughter ever got.

Christina didn't sit down until Van had left the dining room. "Isn't she great?"

Erin nodded. "I like her." Van was easy to talk to and clearly adored Christina, who adored her back. A much better match for her than Erin ever would have been.

Christina rested her elbows on the table. "Thanks for trying so hard. I know it's difficult for you right now."

"Yeah." Erin stirred her ice cream. "Mom says I'll feel better in time, but how long? I can't stop thinking about her."

"I can't believe she dumped you."

"I can't blame her. I used her, I lied to her."

"I'm sure she was hurt, but it sounds more like it was about money. You having so much of it."

Erin had told Christina about Lily's misgivings.

"There's nothing you could do about that. It's not your fault you're wealthy. She wasn't thinking about it the right way, anyway."

"What do you mean?"

"Let's say you have one-hundred times more money than she does. I know it's way more times than that, but one-hundred makes the math easy." Christina traced the number one hundred on the tablecloth with her finger. "You paying a five-thousand dollar fine is equivalent to her paying a fifty dollar fine."

Erin quickly swallowed the ice cream she'd popped into her mouth. "I don't think math like that will persuade her. It's a pride thing."

"What I'm saying is that the five-thousand dollars doesn't feel like anything to you because money isn't a scarce resource for you, like it is to her."

"But we're talking about money. There's emotion attached to it. People aren't always rational about it. Don't get me wrong. I understand what you're saying. It's just not that simple."

Christina huffed a sigh. "I think she was silly for letting you go over it. I mean, who breaks up with someone because they have money?" She shook her head. "Why didn't you tell her about McMillan Park?"

Erin had thought about it. She'd been bursting to tell her. But then she'd realized that if she told Lily about it, and Lily had forgiven her, she'd always wonder if it was because of the park, if Lily had felt obligated to give them a chance. She hadn't wanted to wonder if their relationship was a *quid pro quo*.

"I want her to be with me for me," she said to Christina.

"Sure, but why not use everything you can to get her back. Call her and tell her about the park."

"I don't want her back because she approves of a project I proposed. I want her to be with me, to love me, for me. And she clearly doesn't." She pushed away her remaining ice cream. "I didn't propose that we keep the park as a park for Lily. I did it because it's the right thing to do. Lily helped me to see that, yes. And sure, I knew it would please her. But that's not why I proposed it. It just happens to be what she wants too."

"I see." Christina paused. "So you're not going to try and get her back?"

Erin had agonized over whether she should try. "No."

Christina's eyes widened.

"If I don't accept it, respect her decision, I'll be crossing into creepy stalker territory." Fortunately she'd have plenty to keep her busy. College, if she was accepted into the astrophotography program, and working with Royce on the park project. Though she sort of wished she wouldn't be involved, because the park would keep Lily front and centre in her mind. On the other hand, she believed in her proposal. Maybe knowing it would make Lily happy would help her move on, at least make her feel as if she'd made it up to her in some way.

"You know I'm here for you."

"Thanks."

"She could still change her mind and call you."

"No, she can't."

Christina frowned. "Why not?"

"I cut off my phone."

"You cut off your phone?" Christina shrieked. "How will you survive without a phone?"

"My undercover phone."

When Christina appeared confused, Erin told her about her other phone, the one she'd used as Erin Bartlett. "I kept staring at it, willing it to ring, so I cut it off. I need to accept it, try to move on. I needed to make it real."

"So if she changes her mind, there's no way for her to contact you."

"It's been over two weeks, Christina. She's not going to change her mind. She was very clear about not wanting me." Tears sprang to her eyes. "Crystal clear."

"I'm sorry." Christina rounded the table and gave Erin a hug. "You'll find someone else. Someone as special as Van."

Erin couldn't imagine being with anyone except Lily. If only she could stop thinking about Lily, longing to be with her, to hear her voice, smile into her bright eyes, hold her hand, eat the eggs she'd wanted to make. Wanted to. The promise of more, the hope for a life together, was all in the past now. That brief glorious time in her life was over.

∼

DEAD ON HER FEET, Lily left the Golden Goose on a break during her second shift of a double shift. Now she was square with Carlos for when she'd called in sick. Normally she'd be looking forward to going home and falling into bed, and be asleep before her head hit the pillow. But despite the exhaustion making her body feel heavy, tonight she'd lie awake, her mind going around and around and around in circles about Erin. For all her thinking, analyzing, and arguing with herself, she only knew one thing for sure: she missed her. And that thought would launch her into another thought cycle.

Did that mean they should try? Or was that too simple? After all, she wasn't sixteen. Their feelings weren't all that mattered. Or were they? Had she just not been ready to let Erin off the hook? Or was she being an adult? Mature?

Damn, she wanted to call Erin, to hear her voice, to say, "Okay, maybe I was a little hasty. I do care about you. I think I love you too. It's just we're from different worlds, and I'm worried it won't work out." No, she couldn't admit to that last part. She'd say something like, "We're from different worlds but that doesn't mean we shouldn't try. If you still want to." It had been three weeks now. Erin might have moved on already, but if she had, that would answer the question. Lily would feel foolish for reaching out, but she could stop wondering.

Knowing in her heart of hearts she'd made a decision, she pulled out her phone. She'd call Erin right now, on her break when she couldn't talk long. She brought up her contacts, dialled Erin.

"The number you have called is no longer in service."

What the hell? She tried again.

"The number you have called is no longer in service."

Already?

She brought up Sandy's contact, jabbed the call button. "I was right!" she said, before Sandy even had a chance to say hello. "She's already disconnected her fucking phone."

"I assume we're talking about Erin," Sandy said calmly.

"I called her. I knew I shouldn't have. Jesus, I'm such an idiot." And now her voice was shaking and her eyes were moist.

"Take a breath, Lil. Okay, she cut off her phone. You're talking about her fake one, right?"

"Yes."

"So call her real number."

"I don't have it."

Silence, then, "Why not?"

"She offered it to me but I didn't take it. I was breaking up with her, after all. I told her not to call me again." She could see Sandy's "you're an idiot" expression.

"You have to be the most stubborn person, I swear to god," Sandy said. "And the most determined to sabotage any good thing that comes your way."

"I don't need this shit right now, okay?" She wiped away a tear. "At least I know now."

"You don't know anything. So she cut off the phone only you were using. It's been almost a month."

"A little over three weeks."

"Yeah, almost a month. How long did you expect her to keep hoping you'd call? You broke up with her. You told her not to call. You refused her real number. You have no idea why she cut off the phone. Maybe it was hurting her too much to hang on to it."

She felt a glimmer of hope, but then told herself Sandy could be wrong. Erin might have cut off her phone because she'd moved on. She might already be dating someone else.

"Do you want to talk to her or not?" Sandy asked.

Damn. Fuck, damn, shit, and everything else. "I can't stop thinking about her."

"Okay, so we have to figure out how you can get in touch. I know one way."

"What?"

"Go to Hunt and Bishop."

"What, just walk in and say, 'Oh, hi, I'd like to speak to Aaron Hunt's daughter? Can you give me her phone number?' That'll work."

"Maybe you can leave something for her at reception. She must go there sometimes. Or maybe you can ask someone to call her."

"It's not like everyone at Hunt and Bishop will have her phone number."

"Aaron Hunt does."

"No way. Come on. There's no way they'd let me near him, even if I tried." Not only that, she doubted Mr. Aaron Hunt would put her in touch with his daughter.

"You're probably right. But leaving her a message might work. How else are you going to get in touch?"

"I could email Hunt and Bishop through their website."

"Could take a while, and they might just delete the email."

How else could she get Erin's attention?

"It won't hurt to try the Hunt and Bishop route," Sandy said. "Maybe they'll toss your message in the garbage. Maybe they'll give it to Hunt. Maybe they'll call Erin and tell her there's a message for her. It's worth a try, and if it doesn't work, we'll figure out something else."

"She told me she lives in the Harbour Valley area."

"Even if we could figure out which house is hers without someone calling the cops on us for driving aimlessly around that neighbourhood, showing up on her doorstep might not be the best way to go."

"True, but I might not have much choice." Staking out stores with telescopes could take years, and the college program Erin said she was applying for didn't start for several months.

"You have a choice now. Are you afraid they'll call the cops if you go into the Hunt and Bishop building?"

"No. Not really."

"If you don't want to do it, I can."

"No, it has to be me. I'll do it."

"When?"

"Tomorrow."

Sandy cheered. "You're doing the right thing."

"Am I?"

"Even if it doesn't work out, you'll know you tried. Because you're driving yourself nuts. And me, by the way. Look, you were upset and angry and hurt when you broke up with her. She'll understand that."

Lily wasn't so sure. If she managed to get in touch, Erin might say, "What, now you want to be together? Why would I want to be with someone who can't make up her fucking mind?" Actually, Erin wouldn't express it that way, because she was gentler, kinder.

Lily wanted to cry, sit right there on the pavement and weep until there were no more tears.

"I have to go," she mumbled to Sandy. "I'm on break."

"I'm with you on this," Sandy said. "You can do it."

They hung up. Lily pocketed her phone and dabbed at her eyes. When she got home, she'd write a short letter to Erin and seal it in an envelope. Just a request for Erin to call her, and she'd include her phone number, just in case. She'd try not to sound too terse, but she also didn't want to sound needy or desperate.

God, would anything related to Erin not tie her in knots? She was almost looking forward to striding up to the Hunt and Bishop reception desk and making an ass of herself. She'd try anything that might help her regain some sense of peace and put her in contact with Erin.

25

MENTALLY REHEARSING WHAT SHE'D say, Lily approached the Hunt and Bishop tower but stopped walking when she reached the courtyard. What the hell did she think would happen if she walked in and asked reception to pass along a message to Erin Hunt? They'd probably nod and smile, take her letter, and wait until she'd left the building before they did one of two things: tossed it in the garbage or called the cops. On top of that, she was probably the last person Erin wanted to hear from, given their last conversation. If Lily cared about her, she'd leave her alone, not badger her.

No, that was fear talking. She wanted to see Erin. She wanted to figure things out with her, rather than retreat. She wanted to know if Erin was okay. The name, the money, the unfortunate clash of viewpoints when it came to the family business . . . they could work it all out. Together. Lily wasn't going to figure everything out by herself, couldn't think her way into feeling comfortable about it all. Couldn't get Erin out of her mind and wanted to be with her. Really wanted to be with her.

Okay. Deep breath. Move legs. Move.

But they wouldn't.

Damn it! Maybe it was because she expected to hear the wail of a siren, or for Aaron Hunt himself to suddenly appear before her and tell her his daughter was off limits. That she was a nobody and to get lost. Maybe driving around Erin's neighbourhood or staking out every store in town that sold telescopes weren't such bad ideas, after all.

She was about to turn around and go back to the car when a striking woman strode out of the building's exit and into the courtyard, a woman without a single hair out of place and dressed to the nines. She wouldn't look out of place on a catwalk in Paris, not that Lily cared about such events.

Their eyes met. Lily would have looked away, but the woman veered in her direction. She was walking straight towards her. Lily had to restrain herself from stepping back.

The woman stopped in front of her. "Lily Altree, isn't it?"

Shit, she must work for Hunt and Bishop. Lily raised her hands. "I'm not here to make trouble, I swear."

"What are you here for, then?"

"Okay, this is going to sound crazy, but I need to contact Erin Hunt. Aaron Hunt's daughter."

The woman's expression didn't change. "Why?"

"Well, we're, uh, working on a project together, a, uh, community service project," Lily said, her story picking up steam. "After I, uh, protested here, it was suggested I work with her to get a better idea of what your company does."

The woman's lips thinned. "Really?"

Lily kept going, even though it was obvious the woman wasn't buying it. "Yeah. But I can't get a hold of her. I must have entered her number wrong. The number I have is out of service. Would it be possible for you to get a message to her?" She whipped out the letter from her back jeans pocket. "It's just a letter." Her heart sank when the woman didn't take the letter, but she wasn't running back into the building to get security either.

"Do you believe in fate, Lily?"

"What?"

"Fate. You know, destiny."

"Uh . . ."

"You see, I know Erin Hunt. She told me about this project."

"She did?"

"Absolutely. I know she's been waiting to hear from you."

Okay, for some reason, this woman was playing games with her. Either that, or Lily had entered some bizarre alternate universe like the ones in the shows she watched and the books she read, and this was no longer her planet Earth.

"I'll give you her phone number."

"You will?"

The woman fished her phone from a purse that even to Lily's untrained eye, appeared expensive. She frowned at Lily. "Well, get out your phone."

She plucked her phone from her back pocket and tapped in the number the woman read out.

"You *are* going to call her," the woman said sternly.

"Yes."

"I'll let her know. I'll also let her know that if she hasn't heard from you by the end of today, that she's to call you. To discuss that project. You'd better give me your phone number, in case she's misplaced it."

"Sure. Okay." Lily gave the woman her number. "Thanks."

"No problem. Nice meeting you. Since you'll be working with Erin, I'm sure we'll be seeing much more of each other in the future."

The woman sashayed away on her three inch? Four inch? Maybe five inch heels. Lily gazed after her, then realized she didn't know the woman's name, and the woman hadn't offered it. Fate? Destiny? More like someone playing a joke on her.

She looked down at the phone in her hand. If she called the number, who'd pick up? A local pizza parlor. The cops. Some phone sex line. She could try a reverse lookup on the internet. Or she could just call the number. What if Erin picked up? There was only one way to find out who was at the other end of that line.

She called the number.

~

Erin selected another photo for her portfolio and moved it to the folder designated for what she considered her absolute best images. The deadline for the college application was still a couple of weeks away, but she didn't want to screw this up. She needed something to look forward to. Her attempts to muster up excitement had fallen flat, but Mom kept saying she'd eventually feel better. When, though? In twenty years?

Her phone, sitting off to the right of the keyboard, alerted her to a text. Christina.

You can thank me later.

What was that supposed to mean? Then the phone rang. Erin peered at the number. It looked familiar. She considered letting it go through to voicemail, but changed her mind. "Hello."

"Erin?"

She felt as if she'd stuck her finger into an electrical socket. "Lily?"

"Oh my god, it is you. I didn't know if this was actually your number or if someone was playing a joke on me."

"No, it's me." And her brain had better engage soon. "It's great to hear from you."

"Yeah?"

"Yes. Totally." She paused. "I didn't expect to hear from you again."

"You'll think I'm a wishy-washy idiot, but I miss you. A lot."

"I miss you too."

"Can we try to figure this out together?"

Erin's throat thickened. "I'd like that."

"Let's meet. To talk."

Her heart sank. "Last time we met to talk, it didn't exactly turn out great."

"I won't bail on you this time, I promise. I won't be a jerk."

"You weren't a jerk. You were hurt. But let's not rehash all that. Unless you want to."

"I don't. Not in a confrontational way, anyway. I'm not saying we won't have things to work through. But if you want to try, I want to try. Hell, I really want to try."

Erin's lips trembled. "Me too," she managed to say.

"I have to work tonight, but do you want to meet for an early dinner?"

"Sure."

They arranged when and where to meet, then hung up. Erin rolled her chair away from her desk, then leaped up and punched her fist into the air. She hadn't wanted to ask Lily how she'd gotten her number, not wanting Lily to think she was upset about it. She'd never wanted someone to have her phone number more. And she could guess who'd given it to her.

She'd ask for details later, from both the women she loved in different ways. Right now, she wanted to finish fleshing out her portfolio and then get ready for dinner. A dinner she'd never expected to have and wouldn't miss for the world.

~

LILY WAITED OUTSIDE THE family restaurant, trying to keep her nerves under control and not bounce around. Okay, a Mercedes had just turned into the parking lot. Lily's determination to wait where she was fell by the wayside. She strode toward the car. Her heart soared when Erin got out. Everything she'd thought about saying fled. She took a tentative step, then crossed the distance between them more confidently and threw her arms around Erin's neck. When she felt Erin's arms tighten around her, she smiled into her shoulder.

"Here I was, worrying about whether we'd feel uncomfortable," Erin said, when they parted.

Lily laughed. "Me too." But not about this. "Come on, I don't have a lot of time." She grabbed Erin's hand and pulled her toward the restaurant.

They chose a table and sat but didn't say anything. They just grinned at each other until the waitress had taken their orders. "So we're going to try," Lily said, wanting to verbalize it again.

"I want to."

"Me too." She met Erin's eyes. "I'm going to hand the reigns of the Citizens for Responsible Housing group over to Maria."

"I hope you're not giving it up for me."

"No. Not entirely. I've been thinking about it for a while. Most people come and stay for a year or three, then move on. I've been at it for seven, eight years now?" She picked up her napkin, played with it. "I'm seriously thinking about chef's school. Between that, family and friends, you, having time to read and relax . . . I don't have time. And I seriously do need a break from it."

"What are you going to tell Maria?"

"What I just told you, and tell her who you are. The condensed, sanitized view of how things happened between us."

"You mean you won't tell her how much I hurt you because I was too afraid to tell you the truth?"

"Yeah."

She smiled when Erin did. "But I don't want to rehash that. Seriously." She wagged her finger at Erin. "Never do that again, though. Tell a big lie."

"I won't. Believe me."

The waitress brought over their drinks and salads. "I told you I'll be working on a project with Royce, and who knows, I might work on more after that," Erin said. "I can't share confidential company documents with Maria."

"I wouldn't expect you to."

"You can't share anything I tell you, either. Not with Maria, not with Sandy, not with anyone. I want to feel I can discuss the project with you, without worrying about that."

"Erin." Lily gave her a withering look. "I didn't say I want to try because I want to spy."

"Touché." Erin reached across the table, maybe for reassurance. Lily was happy to give it to her. She squeezed her fingers, held onto them.

"I doubt I'll work on projects that will upset Maria—and you—anyway," Erin said.

Lily hoped so. "Can you tell me about this project now?"

"I don't want to tell you about it."

Oh, for fuck's sake. She drew breath.

"I want to show you, take you to the project site."

Her irritation died. "You sure? I wouldn't want to knock over a sign, or anything."

"You're bad, you know that?"

Lily blew her a kiss. "You know, I still owe you supper." She waggled her eyebrows. "And eggs. When will be too soon to invite you over again?"

"No time will be too soon."

"In that case, are you free on Thursday?"

"I am. Are you free on Friday until you have to go to work?"

"I am."

They grinned at each other.

"Let me take you to lunch on Friday, and then to the site."

Lily tensed. Okay, this was it. Time to talk about *the* issue. "If by 'take me to lunch' you mean you'll pay, I'd rather go Dutch."

"If that's what you want."

"I do." She swallowed when Erin looked down at her salad. Maybe this wasn't going to work after all.

～

ERIN STABBED A PIECE of lettuce with her fork and wondered what to say. Money was one of the issues, perhaps the primary issue, hanging over them. But she wouldn't quibble today. This was what they'd have to work on. They had time.

She ate the bit of lettuce and met Lily's eyes. "Then we'll go Dutch." And it was time to change the subject. "You haven't asked me about White Knight at all."

"I haven't received any more emails, if that's what you're wondering."

"I'm not. You won't be getting any more. I know who it is."

"Who?"

"Christina Bishop. Royce Bishop's daughter. You've met her."

"When?"

"Earlier this afternoon." She'd called Christina, heard the story and thanked her profusely. "She's the one who gave you my phone number."

Lily's mouth dropped open. "Fuck off."

"I'm not joking." Erin explained her relationship with Christina, how they were best friends, pretty much sisters, and how Erin had cried on her shoulder about Lily.

"Now I understand why she asked about fate," Lily said. "But why the hell would she leak company documents?"

"It was a passive aggressive thing. She wanted to get at my dad because she thought he wasn't treating Royce well."

"Don't any of you, like, talk to each other?"

Erin chuckled. "She'd tried talking to Royce. He wasn't handling it the way she wished he would. Talking to my dad wouldn't have accomplished anything. So she leaked documents related to my dad's latest project. She wanted to make him squirm, as she put it. To get back at him."

"Nothing like being a pawn in someone else's little scheme." Lily shrugged and her voice dipped. "McMillan Park's a done deal anyway."

It was, but not in the way she thought. Erin couldn't wait until Friday—and Thursday.

"About the fine . . ."

Erin sighed. "You're not paying me back. Nobody else there that day was fined, and you didn't damage any property. That sign they claim you knocked off had been hanging by one nail for months. My dad just wanted to send a message."

"Still, five grand is a lot of money."

"Not to me. I know that bothers you, but it isn't to me, and it's Hunt and Bishop money."

"I doubt you drew it from company accounts."

"No, but everything I have ultimately came from Hunt and Bishop or family companies that preceded it. I didn't earn a dime of it."

"So where the hell does your money come from then?" Lily quickly raised her hand and shook her head. "Don't answer that. It's way too personal right now."

"I don't mind. My parents gave me one hell of a university graduation present. And my grandmother—my dad's mom—left me quite a bit when she passed away."

"That's the grandmother whose house you talked about?"

"Yes."

"Can I ask what happened to the house now?"

"I own it. My cousin's living in it at the moment. I haven't been able to face seeing it much, but I'll have to soon. He's graduating from university and he'll be moving out. I'll have to decide what to do with it."

"Rich people's problems," Lily said. "But real problems all the same," she quickly added.

"I'm a rich person. Even if Hunt and Bishop went under, and it won't, that won't change."

"Well, thank you for paying my fine."

"You're welcome," Erin said, appreciating how difficult it was for Lily to say it.

"I'm sure most people could get used to the rich thing real quick, but I'm not most people. It's not going to be easy for me."

"I'm glad," Erin said, nodding.

Lily frowned. "Really?"

"Yes, really. I'm not saying I don't want you to get used to it, but if it was too easy, I'd wonder if you wanted to be with me for my money."

"Uh, no. I didn't even know when I fell for you, you dork."

Lily didn't need to tell her she wasn't interested in the money. The lack of interest oozed out of the independent, stubborn, adorable woman sitting across the table from her. "The one reason, the only reason, I'm glad you didn't know who I was when we started dating."

"We're still dating."

"We are."

They gazed at each other. Mom was wrong. Erin would never have gotten over Lily, not in a million years. The waitress broke the spell when she came over with their meals.

"This is so nice," Erin said. "Talking to you like this. Answering your questions honestly. I hated lying to you."

"Let's hope that means you won't do it very often." Lily had narrowed her eyes, but her tone was light.

Erin was only in her mid-twenties, but she already knew enough about herself and life to stop herself from saying she'd never do it again. It would be another lie, and Lily would know it. Erin had promised not to tell any more big lies, and she intended to stick to that.

Lily sprinkled salt on her fries. "Do I get to see your place now? Or are you going to keep me hidden from your parents?"

"My mom wants to meet you." Or she would when Erin told her they were back on again.

"When will you tell your father?"

"He's not going to like it."

"Understatement of the century."

"I'll tell him soon. I want to show you my balcony with all my telescopes."

Lily chuckled. "You're such a nerd."

"Takes one to know one."

They smiled at each other, then focused on eating for a while, or at least Erin tried to. She'd put a deadline on it. Telling Dad. Now all she'd have to do was survive the conversation.

~

WHEN ERIN STEPPED INTO Lily's apartment on Thursday afternoon, her eyes immediately went to the table. Unlike last time, it was bare. No tablecloth, no place settings, no candles. Not surprising, given it was only two o'clock. She and Lily were grabbing every spare hour of each other's time, so why wait until five or six, when they were both free right now?

Lily's smile almost made her forget the wine she held. She threw her arms around her and held her close. This time, she hoped to eat some eggs.

"Thanks," Lily said, accepting the wine. "Do you want a glass now?"

"I can wait until dinner."

"Me too." Lily set the wine on the table.

Erin removed her blazer and hung it on the back of her usual chair.

"Good, it came off."

She shot Lily a questioning look.

"Last time, you didn't take it off."

"I didn't even realize. But I'm not surprised. I knew I was going to tell you about everything."

"And you knew how I'd react?"

"Not the specifics. I'd hoped we'd talk." She'd naively hoped Lily would blow up and then they'd kiss and make up. Now she could see how that never would have been possible, not after the big lie. Lily had needed time. Erin was grateful—and lucky—that she'd decided to forgive.

"Have you told your father yet?" Lily's voice sounded casual, but Erin detected the underlying tension.

"Not yet. I'm telling him tomorrow."

Lily swallowed. "You sure you want to stay?"

Surprised, Erin wrapped her arms around her again. "Of course I want to stay. I don't need his approval when it comes to who I'm dating."

"It would be easier to have it, though." Lily's voice sounded muffled.

"It would, but I don't need it." Erin drew back and met Lily's eyes. "We know he won't be thrilled. I'm a big girl. He can't forbid me to date you, and I won't listen to him if he tries." She paused. "You'll have to meet him."

"Yeah." Lily kissed her and drew her into a hug again. "But I don't want to think about that today."

Neither did Erin.

Now it was Lily's turn to draw back. "Okay, so any bombshells you want to drop before we spend the rest of a lovely day inside my lovely apartment?"

"Nope."

"What about that project you're so secretive about? You haven't bought my parents' subdivision and plan to knock down their house or anything like that."

Erin forced a frown. "Where do they live?" When Lily's eyes widened, she grinned. "Just kidding."

Lily playfully slapped her shoulder. "Don't do that."

She didn't resist when Lily pulled her closer, locked her lips on hers, parted them . . . everything faded away except the two of them.

When they came up for air, Lily cupped Erin's face for a few seconds, then gripped her collar. "I don't have to start dinner for at least a couple of hours." She gently tugged on Erin's collar and walked backwards, taking Erin with her. "I'm sure we can find something to do."

"I'm sure we can," Erin said, the simmering heat within her exploding into a raging fire.

"I don't think you've seen my bedroom."

She continued walking in the direction Lily was pulling her, her eyes on Lily's face, trusting her to lead. "No, I haven't."

Lily pulled her through the open doorway. "It's about time you did."

A big tug this time. Erin fell onto the bed, on top of Lily. They shared a quick grin, then melted into one another.

They ate a late dinner.

26

IN THE PASSENGER SEAT of Erin's car, Lily tried to figure out where they were going. She'd thought Erin would drive her to one of the wealthier neighbourhoods. Now she wasn't sure why. After all, Erin had said she'd be working with Royce Bishop, not her father, and that Bishop was interested in affordable housing, or at least he wasn't fixated on luxury condos only the rich could afford.

Erin turned right at an intersection. They were heading into the Iron Court neighborhood. Hunt and Bishop had already bought McMillan Park. Maybe they planned to take over the area. Erin had said she wouldn't work on a project Lily wouldn't like. Maybe she'd misspoken, because Lily would not be pleased to see her destroy this neighbourhood.

Deep breath. She couldn't freak out over every project and assume the worst. If this skydiving without a parachute relationship had any chance of working, she had to trust Erin. That didn't mean Erin would never hurt her or say or do something she didn't like, but there had to be trust between them or they were doomed.

Erin hung a left. Lily realized they'd be driving by McMillan Park. She was about to open her mouth and say as much when Erin pulled over and parked. Her blood pressure shot up. Her hands clenched. If Erin told her she was in charge of McMillan Park and would oversee its destruction, Lily would . . . she'd . . . Had their time together since Erin had arrived yesterday, their glorious time together, been a lie? Again?

She jerkily got out of the car and fell into step with Erin, struggling to control her breathing. "So, why are we here?" she managed to say.

"I'll tell you inside the park."

Lily gave her a sidelong glance. Erin looked calm. She wasn't grinning evilly in anticipation of blowing Lily's world away. Again. Trust, remember. Trust.

The gate was still locked. The Hunt and Bishop sign still sported an image of a high rise. Erin pulled out her phone. "I'll call the guard." She said a few words, then dropped her phone into her blazer pocket.

The guard must have been near the gate. He arrived within a minute and unlocked it for them. "Good afternoon, Ms. Hunt," he said.

"Hi, Mike. I don't know if you heard, but Royce Bishop is the lead on this now, and I'll be helping him out."

Lily wanted to cry, punch her, scream . . . but she'd hear what she had to say. Trust had better come through.

"We got the memo," Mike said with a smile. His eyes slid to Lily, then back to Erin. "But, uh . . ."

"Is there a problem?" Erin asked.

"No. I mean, I don't know. Security sent us a list of people to watch out for. I know you were here with your friend before, but . . . "

Erin turned to Lily, met her eyes. Despite her anxiety, Lily couldn't help exchanging a smile with her.

"She's with me," Erin said. "Don't worry. I take responsibility for her."

"I'm sorry. I didn't know what to do."

"You did the right thing." She gently touched Lily's elbow. "Let's go inside."

Lily followed her into the park, convinced Erin would not, couldn't possibly, start talking about when construction on the building would begin and how much she was looking forward to it. Hadn't she heard a word of their conversations about this place? About how it was the only green space for blocks. About how the city should have invested into revitalizing the park, rather than selling it. About Jay-Jay. Lily wanted to weep, but grabbed a hold of herself. Trust. She believed she knew the woman walking next to her, knew she would not, under any circumstances, bring her here to rub her nose in it.

"So you're taking responsibility for me, eh?" she said, wanting to lighten her mood. "What will you do if I start attacking the equipment?"

Erin cocked her head. "Wrestle you to the ground?"

"It might be worth it," she said, forcing a chuckle.

She felt Erin's arm slip around her shoulders. "Okay, so that conversation with the guard kind of ruined the surprise a bit," Erin said. "Royce is leading the project now, and I'm going to work with him part-time. Which means it's changed a bit."

Lily slipped her arm around Erin's waist. They walked toward one of the sandboxes she and Jay-Jay had spent many happy hours playing in.

"I mentioned Christina was trying to make my dad squirm because she was upset at how he and Royce weren't seeing eye to eye. Royce wanted to build affordable housing here."

"Is that what you're going to do now? Build affordable housing." That would definitely be an improvement over the original plan. Lily would still miss the park, still wonder where to sit on Jay-Jay's birthday. But at least the people in the neighbourhood could afford to live here.

"Not exactly."

They'd reached the sandbox. When Erin let her go, Lily apprehensively turned to face her.

"When I came out to that first protest, I'd never thought about how my dad's projects affect neighbourhoods and the people in them. Honestly, I'd never thought much about the business at all. Then I met you, and you taught me a few things. I'm not saying we agree on everything, but I did listen."

Erin gripped Lily's shoulders. "During our last conversation here, you said you didn't know why developers never gave anything back beyond writing cheques. That got me thinking. I came up with an idea, and I convinced Royce to talk to my dad about it. We're not building anything here. We're going to invest in the park, as a "giving back" project, for lack of a better term. It might be the first of more such projects. It'll depend on how this one goes."

Tears sprang to Lily's eyes. She hated crying in front of people. "I think a bug flew into my eye," she said, furiously rubbing at both eyes, knowing she wasn't fooling Erin and not caring.

"We had to talk to the city about rezoning it back to what it was before. Once they heard what we wanted to do, they were happy. Honestly, they would have been happy with anything. This land isn't their responsibility anymore."

"So it's still going to be a park, then."

"Yes. I have to give credit to my dad, who gave up his project. More for Royce than me. It's the olive branch that's got them talking about joint projects again. Anyway, we're in the planning stages, but I already know there will be a new bench right here near the sandboxes."

Lily's throat felt so thick she was afraid of what her voice would sound like. "I don't know what to say," she croaked. "Which doesn't happen very often."

"Say you love it."

"I love it!" She threw her arms up and danced a jig. "I fucking love it! And I—" She stopped herself, then thought to hell with gravity and the ground. "I love you."

Erin blinked rapidly. "I love you too," she whispered.

Then they were in each other's arms, in one of Lily's favourite places. She could almost hear the orchestra and see the rainbows. Hey, she had to let her inner sixteen-year-old out every once in a while. She was old enough to know the universe wouldn't take long to throw something at her that would chase the sixteen-year-old into hiding again. Like meeting Erin's father. Aaron Hunt, the one who'd given up his project and didn't know about her yet and had probably sent her photo to the guards.

She drew back, wiped away Erin's tears with her thumbs. "Why didn't you tell me about this before? You knew about this a while ago."

Erin swallowed. "Don't take this the wrong way, but I didn't want you to forgive me, to take me back, because of this. I know you wouldn't have. You're not like that. It's me. My insecurities. My doubts. About me."

Lily hugged her, so tightly she heard Erin squeak. She loosened her grip. "I'm here for you, and only you. If you lost everything tomorrow and your damn company went under, I'd still be here." She let Erin go and cleared her throat. "You said you planned to put in a bench." She bit her lip, to stem more tears. Then she forged on. "Any other plans on the drawing board?"

"We're only just talking about it now, but a few ideas have come up."

She took Erin's hand. "Tell me."

Lily walked through the park with Erin, listening to her ideas, smiling at her enthusiasm, savouring the feeling of Erin's warm hand in hers. She tried not to think about later, when Erin would tell her father about them. When her inner sixteen-year-old might have to retreat in a hurry.

~

ERIN HESITATED OUTSIDE DAD's home office, then stepped inside. Dad was sitting at his desk, typing away on his laptop. She approached him but didn't sit down. She wanted to stand for this conversation, use every advantage she could, no matter how trivial.

He looked up, then motioned toward whatever was on the screen. "I got the email about the McMillan Park sign. You should be there. We should all be there."

"You want to be there?" Her voice conveyed her surprise.

"Sure. It was your idea, and you'll be working with Royce on it. At least you'll be doing something for the company." He leaned back in his chair. "We'll go to the site, then have dinner at the country club."

Erin seized the opening he'd given her. "Can we go for lunch at the country club and then go to the site?" The email had said the sign at McMillan Park would be changed at 2:30 p.m. "I'd like someone else to join us, and she won't be able to make dinner. She works most nights."

His brows drew together. "Someone else, eh? You've never wanted to invite anyone to eat with us before. You introduce me to someone, I say hi, and I never see them again. I was starting to think it was me. Then I thought you'd be with Christina, but you know how that turned out."

She chuckled nervously. In university, she'd believed she'd fallen in love a couple of times. Now she realized she was wrong. She'd never felt as strongly for anyone as she did for Lily. "I'm serious about this one."

"Tell me about her."

"You already know her."

"Really?" He frowned in thought. "I don't know. Tell me."

"It's Lily Altree."

He stared at her, then barked a laugh. When she didn't laugh along with him, he stared at her again. "Are you fucking with me?" He pushed back his chair and stood, taking away her advantage. "Are you fucking with me?" he shouted, looming over his desk.

"No. I got to know her and we've become close."

"Lily Altree." He plopped back into his chair. "There are . . ." He typed something on his laptop. "Seven, almost eight billion people in the world. Let's say half of those are girls. That's four billion girls.

If ten percent of them are like you, that's four-hundred million girls."

"It's probably closer to one or two percent."

"That's still forty million girls. You have forty million girls to choose from, and you choose Lily fucking Altree?"

"I didn't exactly choose her. It just happened."

"Lily fucking Altree." His eyes bored into her. "Why?"

"What do you mean?"

"What's she got? Why are you with her?"

She was going to say she couldn't control who she felt attracted to, but that wouldn't satisfy him. She could say she couldn't explain love and neither could he, but that wouldn't work either.

Rocking on her heels, she gave his question some thought. "She's passionate about things. She's a hard worker."

"Give me a fucking break. She's not interviewing for a job. What made you walk in here and tell me you're with her even though you knew I'd hate it?"

"We have a ton in common. I'm totally comfortable with her, meaning I don't feel I need to impress her. But I want to." She nodded, more to herself than to him. "She makes me want to do something with my life. I want to make her proud."

Dad's expression wasn't giving anything away. "What does she do?"

"She waits tables."

He winced. "Jesus Christ."

"She wants to go to chef school, and she'd make a brilliant chef. She'd give Michael a run for his money. But if she wanted to wait tables for the rest of her life, so what? It's honest work."

"How do you know she's not with you for your money? Because, come on. Lily Altree? And you? The most mismatched couple in the city, if you ask me."

"You don't even know her."

"I know enough. And you should know better. Of course she's with you. As soon as she found out who you are, she must have been all over you."

"She wasn't," Erin snapped.

Shock flashed across Dad's face. She couldn't remember the last time she'd snapped at him. But he was attacking Lily, who wasn't after her money, to the point that she'd made Erin wish she didn't have any.

"Lily doesn't care about my money." Not in the way Dad meant, anyway. "You can think I'm crazy and deluded and naïve if you want, but I know the truth." Not wanting to provide him with ammunition, she wouldn't tell him how Lily had reacted when she'd revealed her true identity to her.

Dad shook his head, then picked up a pen and threw it down. "Is there anything I can say that will make you change your mind about her?"

"No."

He looked up at the ceiling.

"Can't you give her a chance? I think there are a lot of things you'll like about her."

"I'd find it easier to like her if we weren't on opposite sides of the argument."

"Just the one argument, Dad." That she knew about.

He groaned and ran his hand through his hair, then his eyes narrowed. "How long have you been seeing her?"

Erin clasped her hands behind her back. "A while."

"Behind my back."

"You knew I was meeting up with her. Okay, I didn't tell you every time. But I'm sure you didn't tell your parents the moment a friendship with a woman changed into something else."

"We're not talking about me," he said levelly.

"I didn't tell you because I knew you'd want me to stop seeing her."

"Damn right I would have."

"You needed me to find out who White Knight was."

"Oh, so you didn't tell me because you wanted to keep helping me."

"Something like that," she mumbled. Now that she was being honest with herself, she knew she'd been afraid, terrified, of losing him. Of losing Lily. Lying about the important stuff had gotten her nowhere. "I was afraid you wouldn't love me anymore," she whispered.

Dad's mouth opened. She braced herself for whatever he was going to yell.

He swallowed and his face softened. "I will always love you, Erin. I might want you to stop lazing around on your ass. I might sometimes wonder what the fuck you're thinking. I might want to shake some sense into you when you're not making any. Like now, for example. But I will always, always love you."

Her eyes glistening, she rounded the desk and hugged him. Maybe she was delusional, because when they parted, she thought she saw tears in his eyes too. He ducked his head for a second, and when he raised it and smiled at her, the tears were gone.

 The tension between them had broken. Dad met her eyes. "I'm not going to sit here and be all, 'as long as she makes you happy.' But it's your life. Invite her to the sign change and lunch beforehand. Bring her here first. I want to talk to her."

"Dad."

He held up his hand. "To clear the air. You're expecting me to munch on hors d'oeuvres and make nice with her at our usual table. I want to talk to her first."

Erin didn't like the sound of that. But if an uncomfortable conversation with him would drive Lily away, they weren't going to make it. "I'll let her know."

"You do that." He turned his attention back to his laptop.

Erin was on her way out the door when she heard him mutter something under his breath. "Lily fucking Altree."

27

Lily gazed at the sprawling manicured garden below her, wondering how large the Hunt Estate was.

"Fifty acres," Erin said, when Lily asked. "Most of it wild."

"Great view." She turned away from the balcony rail, counted five telescopes set up in a row. "What do you do, run from one to the other?"

Erin smiled. "It depends on what I want to look at."

Lily pointed to the one closest to her. "Isn't that the one you spent so much time fiddling with at the store?"

"I went back and bought it the next day. Sorry, I should have told you."

There were so many little lies and omissions that Erin couldn't keep track of all of them. Lily didn't voice her thought. She'd put Erin Bartlett behind her so she could move forward with Erin Hunt, and if there was one thing she hated, it was bringing up stuff that had already been discussed and handled.

This house and estate, though. Lily knew her worth wasn't related to how much money she had, but it was difficult not to feel small on a fifty-acre estate, standing on the balcony attached to her girlfriend's private apartment, the apartment that was larger than hers. Hell, the walk-in closet filled with blazers and blouses and business suits and flat dress shoes was bigger than her bathroom.

And here she was, waiting to be summoned by Aaron Hunt so he could try to get rid of her. If he failed, they'd all be off to the country club. Maybe she was crazy.

Erin wrapped her arm around Lily's shoulder and squeezed her. "I'm so glad you're here."

"Me too," Lily heard herself say. And she was, because Erin was here. That was what counted. Erin. Their relationship. It didn't matter if they were standing in Lily's rinky-dink apartment or on a balcony attached to a mansion sitting on a fifty-acre estate. What mattered was them. Something Lily suspected she'd have to remind herself of quite often.

"Erin?"

They both turned toward the voice. Erin's mother peered out the open balcony door. "Your father wants to see you."

Lily stiffened. Her hands were suddenly clammy.

"Thanks, Mom."

Erin's mother, who'd told Lily to call her Frances or Mrs. H., gave them an encouraging smile. Lily appreciated the gesture. The woman had been nothing but polite, making Lily wonder what she really thought.

She gripped Erin's hand as they strode through her apartment and down the carpeted hallway, its plushness swallowing their footsteps. She'd taken off her shoes in the grand entryway, of course.

Her heart pounded in her ears when Erin pulled her through an open door. There he was. Aaron Hunt. If she'd ever wanted to throw darts at someone's face, it would have been his. He was wearing a gray three-pieced suit. Lily had put on one of her two pairs of dress pants for this. She wished she was in her jeans, because right now, she felt as if he already had the advantage. They were in his world.

"Dad, I'd like you to meet Lily." Erin turned to her. "Lily, this is my father, Aaron."

Hunt stood and extended his hand at the same time Lily extended hers. Both determined to be polite, then, for the woman they cared about. His handshake was strong, but he didn't crush her fingers. He motioned to the guest chairs. "Have a seat."

"Not you," he barked, when Erin went to sit. "If you don't mind, I'd like to have a private chat with our guest."

Erin's concerned eyes met Lily's. "I'll stay."

Hunt glared at her. "I want you to leave."

"I'll be fine," Lily murmured, even though her fingernails were already digging into the chair's leather arms. Erin's refusal to leave was irritating him. Lily didn't want him agitated right out of the gate.

"I won't bite," Hunt said to Erin. "Close the door behind you."

Erin hesitated another few seconds, then rested her hand on Lily's shoulder. She did as her father had asked and left the room.

Hunt lowered himself into his chair and gazed at Lily. "It's just you and me, so you can be honest. Why have you latched onto my daughter? She tells me it's not because of her money, but I find that hard to believe."

Lily almost shot up from her chair, but that was what he wanted. She wouldn't make it that easy for him, and she didn't care if he noticed how white her knuckles were. "Is this the part where you ask me how much money it will take for me to go away?"

He snorted. "I know it won't be that easy. But come on. You. My daughter. Out of all the women you could be with, you end up with Erin. Don't tell me it's not about," he waved his arm around, "what she can offer you."

"I don't care about your money. It's more a detriment to our relationship than anything else."

His eyes widened. Good, she'd surprised him.

"Why in the hell would money be a detriment?" He flung his finger toward her. "Maybe there's a planet out there where wealth doesn't matter, but it does on this one."

She wished she hadn't said anything. She could make something up, but she had the feeling this conversation would set the tone between them for however long they had to try to get along. She hoped that would be a long time. After Erin had warned her about her father wanting this conversation, Lily had repeatedly reminded herself that pissing him off, lying to him, brushing away his questions, tweaking her nose at him, would only hurt Erin in the end.

"No answer, eh? Because you're lying about Erin's wealth being a bad thing. I'm not surprised."

Okay, that was it. He was calling her a liar, after his daughter had lied about her identity? How did she ever think this was going to work? She should have listened to herself, not glossed over the blatant problems her and Erin's different backgrounds would cause. "It was nice meeting you," she said, rising and heading for the door.

"Bye-bye, then. I'll tell Erin you remembered an appointment and couldn't join us after all."

Erin. Lily stopped herself from yanking the door open and spun to face him. "That's what you want, isn't it? For me to walk out and tell your daughter to go fuck herself. I'm not going to do that." She marched over to the guest chair and plunked into it again. "After Erin told you about us, I'm sure you researched me."

He shrugged.

"You know I'm pretty much broke, and I know that means I could hold Erin back. So don't tell me I'm here for your fucking money. I wish I had my own money, but money I'd earned. I don't want yours."

He leaned back in his chair and studied her over his steepled fingers. "How will you hold Erin back?"

Seriously? She had to explain it to him? "She'll want to go on a vacation to Europe and I'll have to say no because I can't afford it. She'll want to eat dinner in a five-star restaurant. Same thing. If we ever move in together, our options will be limited."

"Oh, for fuck's sake." He rolled his eyes. "I have a very simple piece of advice for you. You want to hear it?"

She could hardly wait.

"Get. Over. It. Or your relationship with my daughter will be a very short one. She says she wants to take you to Europe. Say yes.

She wants to wine and dine you. Yes. She wants to move you into a luxury condo with her. Yes, yes, yes. She said you want to go to chef's school."

Lily nodded, wondering what else Erin had told him.

"Let's say you go, and you become the best fucking chef the universe has ever seen. You'll still never have as much money as she does. Never. So you can say no and hold her back—for nothing. Or you can say yes and not hold her back. See how simple it is?"

She drew breath.

"Don't tell me about your pride, or how you need to pull your weight, feel you're contributing, or whatever other bullshit you're telling yourself. What will not going to Europe accomplish except to make her, and by extension you, miserable? You think you'll have a better time staying home with your pride? That you'll feel good about yourself because, ha! You're paying your fair share?"

He shook his head. "The money thing . . . it's never going to change. So you either accept that she'll always win the money competition and you can both have nice things, or you hold her, and yourself, back." He pointed over her shoulder at the closed door. "If you don't accept the money, embrace the money, you might as well go home right now. Your relationship's already over."

She didn't know what to say. She hated to admit it, but he was right about their relationship being a short one if she couldn't get over the money thing. She'd think about it later, when she didn't feel like her relationship with Erin was on the line.

"Maybe you believe me now that I'm not with Erin for," she waved her arm around. "this. And I resent the question. Not for me. For Erin. Because it implies there's nothing interesting about her other than her money. I disagree. She's kind, she's nerdy—a plus in my book. She listens, she's trying to make her way through this world, like everyone else. She doesn't pretend to be perfect. She's cute. And I want to be with her. I wouldn't care if she's broke." Lily gulped down some air. "It will be easier for us if you let us be."

"What do you think I'm going to do? There's nothing I can do. She's chosen you." He folded his arms. "I'm not entirely pissed off about it.

"You're not?"

"I've been trying for a while to get her interested in doing something. Anything. Nothing I've said or done has worked. You come along and she's applying for this astrophotography program at college. Not doing what I would have wanted, but she's also going to help Royce out on their charity project, which is why I'm supporting her "give back" idea." His eyes narrowed again. "You must have something, something good for her. So for now, I'll go along with you and her. But listen very closely."

He leaned forward so much Lily thought he'd end up on top of his desk. "My daughter is very important to me. You do anything to hurt her and you'll deal with me. I'm not talking about the usual crap." His voice climbed an octave. "Oh, you think I'm fat. Oh, boo hoo, you don't like my haircut." He sliced his hand through the air. "Not that crap. I'm talking malicious with intent to hurt crap, like she finds you in bed with someone else, or you bad talk her behind her back. I find out any of that shit's happening, and I won't only remove you from her life, I'll crush you. Do we understand each other?"

Lily cleared her throat. "We do."

"You still want to be with her?"

"Absolutely."

"Then if anyone asks," Hunt stretched his arms wide, "I'm over the fucking moon about this relationship." He straightened his tie. "I'm glad we had this chat. You should go and tell my wife and daughter I'm just finishing something up and I'll be there in a couple of minutes."

Lily's fingers felt stiff as she uncurled them from the chair's arms. She'd survived the inquisition intact. Received the king's approval. Swallowed retorts for love. Sat through advice she'd ponder later.

She was about to open the door when his voice cracked behind her. "One last thing."

Lily turned around.

"You didn't think you'd get away without us talking about your protests against my projects."

She'd hoped to.

"For Erin's sake, I'm going to be generous, extremely generous, and say what's in the past is in the past. After all, nothing you ever did changed anything."

Her jaw tightened, but she bit her tongue. What he'd said wasn't true, anyway. She'd never changed his mind, but she had changed his daughter's. Not every Hunt was an asshole.

"I will support you and Erin. You will support the family business. Whenever you talk about Hunt and Bishop, you will say positive things. If you can't manage that, you will say, 'No comment'. If you are anywhere near a Hunt and Bishop site, you'd better be wearing a fucking hardhat because you're there with Erin or myself or Royce. Hunt and Bishop is off your shit list. Find something else to bitch about." His eyes went back to his laptop. "Now you can go."

Lily wouldn't tell him that she'd understood it wouldn't make sense for her to date a Hunt and continue to protest against Hunt and Bishop projects. She certainly wouldn't tell him about the disappointment and reproach in Maria's voice when she'd told her about Erin and why she was leaving the group and wanted her to take it over. Maybe she *had* sold out. Or maybe she'd simply fallen in love and wanted a bit of happiness.

There would be other causes. She was already thinking about working to get drunk drivers stiffer penalties. She'd tried in her late teens, but it had been too soon. She was ready now.

Lily had hoped to make it through this chat without him forbidding her to see Erin and throwing her off this estate. She'd succeeded and would take the win. And remind herself often that she wasn't dating him. She was dating his lovely daughter, who was probably worried about whether she was still in a relationship.

She didn't have to search the mansion for Erin, who emerged from the next room as soon as Lily stepped into the hallway.

Erin searched Lily's face.

"We have his blessing." Lily broke into a grin when Erin smiled.

"I hope he wasn't completely rude."

"Parts rude, parts advice, parts burying the hatchet."

"You're still going to lunch with us?"

Lily took Erin's hands and kissed them. "I'm still going to lunch with you. Where's your mother? He said he'll be a few minutes."

In response, Erin took her hand and tugged her toward the stairs.

Lily willingly let her lead. They were on her turf, after all. They'd drive to the country club in who knew what luxury car, make small talk over the silverware while being waited on by servers in crisp white aprons, or at least that was how she imagined it. Tonight she'd be the one in the slightly crumpled apron serving dinner to people who didn't live in mansions.

She'd done it. She was all in. She'd jumped off the cliff, out of the plane, was soaring right now, but gravity was a thing. There would be times when she'd feel the ground racing toward her, but right now, she'd enjoy the fucking awesome ride her love and optimism were taking her on, and remind herself that gravity might pull at her, but she wouldn't fall, not while Erin was holding her hand.

~

ERIN STOOD BETWEEN DAD and Lily and watched a workman remove the sign with the image of a condo from McMillan Park's southern fence. She slipped her hand into Lily's when the new sign went up, the one that read, "McMillan Park Revitalization Project. Sponsored by: Hunt and Bishop." No images of buildings. Instead, there was a tree shading a sandbox and a swing set.

She felt Lily's squeeze, looked at her, and had to resist grabbing her and hugging her tightly right there and then. That would come later, when Mom and Dad and Royce weren't here.

Royce came over and shook her hand, then clapped Dad on the back. "You did good, Aaron, approving this. Erin's vision," he said, smiling at her. "I brought a photographer. He'll take a picture of me and Erin for the article in the paper."

"Not Erin," Dad snapped. "I don't want any photos of her in the paper."

"She's part of the business now," Mom said.

Erin wasn't sure she wanted her face out there just yet. "I'd rather not be in the photo. I'm only helping out part-time." She turned to Dad. "I think it would be good for you to be in the photo too."

He shrugged. "Sure, why not?"

As Erin watched the photographer adjust Dad and Royce's positions, Lily leaned into her and said, "This is weird, standing here at a Hunt and Bishop publicity shoot."

"And not holding a sign?"

Lily chuckled. "And keeping my mouth shut."

Dad strolled back to them. "Done. Let's go."

Erin fell into step behind her parents, wanting to walk behind them with Lily. A flash of red caught her eye. Her mouth dropped open. The guy in the red convertible, with the blonde riding shotgun. The convertible glided by and stopped at a nearby red light. Erin wanted to sprint over to them and apologize for assuming their relationship wasn't real, that for the blonde, it was all about the convertible and whatever else the guy had.

"What are you looking at?" Lily asked.

"I was just thinking that when I get tired of the Mercedes, I might buy a convertible."

"Are you ser—" Lily blinked. "We could lie in it and stargaze."

Erin wrapped her arm around Lily's shoulders and pulled her close. "I love that idea. And I love you."

"I love you too."

They walked back to the car, arm in arm, lost in their own thoughts. For the first time in a long time, Erin felt comfortable in her own skin and excited about the future. The one she'd share with the adorable woman next to her, the woman who loved her for her.

Other Books by Sarah Ettritch

Thank you for reading *Love Me for Me*.

If you enjoyed the book, there's a good chance you'll like *The Missing Comatose Woman*, featuring lesbian PI Casey Cook.

Private eye Casey Cook lands her first case, and it's a doozy: find a missing comatose woman. Eager to prove herself, Casey does whatever it takes to get answers, from pretending to be pregnant to fawning over a hairless cat.

As she runs into one dead end after another, Casey wonders whether she should have left her retail job. Determined to show that she can do the PI thing, Casey refuses to give up, chases down every lead, and snags herself a girlfriend along the way.

Available at online bookstores (or request it at your local library).

The Salbine Sisters Series

Playing With Fire
The Salbine Sisters
Rose and Nora
Salbine's Embrace

(to get *Playing With Fire*, sign up for Sarah's email list at sarahettritch.com/salbine)

The Rymellan Series

Disobedience Means Death
Shattered Lives

The Triad
Identity Crisis

The Deiform Fellowship Series

The Atheist
The Cult
Unseen Bonds
Scarred Souls

The Daros Chronicles

Pawns and Puzzles
Fate or Folly

Other Titles

Threaded Through Time
The Missing Comatose Woman
Their Last Hope
The Voice in My Head
The Perfect Christmas Gift

Thanks for reading!